HOW TO BE A BADASS WITCH

HOW TO BE A BADASS WITCH

HOW TO BE A BADASS WITCH™ BOOK THREE

MICHAEL ANDERLE

LMBPN Publishing
PMB 196, 2540 South Maryland Pkwy
Las Vegas, NV 89109

First US edition, December 2020
ebook ISBN: 978-1-64971-382-7
Print ISBN: 978-1-64971-383-4

THE HOW TO BE A BADASS WITCH BOOK
THREE TEAM

Thanks to our Beta Team

Rachel Beckford, Kelly O'Donnell

Thanks to our JIT Readers

Dave Hicks
Wendy L Bonell
Jackey Hankard-Brodie
Diane L. Smith
Daryl McDaniel
Angel LaVey
Dorothy Lloyd
Veronica Stephan-Miller
Deb Mader
Jeff Goode
Paul Westman

If We've missed anyone, please let us know!

Editor
The Skyhunter Editing Team

*To Family, Friends and
Those Who Love
To Read.
May We All Enjoy Grace
To Live The Life We Are
Called.*

CHAPTER ONE

James flexed his hands and cracked his knuckles. "Showtime."

He stood with Mother LeBlanc amid the red rocks in the blinding sunshine, watching two black SUVs come to a halt in front of them. Beyond, the city of Las Vegas glimmered, an oasis in the middle of the desert.

The vehicle in the rear stayed closed. Presumably, it was full of auxiliary agents whose function was to guard against any attempt by the two thaumaturgists to escape. The doors of the one in front opened, though, and out stepped a pair of agents, a man and a woman.

In his head, James had built up a mental image of what the feds would look like: tall, perhaps, but certainly imposing. Built like athletes. Grim and exuding an air of competence. His vision had been influenced by popular media.

Whatever the case, it was wrong. Both agents were average, unremarkable-looking individuals, thirty-ish, with conservative haircuts. The woman's hair was auburn; the man's, sandy brown. Each was of middling height for their respective sex. Moreover, they didn't look grim. They were smiling wryly.

They stopped several yards from James and Mother LeBlanc,

and James felt his companion's amusement radiating through the air. She gave no outward sign of it, however.

"Hello." The male agent nodded at both of them. "Agent Thom Richardson, FBI."

The woman beside him nodded as well. "Agent Heidi MacDonald."

"James Lovecraft," James said. "Nice to meet you, Richardson and MacDonald." He was trying not to laugh. Being a slight, bespectacled man in his mid-thirties, he probably didn't look the way *they* expected, either.

LeBlanc raised her hand in greeting. "You may call me Mother LeBlanc," she said gravely. "Good day."

James noticed that the agents seemed to take Mother LeBlanc more seriously than they took him. He was not surprised. She was a black woman who looked only twenty-five or so, though she was far older, in truth, and she always wore a voluminous, multicolored dress whose folds and swirls were both attention-grabbing and concealing. Though her appearance was disarming in some ways, she likely was closer to how most people might picture a miracle-worker, and her New Orleans accent didn't hurt.

Agent Richardson cleared his throat. "That was an impressive display back there at the Wells Fargo Tower. I've seen a lot of weird shit in my line of work, but I never expected to see actual *magic*." His eyes narrowed slightly. "Or at least, what *appeared* to be magic."

MacDonald shot a sharp glance at her partner, then looked at James and LeBlanc again. "We'd like to know more about how you pulled that off. The nature of your abilities, and how the incident might be related to a recent string of incidents that have popped up on our radar, so to speak."

James considered how to respond.

LeBlanc did not waste that time. "Thaumaturgy," she said simply. "The working of miracles. We draw upon the divine ruling powers of the universe to effect things that would not otherwise be possible. It is a reduced tradition, but it still lives."

The agents blinked.

James nodded. "Now that she has explained, we have our own question. Why are you interested?"

It was rhetorical and not. Any person would be fascinated by the revelation that magic was real, but James was genuinely interested to know what the FBI hoped to do with this knowledge.

The agents looked at one another, then back at the two thaumaturgists.

"Well," Richardson pointed out, "it allowed you to stop a major bank robbery with relative ease. That seems useful."

"And we have reason to believe you're not the only ones who can do this," MacDonald added. "Such as, for instance, the person who was robbing that bank. But many other unexplained phenomena have come to our attention very recently, and there might be some loose cannons out there. We're interested in securing your cooperation to contain the situation so as to ensure that no one gets hurt."

The thaumaturgists briefly locked eyes again.

James took point. "Pardon me, Agent, but was that a veiled threat?"

MacDonald frowned. "No. It was a legitimate request for aid."

"What we *want* is to contain a potentially explosive situation," Richardson added, "and figure out what the hell is going on. If you can appreciate our position, there's no need for threats."

"Ah," Mother LeBlanc clarified warmly, "so you are not threatening us...*yet*." Her smile remained, but James doubted that anyone would pick a fight with her after seeing her expression.

There was a pause.

"Our role is to protect our citizens," Agent Richardson said finally, "and we take that very seriously. We don't want that to be accomplished under duress, but if you're asking if we'll use any means at our disposal to find out what's going on and protect innocent lives, the answer is yes."

"I see." Mother LeBlanc looked at each of them in turn. "And what, exactly, do you think you can do if we decide to decline your offer?"

The agents bristled slightly. Their self-control was good but not perfect.

James smiled at them. "Oh, sure, if you decide to throw half the heavily-armed, scary government guys in the country against us, it will make our lives more *difficult*…but that's not to say your victory would be guaranteed. You saw what happened back there."

The agents were not happy; that much was clear.

"We would be willing to agree to an equal partnership to accomplish our shared goals," James said simply. "But we are not interested in being deputized by you or under your control in any way."

"What would you say are our 'shared goals?'" MacDonald looked at James and LeBlanc as if hoping to find a breach in their unity. The breeze whipping across the desert ruffled her hair.

"We ourselves were in the process of tracking down several individuals who displayed magical potential," LeBlanc explained. "We want to ensure that none of them are unstable. This is, in part, to divert excessive attention from thaumaturgists, but also out of compassion for persons in the grip of powers they don't understand—or others whom they might unintentionally harm."

"So, we do share goals," Richardson said. "We both wish to make sure that those powers will not harm innocent civilians." He looked over their heads at the Phantom. "Has it just been the two of you driving a Rolls Royce all over the country?"

Mother LeBlanc nodded before James could say anything. He was busy bristling at the application of the word "just" to his beloved Phantom.

"Then perhaps our resources could help you to move around

more efficiently?" Richardson suggested. "Of course, we'd like a certain amount of information-sharing in return."

Negotiations began in earnest, and the four gradually reached an accord. The thaumaturgists would offer a baseline explanation of how their powers worked. They would also permit limited observation in exchange for the FBI's assistance in containing and covering up problems or awkward incidents. Largely, they were in agreement.

With one notable exception. As they prepared to go back to their respective vehicles, MacDonald said smoothly, "And of course, it would be beneficial to have an organized program in place to develop those latent talents."

"The *last* thing we want is to be involved in some kind of super-soldier program." James had to give her credit for upselling, but he wasn't going to agree to something so hare-brained. She was suggesting precisely what thaumaturgists had feared for the past century or more.

"Indeed," Mother LeBlanc agreed. "If that were your true goal, we'd have no choice but to wipe your memories clean." Her eyes flicked over the group. "You all would be left standing on this hill without the slightest idea of why you're here or of anything that has happened in the last two days."

James could only think of the agents' resulting expressions as "deer in the headlights."

"No, no," Richardson said hastily. "Of course, that's not what we meant. MacDonald was simply saying that we think magicians—thaumaturgists?—should be trained how to do things right if they're going to practice magic. Surely it doesn't help *anyone* if more of them turn out to be bank robbers."

James allowed his face to break into a shit-eating grin. "Indeed."

The two groups took their leave of one another for the night, the FBI agents promising to play down what had occurred in Las

Vegas, and all of them agreeing to set out the next morning for Los Angeles.

"They do have a point," LeBlanc said to James as they drove away. "If everyone in the country—or the world—who has the aptitude was exposed to real magic, the planet might change forever. If we *have* touched off a sea change, we'll need to find some way to handle it."

James grimaced. "If so, we can only hope that change is for the better. Anyway, first thing, I want to get a mechanic to look at the car. A close second is, before we worry about everyone else, we need to finish tracking down all the people who read that goddamn book of ours."

"James, that's the *first* priority, not the second."

"We're not setting out until tomorrow morning," James pointed out. "I have time."

"Very well, but if it's out of commission, we go without it."

James grinned. "It'll be back in fine form by then. This is one of those times when having boatloads of money really pays off."

"I think that's most times."

"You're not wrong."

"I don't know what it is, but something about animal fat makes it much more satisfying than other forms of nutrition." Ted looked down at his empty plate and sighed happily. "Especially in the morning."

"Uh-huh." Christian stared down at his own plate and tried to muster an appetite.

A month ago, the two of them had found a greasy spoon that could best be described as a place designed to cure hangovers. The coffee was unusually strong, the pancakes were the size of hubcaps, and the thick breakfast sandwiches featured homemade bread. The two men had vowed to return only when circumstances demanded a strong pick-me-up.

That day had arrived.

As Christian pushed his food around with his fork, Ted raised an eyebrow.

"You suck, by the way."

Christian groaned and sank his face into one hand. "Don't."

Ted ignored that. "You've been getting on *my* case about having a drinking problem because I had a bit too much to drink one time at the Mermaid—"

"Mmmf."

"—and now you can't remember *any* of your dates with one of the hottest women in California." Ted jabbed a fork at his friend. "Oh, come on, give me your pancakes if you're not going to eat them."

Christian shoved his plate across the table and dropped his head onto his crossed arms.

"Drink your coffee," Ted advised.

"If I do, will you have mercy until it kicks in?"

"Fine."

Christian raised his head and pulled his cup over. He added liberal amounts of sugar and cream, then drank the thing down in one long, scalding pull.

TV sets had been installed in the upper corners of the walls near the ceilings, and the one facing Christian's and Ted's booth was currently playing a repeat of the morning news. They'd ignored it for the most part, but during the brief silence, something grabbed their attention.

"And next," declared the newscaster, "we have an update on the ongoing story of LA's new 'superhero,' as everyone seems to be calling him."

Chris looked up, bleary-eyed, and focused on the image. "Oh, God," he mumbled.

Ted craned his neck to examine the screen, too. "Ah, that crap again. Didn't they find out that he's actually a gangster or some shit?"

His friend shrugged.

The woman with the microphone, her face pleasantly neutral, continued, "The individual known as 'Motorcycle Man' has continued to confound both authorities and the local community. Some call him a hero. Others say he's a vigilante who has done more harm than good by interfering in situations better handled by the police."

The segment cut to a brief interview with a dark silhouette in a shadow room, which the caption identified as an LAPD officer speaking on condition of anonymity.

"Frankly," he began in an electronically distorted voice, "we're flummoxed by the whole situation. The signs are pointing to this individual being involved in the recent uptick in gang wars, and he is probably affiliated with the so-called LA Witches. The strange thing is, no one ever heard of them before two weeks ago. We have contacts in law enforcement all over the United States and even internationally in Canada, Mexico, and Europe, and none of them have any idea who those people are. No leads, no answers."

Ted shook his head as he stared at the screen. "People used to say LA was the city where all the crazy people gravitated, but I'm pretty sure we've crossed the craziness event horizon by this point. Superhero gang members. Are we still living in real life, or is this an evil virtual-reality simulation or something?"

Christian felt a faint rumbling in his brain, and he raised his fingers and massaged his temples, trying to think. The coffee was helping, but there was still a dense fog over his mental processes.

He knew that he knew something, but he didn't know what. Or did he? It was as though he was *supposed* to have knowledge to contribute to the subject of Motorcycle Man, but he'd inadvertently blotted it out by drinking too much.

Except that he hadn't drunk much lately. Or had he?

Ted refilled Christian's cup of coffee from the insulated pitcher on the table, then he pushed the plate of pancakes back, having not eaten any of it yet.

"Thanks," Christian said. He cut a bite of pancake, stared at it for a moment to gather his strength, and then shoved it in his mouth. He swallowed, suppressing his stomach's inclination to roll over with an effort, and then sighed. "I'm confused all the time lately. The whole city is going crazy, work is as ridiculous as ever, and I have only the vaguest idea of what's going on with Kera. Like, I remember my plan for when I'd meet up with her, but…"

Ted looked at him askance. "You could call her."

Christian grimaced. "I *could*, but for whatever reason, I feel like I *shouldn't*. Call it a hunch." He shook his head. "And that's the problem. Everything feels like *hunches* now. I can't remember *why* I think anything." He resisted the urge to pound the table with his fist out of pure frustration. "I've never gotten blackout-drunk in my life, and all of a sudden, there's a night that's just *missing*. I don't have a hangover, I swear! I just…"

He didn't have the words to describe this or how terrifying it was. His thoughts skittered away from certain topics, while parts of last night were a complete blank. He couldn't remember going out to dinner or having a drink.

He couldn't remember anything.

Then his phone buzzed. Blinking, he pulled it out and looked at the screen. It was a text message from none other than Kera.

Christian read it, and his mouth dropped open. He could not keep himself from responding out loud. "What the *hell?*"

Kera sat at the small dining table in the warehouse she had converted into an apartment. She was perfectly still, and her eyes were fixed on the screen of her phone—specifically, on the message she'd sent to Christian about two minutes ago.

She sighed, read it to herself for the sixth time, and wondered if she had made the right choice.

Christian,

I want you to know that I have no hard feelings about what you said last night. It was still good catching up with you, and sometime in the future, I'd like us to be friends. But I don't think I can do that right now. Not for a while. I need some time.

Take care, Kera

She'd performed the memory-wipe spell enough times by this point to be confident that it had worked. It was still difficult to control how many of a person's recollections she deleted, so she tended to err on the side of caution. In this case, she'd asked the miraculous forces to intervene in his memories somewhere before he'd noticed her.

Confusing Cevin had been one thing—a very temporary way to keep him out of danger. Wiping the memories of the gang-bangers hadn't bothered her, either. They'd been trying to kill her, after all.

But this...this was far more personal, and it made her feel vaguely sick to her stomach.

She couldn't think of any way around it, however. Christian would always have his friends' backs—and his girlfriend's back. He wouldn't let her go into danger without help and support.

This meant that if she kept trying to date him *and* use her powers, he was going to get hurt eventually. To pretend otherwise was to put his life in danger. Even if she managed to keep him from trying to help her, the odds were good that the gangs would track him down.

She refused to be the reason for his painful death. She wasn't going to be able to forgive herself for asking him out or for getting him embroiled in this mess when she knew there was something weird going on, but at least she'd done the right thing now.

Funny how the phrase "the right thing" made her want to scream, cry, and vomit everywhere. She didn't think *she* would ever forgive someone who had wiped her memory for her own safety.

But it was probably better if Christian never forgave her.

In the meantime, it was better if Christian thought *he* was the one who'd called this off. If he—and Ted—believed Kera had called things off, they might hang around and refuse to accept defeat.

No, it was better if she dropped off of Chris' radar for the foreseeable future. So many things could go wrong, and she wasn't sure she had it in her to make sure they went right.

Kera stood, left her phone on the table, and trudged over to the refrigerator. She was always hungry these days. Even now that she had learned how to channel magic only when doing a spell, she was still using an incredible amount of energy.

Like any athlete, she needed to replenish that energy. She'd dropped a lot of weight quickly and wanted to get things back under control. The first stop on that train was ensuring her ribs did not stick out anymore.

She opened the fridge door, pulled out three armloads of food one by one, and took it all back to the table. About half of it was leftover Korean and Italian food made for her by Mrs. Kim. The rest was an amalgamation of grocery store stuff and leftover takeout. She put some of it in the microwave and started eating some of it cold.

To her consternation, she could not keep her mind from drifting back to Christian.

After she'd mind-wiped him, she had promised herself that she would come clean and tell him the truth of what was going on. Perhaps explain it at dinner with the Kim family to put him at ease and so they could back her up.

But...no. That was how she *wanted* things to be. She had to act on the way things really were. She was dabbling in powers most people had never heard of and had taken the plunge into a world most people didn't understand. The Kims knew some of it, and they were willing to stand back.

She couldn't let others get hurt on her behalf.

It was the smart decision, whether she liked it or not.

Her phone buzzed to tell her she had a text, and her gut tightened when she glanced at the screen. It was Christian.

Scowling, she opened the message and read. Christian was confused as to what she meant, but he was restrained and respectful, asking for clarification and agreeing that he held no hard feelings, either.

Kera's hand balled into a fist. If he'd been a dickhead about it, cutting him off would have been easier.

She started typing a response.

Christian, you told me you didn't think it would work out. I can understand why you wouldn't want to...

She stopped, deleted everything, and thought it over.

Christian, you don't have to play nice. I know you're not interested in me. Maybe you're having second thoughts, but...

She deleted that, too.

"Ugh." Kera sighed and rubbed her face. She left the phone sitting where it was and went back to her meal. Proper nutrition might be exactly what she needed right now.

By the time eighty or so percent of the food was gone, she was crying. Again.

Dammit, this wasn't *fair.* She knew it was the right decision, so why couldn't she make her heart understand that? She had no desire to spend the rest of her life alone, yet the way things had been going, having people close to her was an invitation to catastrophe.

Kera exhaled and looked at the rest of the food. She didn't really feel like eating, but she needed all the calories she could get. The important thing was to do what had to be done.

Not what she wanted to do.

Kera tossed her phone on the far side of her bed, where it slid under her pillow, and tore into the last of her private banquet, staring at the far wall.

CHAPTER TWO

"What happened the other night," Pauline Smith said, "was unacceptable. Not to mention embarrassing."

Johnny Torrez kept his face stony, but the muscles along his jaw tightened. His black hair was slicked back, and his fingers drummed on the table. He adjusted his tie. He was of average height and lean build, and he had learned long ago that it generally suited his purposes if people underestimated his intelligence.

For instance, Pauline had recently decided that Johnny's handling of a business rival had been insufficient and sloppy. She had taken on the planning role in an attempt to show him and the two other members of their team that she had what it took to lead and he did not.

Her own efforts had also failed miserably; several groups of local gang members had fought a single member of the LA Witches at her instigation and failed to take her out.

Johnny wished they'd managed to take the little bitch out, but he knew it was good in the long run for Pauline to see that she *wasn't* more competent than he was. He wasn't failing at an easy task, as she had first assumed.

An unexpected side effect of the whole thing was that he was developing a certain respect for Pauline. He'd thought she was a lunatic in the early days of this gang, insisting they wear suits, going after yuppie office workers, but it turned out she had more of a bloodthirsty streak than he'd guessed.

"We need to act decisively," Pauline said and raised her chin. "As the newest group, we are a convenient scapegoat for the other gangs, so they have decided to blame the LA Witches' ascendance on us. Accordingly, they are doing everything in their power to keep a low profile and have informed us that they will not help."

Johnny glowered. Beside him, Lia and Sven looked like they thought they should say something, but they weren't sure what.

"We knew this would not be easy," Pauline told them. "A new social order always faces resistance. I simply did not believe it would start so soon. If anything, I see this as an indication of our success."

Johnny's eyebrows shot up. Every time he thought Pauline was making sense, she managed to throw a little extra crazy into the mix.

"We knew we would need to show the city what we can do." Pauline was standing taller now. Her eyes were shadowed from lack of sleep, but she did not allow her exhaustion to creep into her posture or speech. "We have the opportunity to do that now. We face an enemy all of the other gangs know they cannot defeat. We *will* defeat them and establish ourselves at the top of the hier-archy. Is that understood?"

Everyone nodded.

"So, what is Step 1?" Pauline asked them.

She was waiting for a specific answer.

"Research?" Lia tried finally.

"Yes. We need information about what these LA Witches can do and what works against them." Pauline crossed her arms. "So…"

"So we find some cannon fodder and see what works," Johnny said bluntly.

Pauline smiled.

"Where are we going to find cannon fodder?" Sven objected. "The other gangs won't work with us."

"None of the top ones," Johnny said. "But there are always a few wannabe-badasses who need a little extra cash."

Pauline nodded. "Exactly. I want a list from each of you with ten suggestions for tactics or technology to try against the LA Witches. Johnny, you will be in charge of recruitment. Dismissed, everyone."

Doug Lopez and Mia Angel sat in his office, reviewing their photos of the ravaged street corner they had seen the night before in South Park, somewhat east of the LA Convention Center. The whole street had been pretty well trashed. The damage was not quite up to the level of a major riot or a warzone, but it was bad enough that he felt sorry for the homeowners and the business proprietors in the immediate area. The gang had stormed down the road, wrecking things and causing general mayhem, only to be confronted by a certain enthusiast of two-wheeled motor vehicles.

The fight appeared to have been pretty one-sided. Motorcycle Man had been drawn into an ambush, which had turned into a brawl, which had turned into a massacre.

By the time they arrived—after circling back around from their semi-successful car chase—the police and the EMTs had converged on the scene and were carting away injured gang members by the dozen.

"It was *way* more people than we should have seen," Doug said finally. He leaned back in his chair and tapped his pen on the desk. "I'm wondering if, rather than the normal back-and-forth between rival gangs, this is a situation where *all* the local gangs are—har har—*ganging up* on Motorcycle Man. Like, he's declared war on crime in Batman-esque fashion, so they've formed an alliance to obliterate him."

Mia glared at her partner. "Couldn't you have come up with that brilliant insight *before* I was ninety percent done drafting the article?"

"Meh." He gave an elaborate shrug. "We'll save it for the next one. There's no way this is the end of the line on this. Motorcycle Man wasn't one of the people they carted out, which means he's still out there—which means those people have a *serious* grudge now."

One of their photographers had been passing by as Doug spoke, and he popped his head into the room.

"This shit is getting crazy, man," He said. "Like, every time I see someone in a black leather biker's outfit now, I wonder if it's Motorcycle Man."

"Yeah, I think we all are." Mia shrugged. "Part of the fun, right? Is it one guy? Is it a whole group dressing the same?"

"The other day," Duane went on, ignoring her, "I saw this *super* hot chick—like, with a figure that should not be *allowed* in tight black leather for the sake of other people's health—at this convenience store downtown. I spent some time wondering if it was her."

Doug looked up. Generally, Duane's commentary wasn't required listening, but anything that might point them toward Motorcycle Man was worth consideration.

The photographer went on. "I mean, yeah, I know it's *not* her, but wouldn't that be fuckin' cool? Superheroine biker chick, all, like, photogenic and shit? Man!"

Doug sighed. It appeared this was not going to be useful, after all. He forced a smile as Duane wandered off, then rolled his eyes at Mia.

To his surprise, she looked thoughtful.

"Do you remember," she began, snapping her fingers, "at the hostage situation at that condo, the kid said something about the biker guy's chest being all padded?"

"Uh…" Doug looked blank, then, "Sure? Yeah, okay, I remember that."

"Duane might be on to something," Mia told him seriously. "Our vigilante might be a woman who dresses down to conceal what she looks like, including her figure."

"I mean, could be." Doug ruminated on it, scratching his ear. "This person can lift cars, jump into and out of burning buildings from the second or third story, and take out small armies of gang members single-handed in personal combat. As far as I'm concerned, nothing is impossible at this point."

Mia nodded. "Yeah. Pretty sure you guys' Y-chromosome doesn't grant you *that* much more upper-body strength."

"Usually not," Doug admitted. "So, that's a new wrinkle, but does it equate to an actual *lead?*"

His partner scrunched her face. "Duane!" she shouted. "Could you come back here for a sec?"

After a moment, the photographer poked his head back into the room, looking pleased with himself. "Yeah?"

Mia asked, "This female biker you saw. Do you remember where the place was?"

"Uhh," he began, "a Korean grocery store downtown, near Little Tokyo. Umm. Kim's, I think it was called?"

Doug scowled. "That's one of the most common Korean surnames, so it might not narrow it down much. Still, thanks."

Duane returned to his work, and Doug started typing quickly on his laptop. "I'm on it. Doing a search in Koreatown would be Needle-in-a-Haystack Central, but in the area he described, we might have a shot at it. Hopefully, Duane wasn't too stoned when it happened."

The other journalist shrugged. "More things in Heaven and Earth…"

CHAPTER THREE

Kera hurried along the sidewalk. Part of her wished she was riding Zee, but she needed to work off some nervous energy, and it was probably best not to take the chance of being recognized as Motorcycle Man.

She had made the decision to keep Chris at arm's length, but that left a lot of other questions. Unable to answer them on her own, she decided to go to people she knew had some knowledge of the world she was now a part of.

The Kims.

The bell rang as Kera pushed through the shop's front door. It was an unassuming place, clean and welcoming, not as well-stocked as a full-sized store, but sufficient for most people's needs. Behind the counter was Sam, Mr. and Mrs. Kim's only son, who was sixteen.

"Hi, Kera," he called. "Here to buy something, or did you want to talk to my mom and dad?" He was blushing and obviously trying not to stare too hard at her.

Kera smiled at him gently. It had been clear for some time now that he had a crush on her, and she didn't want to make him feel any more awkward than he already did. After all, she remembered the hell of being a teenager all too well.

"Hi, Sam. Yeah, I was hoping to talk to your parents. Are they around?"

Before the boy could answer, his father appeared from the rear hall. "Kera! Hello. I overheard. What do you want to talk about? I will have to watch the store soon so Sam can do his homework, but I have a little while. Ye-Jin is here also. She's doing okay, more or less."

Kera nodded. "Sounds good." She waved at Sam as she went by. He blushed harder and waved back.

Kera followed Mr. Kim down the short, dark hallway into the family's living area.

There was a staircase leading to their quarters on the second floor, as well as a back door that opened onto a courtyard with an outbuilding. The whole domicile was cozy if minimalistic, with potted plants in almost every corner.

Mr. Kim gestured at the stairs. "Ye-Jin is resting, but she will be happy to see you. We will talk first, then perhaps you can train with her."

Kera smiled. "I'd like that." Mrs. Kim had helped her hone her proficiency in martial arts, which was allowing Kera to take on gangs without relying entirely on magic. Using magic all the time would make her lose more weight than she could afford.

They climbed the staircase and found Mrs. Kim lying on her couch.

The older woman's face lit up. "Kera! Hello."

Kera went over to the couch and took Mrs. Kim's hand, clasping it and feeling its warmth—as well as trying to sense the woman's level of health. It seemed that the work they had done two weeks ago to reverse the progress of her cancer had helped a great deal.

Mr. Kim brought two chairs over and sat in one, gesturing for

Kera to take the other. "What did you want to talk about?" he asked.

Kera paused. She didn't want to sound ridiculous, but there was only one way to say this. "The rest of my life," she said bluntly. "I…well, you might say I'm trying to come to terms with something. I don't think I can have a normal existence if I'm going to embrace my abilities. I feel like I'm heading into something I'm totally unprepared for. I don't want to bring up bad memories, but I was wondering if you could tell me more about what happened to you back in the old world."

Mr. Kim sat, rubbing his chin, then locked eyes with his wife. Kera could not tell what was passing between them, but the years' worth of understanding and trust made her ache.

She was never going to have that, was she?

Finally, Mr. Kim sighed. "Yes, it is true. Once you accept that you are something the world doesn't see very often, your whole life changes."

Kera swallowed and looked down at her lap.

"My reputation suffered in my town," Mr. Kim told her honestly. "People looked at me differently and had different…" He searched for the right word and waved his hand eventually in defeat. "Different expectations. There is a mixture of fear and admiration. They will not think of you as one of them the way they used to, but they also look to you to solve their problems for them."

Mrs. Kim nodded and placed a hand on her husband's knee. He automatically put his hand over hers.

Kera nodded. "I see. What about other people—mentors who are already part of that tradition?"

The man shrugged. "They exist, but they are rare. And you must do things their way. There are good reasons for that—tried and true wisdom—but there is also vanity. Sometimes the masters get too attached to their traditions and miss what the point was originally."

Mrs. Kim added, "Yes. Must respect what has worked before, but also understand that things change."

Kera sat in silence as she thought, chewing her lip. She kept thinking about gangs and the way they formed in a particular area and exerted control but protected their members in exchange for loyalty and conformity.

At last, she spoke. "Someone put this book out. They gathered all the information and wrote it, then published and distributed it. Someone who knew what they were talking about. They were well aware that it could and would train people to practice thaumaturgy…uh, *gatha*." She tried to reproduce Mr. Kim's pronunciation of the unfamiliar word. "Whatever you choose to call it. In every hidden world, every subculture within a culture, there's a pecking order, right? Someone who's in charge. Knowing *that*, I have to assume they'll be coming for me."

Mr. Kim frowned. "Why shouldn't they be friendly? Think about it. They should be proud of you for having learned so much on your own and all you have accomplished."

She shook her head. She supposed he had a point, but somehow she couldn't believe that was the case. "I'm not part of their group. I didn't go looking for them and volunteer to play by their rules."

It was hard to imagine that if people were tracking her down after observing her, they'd have *her* best interests at heart. Her gut told her otherwise. If there was an organization, its primary goal would be to protect itself, then its members.

She was down the list somewhere, and she didn't know how far.

Until she knew what was going on, she didn't want to trust them, and that meant she had to come up with a way of disguising herself and her activities.

"What I need," she began, "is a method to cloak my power so it doesn't, um…send ripples through the magical atmosphere? I don't know how it works, exactly; it just seems like there must be a way they can track who's using magic." She bit her lip. "It makes me think I ought to use magic less often."

The Kims met each other's gaze for a moment before they looked at Kera.

"Maybe you are right," Mrs. Kim murmured.

"Yeah." Kera nodded. "The more I think about it, the more I remember something my dad told me long ago. *'The most important thing to do with any tool is to only use it at the correct times.'* I wanted to make my magic use more efficient. Meld it with my martial arts and make sure I was enhancing my abilities, but now I think I shouldn't be using thaumaturgy when other methods will get the job done instead. That means using weapons, martial arts, and my brain before I go casting spells."

Ten or fifteen seconds of silence passed, then the Kims smiled in a subtle, understated way and nodded at the young woman.

"You are wise," said the man, "not to rely too much upon the strongest tool you have, and the one that will confuse people the most. We are proud of you for coming to that conclusion."

Kera flushed. Their praise meant a great deal to her.

Mrs. Kim added, "Come practice now." She gestured in the direction of the outbuilding, where they had a small *dojang* set up.

"Wait," her husband interrupted. "First she needs to eat something. Don't you?"

Kera grinned. "Yeah, I probably do."

***

James Lovecraft and Mother LeBlanc sat in a small black room on small black chairs before a small black table. The wall facing them was a mirror, obviously of the one-sided variety. The room was also certain to be bugged.

The two made a series of inane-seeming comments to one another, waving their hands or scratching their noses and adding half-assed sighing sounds. To an uninitiated observer, it would look like a harmless conversation. In fact, it was their way of camouflaging the incantations and gestures necessary to cast a joint cloaking spell.

Once it was complete, anything they said would sound like muffled noise to others, and their images would be similarly blurry and indistinct, meaning the federal agents on the other side of the mirror would not be able to read their lips.

Once the spell was complete, LeBlanc gave a sigh and rolled her neck, stretching. "I have my share of concerns and reservations about this whole matter," she told her companion. "We have always avoided contact with the authorities unless absolutely necessary. They come and go while we remain. Not to mention, their motivations are hardly trustworthy."

"True," James agreed, "but then again, we've unleashed something that *must* be stopped, and there's always memory-wipe for covering our tracks. The way I see it, we can either deal with their interference at a time when we most certainly do not need it, or we can handle their involvement and knowledge *after* we have our potential recruits taken care of."

"Not my preferred method, but you make a valid point."

James raised a finger. "By tagging along, we can figure out how much the feds know about us already and plan accordingly."

"Yes." LeBlanc smoothed her billowing skirts. "This will be temporary, however. I have no intention of allowing them to further contact us once the crisis is passed."

James cracked his neck. "Right? I can't believe they want to 'deputize' us. Black suits aren't your look, are they? Although..." He glanced at her, finding the mental image surprisingly agreeable.

His partner narrowed her eyes. "James Lovecraft, I can make you hurt in ways you did not know were possible."

Before he could respond, the door opened, and in walked Agents Richardson and MacDonald. James turned his eyes toward them, smiling as he canceled the cloaking spell with a surreptitious flick of his hand.

He read the agents' moods and attitudes. Though they were trying to appear impassive, subtle twists of the mouth, twitches of their facial muscles, and beads of sweat suggested the truth. They were flustered and aggravated at the failure of their attempts to surveil the thaumaturgists.

And coming into the room with them made them nervous. In other words, James and LeBlanc still had the upper hand.

Both agents took a seat, and Richardson took point.

"We all know the plan," he summarized, "but we'd like more detail on the specific procedures. Not right now, but as we go along. We need a frame of reference for what we'll be witnessing."

"We're curious about one thing in particular," MacDonald added. "From what you've told us and what our research says, the vast majority of new…talent…has been shut down. By you. But why? Why don't you encourage more of them?"

Mother LeBlanc explained with the patient, half-amused air of an adult explaining a new idea to a small child. "It has always been like this. Few qualify. Most people who have any aptitude for magic either have flaws in their grasp of the power or they are unsuited to thaumaturgy from, shall we say, the standpoint of personality and temperament."

"Right," James confirmed. "A lot of them would do something ill-advised. Vigilante justice, for example, stirring up more problems than they can solve, and in general overestimating their own intelligence."

The two agents sat in silence a moment, their brows furrowed in contemplation.

"Is that assessment objective or subjective?" MacDonald finally asked.

The thaumaturgists hadn't expected the question, and they exchanged glances. James shrugged.

Mother LeBlanc gazed at the agent. "Subjective, but let us say that our opinions have been shaped by a great deal of knowledge and experience."

MacDonald frowned. "Still, it seems unfair."

"Life isn't fair," James pointed out. "Do they still teach that to kids?"

MacDonald bristled, and her co-worker jumped in. "Okay, we see the logic to an extent. Perhaps our more, ah, *modern* sensibilities can't fully grasp what is, I'm guessing, an ancient tradition."

LeBlanc nodded. "Yes. It has always been the case that there are only a few of us. Very few."

Richardson nodded and quickly wrapped the meeting up. Clearly, he wanted to avoid an argument.

James, however, watched as the door closed after them and then exchanged glances with LeBlanc. They did not need words to know they were thinking the same thing: they would watch MacDonald closely.

CHAPTER FOUR

Pauline's mouth slowly twisted into a smile as she watched the spectacle unfolding before her. It was pitch-black in the building, and she had taken up a position in a second-floor window with a nice view of the darkened alley below. The window was cracked to allow her to hear, in addition to her wearing an earpiece linked to Johnny's microphone.

Lia had been Pauline's product acquisition specialist since the beginning, but Johnny was the one Pauline had chosen to find talent in the more recent conflict. Although Johnny's plans had so far proved insufficient to deter the LA Witches, Pauline could not help but notice that he was the only one who was taking the threat seriously.

Lia and Sven understood that looking weak was bad, but Johnny felt that on a visceral level. He understood Pauline's hatred for their opponent.

At the moment, Johnny stood facing a large group of LA's more promising young criminals. They had all been vetted to weed out the imbeciles, low-functioning psychopaths, and other unreliable types.

They all looked excited, and that excited Pauline. She folded her trembling hands together and briefly closed her eyes in pleasure.

Her reputation was growing. Not as meteorically as she'd like, but she was not a nobody or a wannabe anymore. On the contrary, whispers were going around the underworld that she was an up-and-comer in Southern California's organized crime scene.

She'd worked hard to cultivate a certain mystique. People knew her alias and had heard stories of her organization's growing power and influence, but no one had seen her in the flesh, and no one knew her real name.

Johnny addressed the troops with an easy nonchalance. "Folks, you will soon be engaging and confronting 'Motorcycle Man' with the intent of taking him out of the picture."

He was still wearing his suit, but he managed to project an image completely different from that of the high-level professional he pretended to be in their downtown office. His posture, his expressions—everything had changed to allow him to fit with the group before him.

"As you'll have noticed," Johnny went on, "that motherfucker has some balls on him, and he's done us a lot of damage. All of us, no matter the organization."

The assembled group nodded and muttered in agreement.

"Now, Vox and Dread and the Union don't want any part of this. They've gone silent. They gave up their territory to those LA Witches. That means, unless we want our streets to go to someone who doesn't even know 'em, we need to take those fuckers down *now*. I need people in Little Tokyo and Chinatown to make sure those areas don't go to anyone else in the meantime."

The assembled thugs nodded.

"You want the bad news?" Johnny asked.

There was some good-natured complaining, and a few people groaned or laughed.

"You all heard what happened at the warehouse." Johnny leaned against the wall and shrugged. "You probably *didn't* hear what happened to one of Vox's contractors, but let's just say it was more of the same, and it wasn't pretty. Those fuckers got busted up so bad they went to a hospital." Doing so, and thus going on the radar, was rare.

"So, you're going to go out in teams and wreak havoc," Johnny said. "But not all at once. Xavi, man, you okay picking a team to go first?"

The other man nodded, and Pauline sighed in the darkened room. She had been right to pick Johnny for this job. Sven's looks meant he was noteworthy in a way Johnny was not, and Lia did not switch between formal and informal speech as easily as Johnny did. Between those factors and Johnny's familiarity with most of the people here, he was the best person to get those gang members to sign up for what was quite frankly suicide.

"So, you've heard Motorcycle Man does some weird mind-trick shit," Johnny told them. "You're gonna do this fight in earplugs."

Xavier and his team frowned as everyone else laughed.

"Hey, if he can't talk to you, he can't get in your head, eh?" Johnny grinned. "If you get the chance, you're gonna either capture or kill this dude. Capturing is preferable, but if you think he's gonna escape, do what you gotta do. One thing we *do* know? You wreak enough havoc, and he'll show up."

More nods from the group. Pauline noted the air of anticipation among them. She supposed that part of it was the usual mixture of eagerness and trepidation that preceded a battle, but there was something else, too. Something almost...fannish. Motorcycle Man was a local celebrity, and they were looking forward to meeting him.

Even if it was as an enemy combatant in a fight.

The gangsters started to banter among themselves and show their weapons off to one another or tell stories of brawls and hits they'd been involved in, but Johnny snapped his fingers and called them back to order.

"Hey. Not done. One more thing; this isn't an isolated job, it's a trial. You want to get in good with the one I work for, this is your ticket."

There was a round of goodbyes, various people clapping Xavi or Johnny on the shoulder, and Johnny doing a circuit to say hello to some of the established members of the group, as well as introducing himself to new ones.

When the crowd cleared at last, Johnny ducked into the dark building and met Pauline on the stairway.

"Good." Pauline nodded at him. "You handled that well. Of course, we have yet to see how well *they* handle *their* jobs. I'll be curious to see if they succeed where we've failed." She stressed the "we" faintly. She believed in owning her mistakes.

Johnny nodded. "Maybe. Maybe not. Xavi's not an idiot. He'll pull his men out if he needs to, which means we won't be sifting through bodies to figure out what went wrong."

"Excellent." Pauline made her way past him down the stairs, letting him take up position at her shoulder. "Before dinner, I think we should observe operations at the docks."

"Sure," Johnny said easily. "Let's make sure they know we'll be able to tell when they skim some."

"Yes." Pauline's voice was cold now. "*Has* anyone?"

"One person. I figure we should take care of him in front of everyone." Johnny's hand slid beneath his coat to the familiar shape of his Beretta. "You want to do this one?"

Pauline did, but she knew it wasn't worth compromising her anonymity.

"I wish I could." She allowed her regret to show. "I'll leave it to you, however. Make it satisfying to watch."

Johnny chuckled. "Will do, boss."

CHAPTER FIVE

James Lovecraft and Mother LeBlanc sat at the table, each wearing the same calm, pleasant, understated smile. After doing some research of their own while the FBI agents conferred with their superiors, the two groups had reconvened.

This time, the venue was less suited for interrogation. They were in one of the conference rooms at the FBI's field office in Las Vegas. There was a potted plant in the corner and a coffee machine with cups and creamer and sugar.

MacDonald and Richardson had come back to announce that the two thaumaturgists had been *invited* to discuss things with the feds as equals, in casual circumstances. The Bureau had abandoned their attempt to treat them like they were suspects in custody.

It was comforting to know they would get to continue working with Agents Richardson and MacDonald since they had a decent rapport with them. Also, it meant they wouldn't have to repeat themselves to a series of half-informed new people. Accordingly, James had mentioned to them that he and LeBlanc had come to their own conclusion, which they would be happy to share with their new colleagues.

Richardson coughed and ruffled his hair before sitting down. MacDonald looked at the pair, nodded, and seated herself as well.

"Okay," the male agent began, "you said you've arrived at an important conclusion about the situation in Los Angeles but wanted to tell it to us in person, and that you and I might be ready to move against the intended targets."

LeBlanc inclined her head. "Yes, that is accurate."

The female agent was having trouble hiding her eagerness. "Please tell us what you concluded."

James took a long, slow sip of coffee, then leaned back in his chair, exhaled, and folded his arms behind his head. He delayed further by sniffing. He was choosing his words, yes, but he was still feeling the agents out, and he wanted to gauge their impatience.

Judging by the faint twitch in her expression, MacDonald was the more impatient of the two.

"Yes," James said. "We heard about the situation with this 'Motorcycle Man' person and about the outbreak of gang wars involving an outfit calling themselves the 'LA Witches.' Based on the intelligence we reviewed on Motorcycle Man's many activities over the last few weeks and our knowledge of how magic works…well, the takeaway is obvious."

LeBlanc finished once it looked like he was going to delay the rest of his response. "It is clear to us," she stated, "that all this is the work of a single person, who may be attempting to pose as a group by obscuring their identity. The coincidences are too many, and the psychic evidence for an entire coven too little for it to be otherwise."

To James' surprise, Richardson laughed. "Well, that's a relief. I'm not sure how we'd deal with a whole bunch of them. The three guys with magic among the bank robbers, not to mention you two, have been enough of a handful."

MacDonald gave him a quelling look, "Be that as it may, the FBI has asked a group of agents to join us in LA. We are to meet with them and then move against this...individual. The flight leaves this evening at 6:30. We'll be there before prime time is over."

James shook his head. "Nope. Out of the question. I insist on taking my car. We just got the radiator repaired, after all."

LeBlanc held back, remaining neutral as MacDonald and Richardson tried to argue that flying would be far faster and more convenient and that if the Bureau had to delay the operation by an extra day, there would be more opportunities for things to go wrong.

James wouldn't hear of it.

"Besides," he added, "if I tried to cast a spell and screwed it up —unlikely, but by no means impossible—the plane would crash with everyone on it, instead of only crashing a single Rolls-Royce with two inhabitants."

He had enough experience that catastrophically failing at a spell to that extent was only "possible" in the same way that it was possible to be struck by lightning twice on different occasions, but the feds didn't need to know that.

Mother LeBlanc seemed inclined to let him proceed with his deception. She shrugged, her multi-hued dress wafting in the air. "I will be riding with him."

Agent MacDonald leaned forward. "Fine. We might be willing to meet you halfway on your admittedly incomprehensible terms. If you won't agree to go now, we at least want to start prepping for the endgame by starting a smear campaign against Motorcycle Man. It will be easier to take him off the streets if the people start to dislike him."

Both thaumaturgists frowned, and James asked, "How are you going to do *that* if I might ask?"

"Oh, we have our ways." Richardson was smiling.

LeBlanc raised a hand. "That sounds like you plan to create even more publicity and draw still more scrutiny to our witch. One of our primary goals was to quiet things down and avoid excess public attention. Attacking the vigilante's reputation might seem wise in the short term, but it could be very foolish in the longer term."

MacDonald shifted in her seat, trying to control her impatience. "The immediate goal of stopping MM from wreaking havoc—or getting to a point where he can escape our scrutiny altogether—outweighs any long-term concerns of that sort. Besides, since you two were the ones who caused all of this, you aren't in a position to complain about 'increased scrutiny' of magic users, are you?"

At that, the New Orleans thaumaturge bristled and glared at the agent, but James laid a gentle hand on her shoulder.

"It was mostly my idea," he told the two of them. "LeBlanc, you were right. We still want to cover this up, not get the whole country talking about it. What we want from you is an assurance that your smear campaign will tone down attention and cause this to fizzle instead of increase scrutiny."

MacDonald made no assurances. She leaned back in her chair and watched him.

James felt it better to get LeBlanc out of the room before she hexed anyone. He smiled at the agents and stood. "We'll be at the Bellagio," he told them. "You can find us under 'Lovecraft.' We will set out for Los Angeles tomorrow morning, first thing."

He hustled LeBlanc out of the room, trying not to make it obvious.

"I am going to turn her into a frog," LeBlanc stated.

"Patience," James told her with a grin. "First, we get their intelligence. *Then* you can turn people into frogs."

"Very well. I'll wait." She gave him a look. "For now."

Kera picked at the remains of the grilled cheese sandwich before returning to her chicken fettuccine alfredo and tall glass of soda.

Non-diet soda. Calories were key.

"Thanks," she told the Kims between mouthfuls.

"Keep eating." Mrs. Kim was not impressed. "You need to gain weight."

"And energy," the man added.

Kera swallowed. "I had a double meal before I came over. Can't believe I'm putting away this much. I appreciate your generosity, but at this rate, I'm going to end up having to roll home."

"Hah!" Mr. Kim scoffed. "You know by now that isn't true. You never put on a single pound."

"True." Kera sighed, pausing to wash the current bite down with carbonated lemon-lime sugar water. "I'm probably the only woman in America ever to worry about whether alfredo pasta will put *enough* mass on my thighs."

Mrs. Kim laughed at that. She didn't laugh often, and the sound was soft and pleasant.

Her husband waved a hand. "Anyway, I have reached out to other people in the Korean and Asian ex-pat communities. Made some, ah, very discreet inquiries, and I learned something that's been troubling me."

Kera raised an eyebrow as she finished the grilled cheese and mopped up some of the white sauce on her plate with the crust.

He went on, "There have been a lot of incidents in the local news of people saying they can work magic and perform miracles all over the country. Then it all dies, and nobody talks about it anymore."

Mrs. Kim reached out to retrieve Kera's empty plates, then she pushed a tray of fruit and chocolate dipping sauce toward her. "Here, eat more. Dessert!"

Kera grudgingly accepted it. "Okay, fine. But the magic thing. Do you think it's connected to what I've been dealing with?"

"Probably." Mr. Kim shrugged. "Most of the reporters and the so-called experts they interview think it's a new nationwide fad of people claiming to have special powers so they can be famous for fifteen minutes. People hearing stupid stuff on the Internet and wanting attention. That kind of thing."

Kera frowned, thinking back to the day she'd seen *How to Be a Badass Witch* listed in Amazon's e-book store. "Right." She waited for more.

Before her husband could speak, Mrs. Kim refilled Kera's glass with soda and said, "We also have leftover spring rolls. You should eat those, too. Need healthy weight! We might not eat them, anyway."

Kera covered her mouth to disguise a burp of consternation. "I'll, um, take them home with me for a snack later, okay?"

"Okay," Mrs. Kim agreed. "But finish your fruit."

The man glared at her. "She already ate enough for five people. Leave her be, woman."

Mrs. Kim snapped something at him in Korean and he briefly went pale, then shook his head. He reclined in his chair, giving up the fight and returning his attention to the subject at hand.

"Kera. We know what is happening is not just a stupid fad. This is real. Magic, or whatever people choose to call it, exists. Its power is as much a part of our world as the water and trees and sun."

For a second, Kera felt as though a droplet of ice water had fallen on the back of her neck. "So, what does that mean? That these random people figure out how to cast one or two spells, then screw up the rest and decide to give it up?"

"No," Mr. Kim responded. "I don't think so. It means that someone is stopping their power. Turning it off like a faucet—one that can't be turned back on."

The people who published the book, Kera thought immediately. It must have been a trap from the beginning. Maybe? Would they go to all that trouble to flush out people with magical potential so they could hunt them down and snuff out their power?

She raised a hand. "Do you have all those stories saved? I want to look at them."

"Yes," said Kim. "They all say much the same thing, though."

Kera closed her eyes. "Okay, but I want to look at the dates and also the locations."

At that, the man gave a slow nod as understanding dawned on his face. "Ah, yes. Come."

He helped his wife back to her couch to rest until it was time to begin training, then he took Kera over to his computer and found the list of articles in his bookmarks.

Kera skimmed the text of each, paying attention to the temporal and geographic data. She opened a map of the US to chart the course of the stories.

They started in the East Coast states. A couple days later, they moved on to Missouri and Texas, then they proceeded into New Mexico and looped around much of the Southwest.

Once again, the icy-water feeling worked its way down her spinal column.

"Whoever they are, they're coming here," she whispered. "They're getting closer."

Kera opened the side door into her warehouse, yawned, and took off her boots. She needed caffeine and perhaps a cold shower.

"Man, eating enough food for eight people and then doing martial arts for an hour is better than a handful of sleeping pills. I'm pretty sure I did sleep better back when I was in karate and cheerleading in high school."

She made herself a small pot of coffee, enough to have perhaps two cups over the course of the next hour. Then she rubbed her eyes and tried to orient her thoughts toward the issue at hand:

How to hide a witch.

As she poured her first steaming mug, she glanced over to

where her bike sat, lean and impassive, by the front warehouse door.

"Okay, Zee," she told him. "I need to find a way to mask my magical signature or whatever. Any ideas? If so, feel free to shout them out at the highest possible volume."

Unfortunately, Zee didn't respond, and studying his sleek profile didn't give her any bright ideas. She sipped coffee and walked over to where a pile of books lay next to her bed. On top of the others was the hard-copy version she'd ordered of *How to Be a Badass Witch.*

"Hmm." She picked up the grimoire and flipped to the lengthy Table of Contents, her finger running down the page as she examined each item. To her lack of surprise, there was nothing that seemed capable of helping her.

Kera scowled and tossed the book back on the floor.

It was by design; it had to be. The mysterious individuals who'd composed and distributed the damn thing must not have wanted their erstwhile pupils to be able to hide. They'd intended to track people down all along.

A thought popped into her head. If the book was still available for sale, its publishers might have a never-ending task ahead of them. What if they only wanted to do a brief cull of America's magical talent?

Kera flipped open her laptop and went to Amazon to check for the volume in question. A search for its title yielded a couple of vaguely similar-seeming books on witchcraft, but not the one she possessed. When she went to her Orders page, the link to the book was now grayed out and dead.

"Shit." She tapped her lips, then pulled up a search engine and typed the title again. A few reviews and forum discussions popped up, some of which looked like they might be interesting. She could not find the book for sale anywhere.

After staring into space in puzzlement for a few minutes, Kera had to laugh. "I wonder if they got more than they bargained for?

Like, maybe they published the damn thing for fun, or money, or to spread the knowledge, but something got fucked up, and now they're trying to erase their tracks."

The laughter faded, and her face fell. If that were the case, these people might be even *more* dangerous.

The one thing I know for certain, she concluded, *is that I don't want them to find me. Or the Kims, for that matter. Having my powers taken away would make life simpler, but I don't know how I could go back to normality at this point. I've been helping people and making a difference. Without magic…*

She didn't want to think about that. As much as part of her just wanted a normal life, she could not imagine how painful it would be to lose her newfound abilities.

As the various possibilities, most of them not encouraging, weighed on her, she found herself wanting to text Christian.

When she'd seen him at the Mermaid a few weeks back, she'd remembered how much she enjoyed hanging out with him. It had always been easy and pleasant. They had picked up right where they left off, but now…

She missed him.

"God*dammit.*"

She needed to stop being ridiculous. No amount of missing him was going to make dating him a responsible choice. It would put him in danger. She hadn't told him he was taking on being connected to the Number 1 target of the LA gangs, and even if she had, how was *that* a fair thing to ask of someone after two damned dates?

Despite her recent workout, the punching bag hanging in her exercise area looked very tempting. She pushed off the bed, did a quick stretching routine, and launched in on the damned thing.

She hit the heavy sack with one roundhouse kick, then another. She imagined her target as herself. Would he ever want to deal with her after all the falsehoods she'd subjected him to? If their positions were reversed, she would have serious doubts about him. It wasn't wise to get romantically involved with people who contradicted themselves, led shadowy double lives, and flat-out lied about shit.

She struck the bag with a flurry of punches, elbows, and knife-hand strikes. "No," she breathed, the words barely coming out with each strike. "I can't have people close to me. Not right now. Not with the witch-hunters or whoever they are on my trail."

The bag swung back at her, and she kneed it at groin level, then gave it a good, solid headbutt. She blinked, mildly dizzy, and staggered back to her couch to collapse on the cushions where Chris had so recently slept.

Who am I kidding? I'm just trying to soften the blow to myself. There's never going to be a safe time as long as I have these abilities. Normal life is lost to me for the rest of my life, isn't it?

Lost to me.

For the rest of my...

"Wait. The rest of my life...how long *is* that?" She'd heard something somewhere, long ago—the notion that magic had its price.

At this point, the question was whether that price was a short life...or a long one.

She looked at Zee for confirmation, and something about the way the overhead lights reflected off his glossy black surface told her she needed to think about it further. Later.

Her phone rang and vibrated. It was still in her pocket, so she slipped it out and glanced at the screen before the first ring finished. It was Cevin, the proprietor of the bar and restaurant known as the Mermaid, and therefore, Kera's boss.

"Hi," she said after swiping her finger across the green icon.

"Hi, Kera." Cevin sighed. "Listen, based on how business has been, it looks like I might have overscheduled us for tonight. I'm sorry to ask this after sending you home early the other day, but would you be willing to give up one more shift?"

She thought it over for three or four seconds. Her parents had promised she'd finally be getting her inheritance, and in addition to that, she had some cash reserves.

"Yeah, sure," she agreed. "I'll be okay."

He sounded relieved. "Oh, great. I'll make it up to you soon. You should be back on normal hours next week, and I can put you at the top of the list to call in if we need extra help if you want."

She told him that going back on a standard schedule would be sufficient. Her extracurricular activities were taking up enough time and energy these days that working a bit less was probably a *good* thing.

They said goodbye, and after she hung up, Kera frowned into the distance, her caffeine-stimulated brain racing again. She really should quit at the Mermaid, but she realized she hated the idea. The work was only okay, but that seemed to be true in most places, and her coworkers were great.

And it was the one link she had to normalcy.

Her phone buzzed again, and she peered at it, then cringed.

It was a text message from Chris, who wanted to talk. That made sense. What surprised her was that he rather bravely admitted he couldn't remember why the hell he had called things off with her, so as far as *he* was concerned, nothing was final yet.

A lump formed in her throat, but she swallowed it and switched to the logistics of the situation. Much easier to deal with than the feelings.

Did he remember her address? Probably not, after the amount she'd wiped from his memory.

She definitely did *not* want him to show up at her place at random, especially if there were people looking for her.

She typed a few responses, trying out ways to get him to avoid speaking to her ever again. In the process, however, she came up with an even better strategy: to simply not reply.

He'd think of her as a total bitch, and maybe he'd decide he was better off without her.

"This sucks," she muttered. "I'm turning into a great person: rude *and* dishonest."

There was no way she could stay cooped up in the apartment with her thoughts, especially since she wouldn't even have work to distract her.

What else is there? Oh, right, she concluded, nodding. *Crime, and how half the time, it seems like I'm the only one who can fight it.*

She looked over to her bike. "You hear that, Zee? We're heading back to the front lines, and I bet we'll find some action. In LA, there's always *something* shady going down."

She didn't want just something shady this time, though.

She wanted names. She wanted to know who was sending people after her.

Since James was carrying two suitcases full of luggage and LeBlanc had none, she was kind enough to open the door to their hotel room.

"Thanks," said James, puffing as he hauled his luggage into the suite and tossed it on his bed. It was a joined complex of two rooms, and LeBlanc gravitated toward the far one. Her multicolored skirts swayed as she moved.

He watched her as she moved, seemingly untroubled. *Must be nice,* he mused, *to have everything you need hidden inside a single garment. If she could pull out everything she needed for a nice home-made chicken soup that one time, it can't be too difficult to produce toiletries and extra pillowcases, can it?*

He coughed before he spoke aloud. "I have to ask, Mother. Does the dress clean itself or something? Or do you have multiple copies of the same dress? I've never seen you wear anything else the whole time we've been on the road."

She looked over her shoulder, giving him a deliberately vague, enigmatic smile, and continued toward her room without speaking.

Typical, he lamented, turning away to unpack his things. Still, she was far older than he was and thus had had plenty of decades to study esoteric spells. It stood to reason that she would know a few tricks he didn't.

Once the pair were finished with their settling-in routine, Mother LeBlanc came into James' room.

"Shall we?" She gestured at the second-story window that overlooked the parking lot.

James just wanted to flop down on the bed and watch TV, but she was right. "Fine. We shall, momentarily. This is a nice place, and I'd honestly rather relax, but as usual, you're *mostly* right."

They left the suite and took the back stairs down to the lot, whose bright lights belied that it was well past nightfall. Then they opened the trunk of the Rolls Royce and pulled out a big red cooler, heavy enough that it took both of them to carry it back up the steps. They *could* have gone in the front and used the elevator, but they didn't want to attract undue attention.

James led the way into the room, backing in as LeBlanc managed the other end of the container. They set it down on the floor near the door that joined the two sub-rooms.

LeBlanc opened the lid; within was the makeshift scrying bowl they'd set up. Originally, they had found it sufficient to link it to the camera that was set to view the first such bowl they'd made—which was languishing in James' study in the mansion in upstate New York.

But the situation had grown more complicated, so they'd leveraged the FBI's resources to make a new device that was small enough to transport with them.

Mostly, they needed to figure out where in LA their mysterious new recruit *was.*

James cracked open a can of soda and took a sip while

LeBlanc activated the scrying spell. "All right," he said, "let's see what we can see, or something. Ugh. My wit is exhausted for the day."

"It usually is," LeBlanc remarked. "But yes."

He shot her a glare and went back to studying the bowl.

The device consisted of a deep, broad metal bowl filled with enchanted water. At the bottom lay a moisture-proof map of the area around Los Angeles. The spell they had set up before leaving upstate New York had shown them that magic was being used in Los Angeles almost every night. They needed to know where and the size of the flares. Now that they could spend some time watching the scrying bowl, they could build up a more accurate picture of what was happening.

It took some time for anything to show up, which was to be expected. Despite the book, magic still was not a common occurrence.

But then emerald flashes, a quick sequence of them, erupted in an area near the coast of Southern California in metropolitan Los Angeles, either the city proper or maybe in one of the adjacent suburbs.

"Again," said LeBlanc, "never just one flare. Our LA thaumaturgist is by far the busiest of our various potential students, and quite possibly the most practiced, at this point." She chewed her lip.

James shrugged. "Should've flown out there, then worked our way back east, but spilled milk under the bridge."

She smiled slightly, but her air of concern did not ease.

"Perhaps it was good to give them time," James suggested, trying to lighten her mood. "Healers are uncommon, and perhaps this one needed…something. Time. Space."

To his surprise, LeBlanc was frowning again, her eyes still fixed on the flashes of light. She had been so pleased by the thought of a healer, but now she didn't seem happy.

A moment later, James knew why.

"Look at that," she said quietly. "The flickers, the way they've moved over time, the tiny pulses of energy. It's like no healing I've ever seen."

James frowned as well. "What are you saying?"

"It looks like no *healing* I've ever seen," she said again, "but…it looks a great deal like martial magic I've seen before."

"Martial magic." James sank back into his chair. "That one flare we saw, though. If that had been damage-focused, it would have been on every news channel in the world."

"Most likely." LeBlanc was not one for ironclad statements.

"So, what the hell are they doing?" James murmured. He took a sip of cola and looked at her. "Do you think that this individual is 'Motorcycle Man?' Rumors have a way of being total bullshit, but the stories about that guy are so persistent that he's pretty much the obvious candidate."

LeBlanc leaned back but kept her eyes fixed on the water and the map. "It's likely, yes. Are we certain it is a man? It could as easily be a woman since the rumors suggest our vigilante wears clothing and a helmet that obscure their features and identity. Not that it matters at the end of the day."

"Whatever," James said with a shrug. "Both sexes are equally capable of being a pain in our asses."

The woman's face was grave with concentration, and her slim, dark hand rubbed her chin. "Consider, James. Since we can be reasonably certain that this is our magic-wielder, their abundance of activity suggests they are not constrained by normal strength thresholds. We may be dealing with the quality of thaumaturge who comes along once in a generation at most."

"Great." James set his can down and massaged his temples. "Let's hope they're nice. Oh, and the news. We should watch it. I've heard you can get information from the news."

Mother LeBlanc flicked her hand toward the wall-mounted big screen TV. "Sometimes," she said as the screen came to life.

A newscaster was wrapping up a story. "And that, Sandy, is

why you teach your kids the importance of using a plunger correctly. Back to you, Enrique."

Next up was the weather report, and the two thaumaturgists sat patiently through it, waiting for something useful.

James finally announced, "I'm going to look through digital print stories concerning our biker and see what I can turn up. Let me know if the TV people get around to covering the subject."

"Of course," LeBlanc assured him. "This part of the country gets beautiful weather much of the year, doesn't it?"

James fired up his laptop and soon found himself plunging down the rabbit hole. As LeBlanc watched the news and kept an eye on the scrying pool, James opened up tabs by the dozen.

It wasn't long until he found a pattern.

"Holy crap." His flagging attention was perking back up. "Everyone's linking to the same articles. The first people on the scene, every time are these two." He scrolled down. "Lopez and Angel. They've been following this guy since the beginning. They have a whole catalog of his exploits, along with eyewitness interviews, timelines of what happened, and postulations by various experts they contacted—stuff like that. They must be chasing a damn Pulitzer."

LeBlanc, who'd reclined on the couch to watch the television news while nibbling on a pastry she'd pulled out of her dress, glanced at James. "Good for them. And for us. Anything useful?"

"Oh," he returned, "all kinds of useful info, but none of it is current. If Motorcycle Man has been up to anything in the last day or so, we haven't heard about it yet. And that's what we really need. Still, reviewing all this stuff ought to help."

As he sifted through the documents and started writing down a list of the most important points, LeBlanc stared at the screen with a curious mixture of complacency and annoyance.

"Come, now, ladies and gentlemen," she said to the program, "you can give us *something*, can't you?"

CHAPTER SIX

It didn't take long for Kera to find trouble—or, more accurately, to hear about it on the scanners. Her hand went instinctively to the side of her helmet as the police radio crackled and a voice began to speak. A woman said something about a string-of-numbers in progress on a street in Westlake South.

In the middle of the communication, another voice began to overlap it. A man's voice reported a different code for crimes being committed in the southern part of the Fashion District.

As the first two voices came to an end, a third spoke up. This one, for whatever reason, spoke in plain language, reporting mass vandalism and possible arson in South Park not far from the Convention Center.

"Holy shit," Kera breathed. She slowed Zee, then checked the lanes and pulled over. The situation was clearly urgent, but her gut told her she needed to stop for a few seconds and think before she acted.

She took a deep breath and went to work deconstructing the problem logically, rationally, and systematically, as she had learned to do in her years of computer science classes.

Three sets of crimes, all of them, if the tones of voice were to be believed, major, and all occurring at once. She was accustomed to hearing overlapping voices, but not like this. Was it possible she simply hadn't been listening long enough to hear something similar? Statistically, these things could crop up.

But each of the three individually was large enough to have required planning. The odds of all three happening at the same exact time and *not* being connected…

She nodded. It was a good bet that they were.

"Well," she remarked, "we *were* expecting people to try to find us, weren't we, Zee? They did it before, twice, and now they're giving it another try. It's a trap, but we've survived traps before. If we *don't* take the bait, innocent people might suffer."

She did a quick mental review of the three locations to calculate which of the incidents was most likely to cause collateral damage. It would help if she knew what the hell the police code-numbers were referring to, and she cursed herself for not having studied and memorized that information.

Somehow, though, she expected it was all low-level shit—the kinds of mischief that would attract attention but wouldn't fast-track the goddamn SWAT team to their location. If they wanted to draw her into a conflict, they needed time to deal with her before the police arrived.

"South Park it is," she concluded. "I dunno if there's anything going on at the Convention Center, but if there is, a bunch of people might be out on the streets. In the other areas, it's late enough that most of the locals will stay in if anything weird is happening. I hope."

She checked the map app on her phone to double-check her route and find the fastest one. The assholes responsible probably wouldn't escalate too much or try to flee if indeed they were baiting her, but she didn't want to delay.

Zee buzzed, then roared as Kera guided him down the streets. They wove in and out of traffic, took sharp turns at borderline-dangerous speeds and angles, and cut through alleys and side streets as needed.

She heard the commotion before she saw it: crashes and bangs, not gunshots, more like things being thrown around and smashed, interspersed with what sounded like fireworks and people howling and whooping aggressively.

Meanwhile, the police scanner reported that the commotion was working its way east, away from the Convention Center. Two squad cars responded that they were on it and would be there shortly.

They're luring me away from the public, Kera postulated. *Clever sons of bitches.*

She inhaled and performed a series of subtle gestures with her hand atop the bike's clutch as she rode while speaking the incantations under her breath. The first was the luck charm, which increased the odds of successfully pulling off actions that might be risky otherwise. For the other, calling upon the divine powers of the universe, she channeled more energy into a slight renewal of her obscuration and glamour spells. Her enemies might not even realize that they'd caught the right person until their asses were already being kicked if she was lucky.

She would use enchantments to bolster her speed, strength, and perception as part of the physical fighting.

She took a deep breath and tried to prepare herself mentally for what was coming.

Then she rounded a corner, and there they were.

About a dozen men between the approximate ages of nine-teen and thirty-two, she guessed. They had been smashing windows, hurling garbage into the streets, lighting Roman candles and tossing them across the sidewalks, and shoving and heckling passersby. A young couple was fleeing to the nearest cross street, having made it past the gang.

Something was wrong. Kera noticed it instantly, but it took an extra second for her brain to process it. They were acting like a drunk, rowdy, stupid mob, but their eyes were bright and alert, and their movements were strangely tight and coordinated.

Yup, she told herself, *it's a trap. Still, they don't look all that tough, do they?*

"Hey," someone shouted, "I think that's him! Get the fucker!" His voice was many decibels louder than it needed to be, as though he were concerned that his friends wouldn't hear him.

Kera didn't have time to wonder why he'd yell at such a volume because while she was skidding Zee to a halt, the dozen men were fanning out in practiced and coordinated formation to encircle her like a military squad executing a precise operation.

Showtime. She bared her teeth in a crazy grin, then jumped off the bike and flung herself at the nearest attacker.

He had a lead pipe and he looked mean, but it didn't look like he had much to back up his meanness. She swung below and around his backhand strike and then brought her foot up in a head-high Tae Kwon Do kick she'd learned from Mrs. Kim, retracting it after her boot crunched against the side of his face.

"Augh!" he exclaimed and stumbled, trying to keep his feet. She hadn't hit him hard, not by her standards, but hard enough that he'd be out of the fight for the next several minutes.

Kera ducked around the toppling body and met the next two head-on as two more moved in behind her. Adrenaline was rushing through her system, but she still noticed a faint pain in her inner thigh and groin area.

"Fuck," she muttered, "high kicks are way harder to do when you're wearing tight-ass leather. No wonder the old masters wore loose outfits."

The pair of guys launching a frontal attack seemed to hesitate. It was tough to say if it was because they were afraid or because they were trying to delay long enough for the other two to attack her flank at the same time they struck.

Kera didn't give them the chance to execute their little tactic. She charged the bigger, thicker man, who didn't have a weapon, head-on. She slammed her helmet into his solar plexus and knocked him on his ass as she raised a forearm to fend off his friend's punch.

Once the second guy's fist connected with her arm, Kera seized it, looped her other arm beneath it, and swung him around while knocking his legs out from under him. She could have broken his arm but refrained; somehow, she didn't suspect that the pricks were trying to kill her or anyone else.

At least, not yet.

And she didn't want to piss them off so much that they wouldn't be willing to give her information.

She spun to face the two who'd come up behind her as three more advanced, barking and waving crude bludgeoning weapons. Everything degenerated into a chaotic flurry of violence.

The gang, whoever they were, had better discipline and coordination than the others she'd fought, yet she found herself triumphing with relative ease. They were holding back; perhaps they intended to capture her rather than maim or murder. She noticed that one had a large burlap sack, and two others had zip-ties.

They staggered aside as she recalled her karate, hapkido, and judo moves with perfect clarity and executed them with stunning speed. She hit three more with confusion and demoralization spells and they swooned and stumbled, easy prey for her fists, feet, and knees.

One man shouted the alarm. "They're not working! Plan B, guys!" His voice too was abnormally loud.

What? What aren't working? Kera wondered, but she was too busy to give it much contemplation.

A gangster tried to flee the main brawl toward a pile of junk on the corner. Kera thought he might have a weapon stashed there, perhaps a gun. She tossed a Firefly spell at his rear, and his pants and lower shirt burst into flames. The magic wasn't strong enough to pose a serious danger to him as long as he remembered to stop, drop, and roll—which he did, cursing in a high-pitched voice as he tumbled across the asphalt.

Kera punched a tall, lean man in the face, grabbed a shorter, squatter one, and threw him into a wall, and suddenly found herself standing victorious over the entire gang.

She had dropped them all in a minute, two at most. None were severely injured, but they'd all be having a really shitty weekend.

"You boys," she announced, "are lucky not to be more messed up than you are, not to mention alive. I know that someone else hired your asses, or threatened you, or put you up to this one way or another. I want some fucking answers."

She spoke in a deeper, rougher register than usual to disguise her voice. It would further their confusion as to whether she was a man or a woman. Probably.

She strode toward one of the men on the ground, who gave a whimper and tried to scuttle backward like a crab. It wasn't very successful. Kera made sure to look around for any new changes to the battlefield—guns, for instance—but saw that the others were backing away as fast as they could.

So much for camaraderie among thieves. They were going to leave their friend to be interrogated.

"Who hired you?" Kera ground out.

The man gave a tiny shake of his head.

"*Who?*"

"We don't—no one knows." He was scrabbling away, his voice far too loud. "New group!"

"Why are you fucking yelling everything?" Kera demanded. Then she saw the earplugs. She came over, grabbed his chin, and pulled one of the earplugs out, then held it up. "What are these for?"

"They said you used mind tricks!" He was trying to scrabble backward again.

She looked around and cursed. The others, the ones who hadn't been as badly injured, were looking like they were thinking of taking another shot while she was confused.

Dammit. She stood up and threw the man away from her and looked around at all of them.

"Tell whoever the fuck sent you," she told all of them, "that they have two choices. They can give up and leave town, or they can deal with me."

Then she raised her arms, called upon the powers that be, and brought down a fog of memory interference on them all. A relatively weak one; she wanted them to remember her warning and that they'd gotten the shit kicked out of them but to be unable to recall many of the details.

They groaned, squirmed, or simply breathed in response. Sirens were getting closer and louder, and it looked like a couple groups of bystanders were moving in to check things out.

As Kera went back to Zee, an object on the ground caught her eye, and she picked it up mid-stride. Another earplug.

She shook her head and tossed it aside as she mounted her bike. "Cute. I mean, I guess they get points for trying something new, but it takes more than dense foam to stop my spells."

On the other hand, it reminded her that she'd begun to get tinnitus again when there were gunshots or other loud noises close to her. She'd had it when she was shooting with her father due to the poor-quality earplugs they'd had then. Grimacing, she sped off down the darkened street.

CHAPTER SEVEN

James was annoyed.

He had succeeded in getting the agents to let him drive himself and Mother LeBlanc to LA in his car. What he hadn't considered, though, was that they would claim not to have a car of their own.

Heidi MacDonald had smirked a little when she'd explained that. "We'd planned to fly, as I told you earlier. There wasn't time to make arrangements for us to procure a motor vehicle. The SUVs we had earlier had to be returned for other agents' use."

Thom Richardson had broken into a big fat grin, meanwhile. "So, looks like you guys will have to give us a ride. Sorry! It's okay, though, we can give you money for gas. That one always gets reimbursed."

The one saving grace was that the drive from Sin City to the City of Angels took only about five hours. Having to babysit two representatives of the FBI for multiple days would have driven James completely mad.

"Okay," he announced as they sped through Rancho Cuca-monga on the 210, "we're almost there. Anyone want to pull over and get something to eat? It might be easier now before the notorious L.A. traffic hits us full-force."

Everyone agreed, and they took a short detour to pick up sub sandwiches for them all. To James' chagrin, though, the place didn't provide either picnic tables or trays that could be mounted on windows.

He turned to glare at LeBlanc, then moved on to Richardson and MacDonald. "Rule. *Do not spill anything on my seats.* In case you had failed to notice, this is a beautiful, much-beloved Rolls Royce. It's not a Honda Civic. You break it, you buy it."

MacDonald scowled. "We're capable of eating neatly, Mr. Lovecraft."

LeBlanc caught her partner's attention. "It's nothing to fret over, James," she reminded him. "After all, you have access to rather better cleaning methods than most people."

James took a careful bite of his steak-and-onion sub. "Just because I *can* clean the seats that way, Mother, it doesn't mean I want to. I thought we'd agreed that magic is best saved as the last resort."

"Too true," she conceded.

The agents both perked up. The two groups had settled into a strange stalemate, where the agents kept asking questions and trying to induce the thaumaturgists to give demonstrations of their power, while James and LeBlanc found increasingly creative ways to avoid doing so without saying *no* outright.

James suspected that LeBlanc had been teasing the two agents with her remark.

Once they finished eating, James carefully gathered the trash before tossing it.

MacDonald seized the initiative. "Okay, what's your plan for when we get into Los Angeles proper? We have one of our own well drawn out, and it might be best if you followed it for the sake of consistency and simplicity."

James turned the key in the ignition before he answered her.

"Well, I thought we'd find a nice place to hunker down, say, a swanky hotel with the most excellent accommodations, available for—"

"Good," Richardson interrupted him. "We had the *exact* same idea, minus a couple of the details. Here, follow these instructions." He handed his tablet up to the thaumaturgists in the front seat.

They glanced at the route indicated on the GPS mapping app.

"Where does this lead?" LeBlanc asked him.

"To a place where we can hunker down," Richardson said obliquely.

His partner added, "Without anyone disturbing us."

James suspected he'd regret it, but he followed their route nonetheless. If they were collaborating, they might as well collaborate.

The suburbs grew denser and more conventionally urbanized as they gradually worked their way into the city of Los Angeles. It was enormous; miles upon miles of sprawl, some of it beautiful and impressive, and a significant portion given over to urban blight. The contrasts of wealth versus poverty, often right next door to one another, were glaring. Still, the place had a certain character to it that James found growing on him as he drove deeper into town.

Although the heavy traffic and slightly hazy air disturbed him.

They reached the end of the route in an out-of-the-way residential neighborhood. No luxury hotels in sight.

"Hey," James demanded, squinting at the agents in the rearview mirror, "what the hell is this place?"

Richardson shrugged. "An FBI safe house. What did you expect? And like I said, the details aren't the same, especially the swanky part. But on the plus side, you'll get to meet a real-life criminal informant we threatened, bribed, and extorted into showing up for the occasion. Doesn't that sound fun?"

Lovecraft parked in the driveway of the old bungalow,

simmering as he thought about how ridiculous his Royce must look next to such a humble abode.

"Yup," he murmured, straightening his glasses, "I regret this."

———

Though definitely not a four- or five-star hotel, the feds' safe house was cozy and clean. Richardson went so far as to make them all a nice mug of tea from the stores in the kitchen cabinet. To James' surprise, the agent seemed to take this seriously, going so far as to steep each person's tea for a different amount of time.

Even LeBlanc looked impressed.

Once all of them had a cup, they went to the living room. The thaumaturges sat on one couch, the FBI agents on another. Between them and off to the side was a big easy chair, which supposedly would soon be occupied.

Richardson checked his phone. "Okay, good. Our informant is a guy named Lamar. He says he'll be here inside of five minutes. He's provided us with useful intel before, and presumably, he will again. He usually has his ear to the pulse of the streets. In return, we ensure that no one finds out what he's doing. You know what they say about snitches."

James nodded.

MacDonald added, "Lamar is, how should I put this, rather crass, but ignore his behavior and manners and focus on the meat of what he has to say. Also, it might help if you try to emphasize that our goal is simply to protect the good people of LA."

LeBlanc only nodded enigmatically.

Moments later, there was a knock on the door, and Richardson went to answer it. He returned with a thirtyish man, lean and rough-looking with a face that was simultaneously squinty with suspicion and calmly observant.

"Hello," James said.

MacDonald interposed herself. "Hello, Lamar. Good to see you again."

The informant snorted. "Fuckin' great, yeah, you assholes are really goddamn impressive with your expensive shades and your suits that you probably hired someone to iron this morning, am I right? Acting like you're all bad with your fuckin' black cars and your Glocks and the government covering your ass."

Richardson turned his head toward the thaumaturgists and put a hand beside his mouth as he spoke in a stage whisper loud enough that everyone could hear him with ease. "Lamar doesn't like law enforcement much."

James nodded. "So I see."

LeBlanc leaned forward and extended a hand toward the young man. "Hello, Lamar. You may call me Mother LeBlanc. How do you do?"

Blinking, Lamar's demeanor softened instantly. He shook her hand and replied, "Nice to meet you, ma'am."

MacDonald raised an eyebrow, her face quizzical.

Lamar shrugged. "You never disrespect an auntie. That's how it is."

"Well," said LeBlanc, "it's good to see that the younger generation still has some manners. Thank you for coming to talk to us, Lamar. We are here to help ensure that no innocent people get hurt. Is there anything you can tell us about the LA Witches? We have heard that they might be involved in some very bad things, and we want to look into it."

Reclining in the big empty chair, Lamar pursed his lips. "I mean, I only heard the rumors. There isn't a lot of reliable shit about them. No one knows who they really are or where the hell they came from."

"Really?" James frowned. He hadn't considered the possibility that even the gangs wouldn't know what was going on. "That's interesting. About when did they first turn up on the scene?"

Lamar scratched his nose. "Dunno. Few weeks ago, maybe? Not that long. It doesn't make any fuckin' sense, man. We ought to know more about them by now. Zero sight or word of any recruiters, weapons buyers, or any connections they got to any other gang. How the hell does a full gang come right out the ass-end of *nowhere* with high-level members, a rep, tags, and *everything?*"

Lovecraft and LeBlanc nodded at one another.

The informant railed on. "Like, it's different from what happens with most newer gangs that are making power plays all over the place. There's this outfit; people are calling them 'the Startup.'" He chuckled at that. "Word is they're run by this Russian business chick people are calling 'Catherine the Great,' but nobody knows who she is. They're doing the usual stuff: rubbing shoulders with high-end clients, buying up two-bit gangs to do their dirty work, shaking down local businesses, that kind of shit. With the LA Witches, it's all different. Doesn't make no sense."

Everyone else nodded, appreciating his words.

LeBlanc caught his eyes again. "Lamar, we are curious. What have you heard about this person known as 'Motorcycle Man' in the media?"

"Oh." Lamar nodded. "Yeah, people been talking about him even more than the LA Witches. I mean, that's because *his* shit's all over the news, right? Most people don't know about the Witches, but everyone gossips about *him.*" He shrugged. "I don't know anything personally. Probably some crazy son of a bitch who thinks he's goddamn Batman, just taking steroids, and then people who can't remember what the fuck they actually saw. Like, people in a car crash? A burning building? Some dude bleeding out? Yeah, sure, I'll believe *those* guys that Motorcycle Man actually *flies.*" He gave a huff and shook his head, then laughed. "*That's* some witch shit, huh?"

LeBlanc and James did not need to exchange glances, and James noticed that both FBI agents suddenly had the air of hunting dogs on point.

"Wait a fuckin' second," Lamar said. "You think he's one of them? Because the people fightin' the witches *do* say they're all leathered up." He frowned at them. "You're not tellin' me…"

"We have no idea," LeBlanc said simply. James marveled at her ability to tell the truth without making it seem scandalous. "We came here to ask questions about the LA Witches, but it seemed unwise not to ask about something else that was so newsworthy."

She did not address the issue of magic, and James was willing to bet that Lamar would forget whatever suspicion he'd had as soon as it came time to leave.

They spoke to him for another few minutes. He mentioned that multiple gangs had a hit out on the mysterious vigilante. Word was, they were drumming up muscle to kill him or otherwise take him out of the picture before he started intruding on their turf instead of just rescuing people from burning buildings.

"It'd be somthin' if he was in with the Witches," Lamar mused, shaking his head. "It'd explain why the Startup is gunnin' for him, too. They're the ones the witches have fucked with the most." He scratched his head.

MacDonald asked James and LeBlanc, "Do you need anything else?"

"Yeah," Lamar echoed, "do you? I got stuff to do later."

LeBlanc smoothed her dress. "No, thank you. You have been very helpful, Lamar, and we appreciate your coming to talk to us. I believe everything will be all right."

"Okay." He stood, shook the thaumaturgists' hands, and gave a barely polite nod to the FBI agents before Richardson escorted him out.

Once they were alone again, the feds looked at their guests, waiting to hear their assessment.

James cleared his throat and smiled. "Well, that was helpful, wasn't it? We found out exactly what we needed to know."

"Namely," LeBlanc finished for him, "that Motorcycle Man is almost certainly the sole member of the LA Witches."

MacDonald's eyes widened with growing eagerness. "You're sure?"

LeBlanc smiled. "Once you accept the reality of miracles, it's the only logical explanation."

Richardson and MacDonald left soon after Lamar, telling the thaumaturgists that they would be gone for about two hours, coordinating surveillance activities with other FBI agents across the city.

James and LeBlanc did not need to confer to agree that they were likely being surveilled within the house. They began a synchronized cloaking spell to ensure that the feds would not be able to hear them, regardless of what sorts of bugs or other technology they might have had planted in the safe house. After a moment's effort, a magical buffer formed around them, invisible to most but obvious to masters of thaumaturgy.

"There," James stated, dusting his hands off. "Much better."

Mother LeBlanc wasted no time. "It is clear to me what we must do, James. Are we in agreement?"

He frowned and reclined on the couch, folding his hands behind his head. "It's less clear to me, I'm afraid. Which, I suppose, suggests we're not necessarily in agreement yet. Let's hear it."

She had seated herself on the big chair where Lamar had been earlier and now crossed her legs, the colorful skirts swishing in the air.

"You know the answer. It is clearer than before. We must blot out this person's power. They are a loose cannon, more dangerous than any other we've encountered on this trip. Not only is the so-called Motorcycle Man clearly someone with exceptional ability, and therefore the ability to do greater harm, but they've drawn so much attention to themselves that everyone in the second-largest city in the United States is talking about their exploits."

James was more surprised than he had expected to be. "Are you certain? This is your healer."

"Not *my* healer," she said quietly. She folded her hands in her lap and looked at him. "James, I do not suggest this idly."

"I know," he hastened to assure her. He *did* know, after all. He could see the pain in her eyes. "A person this powerful, however…shouldn't we *try* to get through to them?" When she had no ready answer, he pressed his point. "This person is doing *good* things with their power, aren't they? Helping people? Not to mention, they're *strong*. A true prodigy. It would be a shame to waste talent like that, wouldn't it?"

"Better a waste of talent," LeBlanc retorted, "than our kind being exposed. James, we saw the magicians at that bank. The more people know about magic, the more will use it, and many will use it badly."

He sighed and sat up. "I knew you'd say something like that. Yes, traditionally, caution is to be prioritized over everything else. But…"

LeBlanc ran a finger over the smooth lines of her chin. "I don't think that this person is evil, James, but they *are* likely to be foolish and ignorant. Most people don't have organized crime trying to assassinate them, do they? That bespeaks a certain flaunting of prudence."

"I will concede that no matter what else happens, we cannot allow another assassination attempt to occur. If it does, then the way things are going, things will spin out of control beyond our ability to contain them. So, what we ought to do is—"

"Shut them down," LeBlanc interrupted.

James coughed. "What we *ought* to do is get them clear of the current mess they're in. As I said, it would be sad to waste all that potential. Have you considered what might happen if we were to rehabilitate them? Allow them to keep their power, but ensure that they know better than to use it unwisely?"

"That," said the woman, "is easier said than done. Most of what we have heard suggests that this individual is under a great deal of strain, much of it self-inflicted by their own foolish decisions. If a person with that much magical talent cracks, the results will be disastrous for everyone."

"Yes, so we remove the strain," James protested. He wanted to tear out his hair. "Bring them into the fold, and we can avoid them cracking. Recruit them for an internship under our close supervision and experienced guidance. Wasn't that the goal from the beginning? Wouldn't it better to salvage something from this experiment?"

As LeBlanc silently weighed the pros and cons, an idea occurred to James. He didn't *like* it. In fact, it was borderline-painful to consider, but arguing for it might be his best shot to sway his friend to his way of thinking.

"What if we ask the council what they think?" he suggested. "Float the idea before them and hear what they have to say. Agree to submit to their standards, which, when you get down to it, are about the same as ours, explaining that the aim is to temper Motorcycle Man's overly proactive and reckless tendencies and instruct them in the smart way of doing things. If they turn out to be unteachable, then and *only* then will we block their power, memory-wipe them, and dump them back into normal life."

Normally, it did not take LeBlanc long to process information or decide on a course of action, but she was quiet for nearly a full minute.

"So be it." Her voice was quiet. "We will contact the others and allow them to weigh in before we make our move."

Lovecraft smiled. "Ma'am, you've got yourself a deal. And in the meantime…"

She raised an eyebrow at him curiously.

"I say we start asking around in motorcycling groups," James said. "The details on the type of motorcycle are maddeningly few. I know there's magic in play, but it's likely they've managed to see *something.*"

CHAPTER EIGHT

By the time Kera got to the Mermaid the next day, she was in a terrible mood. Everything annoyed her, from the traffic to her gloves snagging on her coat. Winter had settled into the endlessly gray phase, which did not impress her either.

She took a moment outside the back door to compose herself before going in.

"Remember, Kera," she said, mimicking her mother's voice as best she could, "you're a witch, not a bitch."

She punched in the combination and stepped into the shadows, only to hear Cevin call her name. The manager came to his door when Kera poked her head in.

"Hey," Cevin said. He looked worried.

Kera did her best not to look as annoyed as she felt. "What's up?"

Cevin grimaced. "I tried to call you, but you must already have been on your way. We're still absolutely dead out there. The violence has scared people off, and the few people who *are* coming in are not the clientele we want."

"Oh." Kera felt a flicker of annoyance that was quickly swamped by relief. She didn't want to be left alone with her thoughts, including the question of how to find the gang that was putting out hits on her, but she also didn't want to have to fake-smile at customers for eight hours. She shrugged. "If you need someone to give up a shift, I definitely can."

Cevin ran a hand through his hair. "I...don't want you to feel obligated. You've really taken one for the team, and—"

"Cevin. It's fine. Seriously." Except it didn't *feel* fine all of a sudden. Kera realized she just wanted to get out of there before she embarrassed herself by looking fearful. She took a deep breath. "I'm, uh...I *am* going to take a bathroom break before I drive home, though. Bye." She whisked off before he could see her expression.

In the bathroom, she splashed cold water on her face and considered it in the mirror. She didn't feel like herself today. Between the black hair and the eye makeup, not to mention the shadows under her eyes, she looked like someone who knew the walls were closing in.

Someone who might not be the hero of this story after all.

Things had gone so well at first, but now she had the sense that the smooth sailing had been the calm before the storm.

On the way out, she bumped into Stephanie.

"Hey." Kera smiled and kept walking.

"Hey," Stephanie called to her back. "You okay?"

"Yeah." Kera knew she had to look back to show Stephanie things were fine. She plastered a smile on her face. "I am. Promise."

"You don't look okay," Stephanie said bluntly. She came closer. "Look, Kera...never mind. You said you were fine. I don't want to pry. I just want to help if you need help."

"I don't mind giving up the shift," Kera assured her.

"Okay." Stephanie nodded. She hesitated, then came to offer Kera a hug.

Kera, to her surprise, found herself hugging the other woman tightly. When she pulled away, there were tears in her eyes, and she swiped at them angrily. "God. I'm sorry."

"Is it…the guy?" Stephanie asked.

Christian. She'd almost managed to forget about him. Kera squeezed her eyes shut and counted to five in her head, trying to regain her composure. When she opened her eyes, Stephanie was staring at her sympathetically.

"Yeah," Kera said tightly. It was the only part of this she could even halfway explain.

"Oh, honey, I'm sorry." Stephanie reached out to squeeze her hand.

"It's for the best," Kera told her. "We, uh, we weren't going to work."

Stephanie nodded quietly, then shot a quick glance over her shoulder at the room, but as Cevin had said, the place was dead. The recent crime spree had done a number on the number of people wandering around Little Tokyo.

Kera sighed. "I should go. Unless you know any way to make sure a guy doesn't show up at your house."

She was joking, but Stephanie's eyes widened. "Oh, no. Are you okay? Did he get creepy?"

"No. No!" Crap. It was the logical conclusion after what she'd said, but it would not be fair to Christian to let the people here think he was creepy or violent. "Promise. It's just, I don't want to see him. I know it isn't going to work, but I don't think he feels the same."

"Aha." Stephanie looked dubious. "Well, you know we've got your back if you need us."

"I do." Kera gave her a smile, this one slightly less forced. "I really *should* go, Steph, but seriously…thanks."

"Anytime." Stephanie smiled at her. "You should go out tonight. Get moving. Dancing, maybe? It helps, I swear."

"Uh-huh." Kera's smile this time was genuine, amused by the

idea of dancing her way through LA's two-bit gang members. "See you soon."

Pauline Smith's impassive mask of professionalism was slipping, and even she knew it.

"What the *fuck* is going on?" Her voice was a snarl. She had worked hard to all but eliminate her native Russian accent, but it was creeping back into her speech. "We walked them through this. They had all the training they fucking needed." She clenched her fingers on the table's edge.

"They had instructions! And there were *twelve* of them!"

There was silence. Lia and Sven were sitting as still as mannequins.

Johnny, on the other hand, was lounging in his chair. He shrugged. "We were pretty sure the first few groups were going to get their asses handed to them. That was the point of bringing in these guys—to try a few things."

Pauline shot him a glare, and Lia flinched.

Johnny didn't. He stared Pauline down. "You saw this happen before. I told you what I saw." He shifted uncomfortably. "What I remember of it."

"You sure you're not just enjoying watching other people go through it?" Pauline snapped at him.

"Oh, I am." His grin looked almost like a snarl. "You thought I was full of shit when I came back here a few weeks ago with my car busted. You didn't want to believe this was as bad as it is, but you're starting to fucking get it now."

Pauline had regained some of her composure. "'It,'" she repeated precisely. "Explain, Mr. Torrez."

"Miss me with that shit." Johnny stared her down. "We keep thinking the problem is prep-work. Throw enough people at it, train 'em well enough, it'll be fine. Truth is, this bitch can take down more people than they should be able to—and when they decide to bug out, they're just gone. We have to assume the next few groups are going to get their asses handed to them too."

Pauline's eyes flared at his disrespect, but she was accepting his words, no matter how much she might not like them.

She turned back to the board for a moment, looking at the company diagrams she had set up—all blandly labeled in case they fell into the wrong hands. She tapped her fingers on her arms.

Then she turned back.

"Very well. Johnny, get the next groups ready to go. Shelve the ideas from Sven and Lia, and make the next one trap-focused. Something immobilizing."

Johnny nodded.

"And next time," Pauline said, "I expect you to be there to oversee it personally."

"I *was* there—"

"In the fight," Pauline snapped. "I'll handle surveillance."

Johnny's lip curled, but before he could respond, she'd moved on.

"Sven."

The big man tensed.

"What the goddamn fuck were *you* doing?" Pauline demanded. "Someone of your experience would have been useful in supervising the whole operation. You should have volunteered. Do you think I respect employees who only do the bare minimum? Successful organizations are the ones whose workers go the extra mile *without having to be asked*."

Sven's mouth opened and closed soundlessly like a fish's. Johnny saw that he was trying to figure out whether to remind her that he'd been told to stand back on this operation. In the end, he wasn't brave enough. He just nodded.

"And Lia," Pauline snapped, her tone still cold and jagged, "you of all people know that results are what's important. I asked you for ideas, and I still haven't seen any fucking good ones. We have several unexplained phenomena going on, and I expect you to have answers on my desk by midday *tomorrow* about how this bastard is pulling those off. *Am I clear?*"

Lia had gone white. Johnny thought she looked angry, but in the end, she only nodded.

A heavy, awkward silence hung in the air while Pauline took three deep breaths. "Very well. To continue with the agenda, reports. Now. Lia, you start."

Each of them spoke in turn. There wasn't much to tell, but the illusions of normalcy and routine it invoked helped them relax.

Pauline folded her hands one last time. "Good. We are moving on to the next phase. The pushback has taken an unexpected form, but it's nothing we can't handle. Sven, Johnny, go make a plan—a good one. Then brief the next group. Lia, you have research to do."

Pauline waited until the three were gone, then she dropped into her chair and let out a stream of expletives under her breath. English might be adaptable as a language, but when the time came to swear, it had *nothing* on Russian.

She was done hand-holding. She had allowed Lia and Johnny to convince her that their setbacks had been unavoidable when she should simply have held the line and demanded results.

Well, she'd start now.

As for Sven...

He was going to have to step up. At the start, Pauline had believed Sven had more of an idea of what was going on than Johnny. Less of a challenger. Knew what was expected of him. Didn't make waves.

He also didn't take risks. If he didn't start being serious about this, Pauline wasn't sure he would get through this operation with his head still attached to his shoulders.

She had no use for people who couldn't get things done.

Johnny stood before the assembled mass of LA's least-fine, as it amused him to think of them, with Sven at his side. The pair of them looked quite different physically, but given their identical dark suits, dark glasses, and ties, it was easy for the group to look up to them as important and respectable middle managers.

By now, the group had heard what had happened to Xavi's team. The ones who were present were uneasy, and several had not come. Johnny had noted who. Many others looked like they wanted to run out on the job.

He'd take care of that immediately after this meeting.

In the meantime, he exchanged looks with Sven, who was hanging back, then looked over the assembled group. They had gathered in a grassy, weedy lot hidden between four- and five-story buildings and conveniently surrounded by a tall, rusty fence.

"So," Johnny said, "earplugs don't work. Now we know."

There was a round of nervous chuckles, but the sound died quickly. They were too tense to be amused.

"What *also* doesn't work," Johnny added, his voice a whiplash, "is a group of grown-ass men getting beat down like little girls on a schoolyard."

There was total silence. All humor had died. Xavi's group had gone from embarrassed to mutinous.

"You want to explain to me what happened?" Johnny asked them.

In response, Xavi rolled up a sleeve to show the marks on his arm. It was early for the bruise to be showing all the way, but from the spread and color, it was going to be a doozy. Whoever had hit him and however they'd done it, the blow had been *hard*.

Johnny didn't waver, however. He just waited. A bruise wasn't an explanation. It was time to start employing Pauline's methods, he felt.

"This wasn't us folding," Xavi told him furiously. "Fucker hits *hard*. He's too fast."

"So, we're dealing with a kung-fu master, is that what you're telling me? Someone with mystical powers? Did you see a long white beard?"

Xavi glowered at him. "Fast enough for it."

"Then we need to be faster," Johnny said. The 'we' was a concession. He looked around. "Who here is faster than Xavi?"

There was a pause, then a few people raised their hands. One or two even stared at Xavi while they did.

"Good. You go next." Johnny didn't spare a glance for Xavi. "I want you on your fucking A-game, you got it? No drinking between now and then. No drugs. No injuries. We know from Xavi's group that this bastard prefers less crowded places, and they respond quickly."

Everyone nodded.

"What we're going for is a trap," Johnny told them. "Something to keep them immobile." He held out a hand to Sven without looking over, and the other man put a sheaf of papers in it. Johnny handed it to a young man who seemed to have assumed command of the second team. "Those are the specs. We'll go tomorrow night to give you some time to prepare. You bring this motherfucker to us in chains if you have to."

"And if they don't?" Xavi asked bitterly.

"If they *do*," Johnny said coldly, looking at him, "they'll have their fucking careers made. If they *don't*, they'll be nobodies."

"Don't forget," Xavi said, "this motherfucker is looking for *you* too."

One of the team members raised his hand. "I can't remember everything I saw, but I'm pretty sure Motorcycle Dude is a *chick*. No shit, bro."

Murmurs went around the group, and three or four of the South Park group agreed. The others didn't know or weren't sure, and the men who hadn't been there snorted in derision.

Sven just chuckled. "That would be a nice change of pace, a beautiful woman in tight leather instead of some ugly fuck. Maybe not beautiful if she's always wearing that helmet, but whatever. Duty calls. Either way, they won't be alive long enough for it to matter."

When he heard Sven say that, Johnny squinted into the distance as something rumbled within his brain—a memory trying to come out but unable to, like a scene from a dream that had been vivid five seconds ago but was now fading.

It had been like this from his first experience with Motorcycle Man—or the LA Witches, whatever they called themselves—and it frankly scared the shit out of him. Brain damage would mean the end of Johnny Torrez. He had always prided himself on his inborn smarts and his accumulated street smarts. They'd saved his life many a time.

It didn't *seem* like brain damage. Just, every time he was supposed to have tangled with this person, he couldn't seem to remember much about it.

He wasn't going to think about it now.

"Whatever this tech is," he said bluntly, "first one to figure it out is gonna be fucking rich. You'll be set for the rest of your life if you do. The bad news is, you're going up against our acquisition specialist, and she's good at finding answers, so I'd get a move on."

He didn't mention that this was how Xavi could restore his reputation. The other man was smart enough to have caught that on his own.

"We'll be there to oversee tomorrow night," Johnny said. "See you then. Oh, and one more thing… We want this fucker to answer some questions, sure. But if push comes to shove, we wouldn't be too upset if they wound up dead."

He left without another word, Sven following at his shoulder.

Gloves off, Johnny thought to himself. *Now we wait.*

Kera had borrowed some books from the Kims, and as she plunged into the first, she found herself stumbling onto things that might prove far more useful than she would have expected.

The book was written in an archaic style, much like the grimoire— perhaps a relic of an earlier time given a brush-up. If she hadn't known better, Kera would have lumped the Kims' books into the category of folk tales from the old country, on a level with her grandmother's belief in the fae.

Although come to think of it, maybe her grandmother had been right. After all, magic was real.

Kera decided to shelve that for now. If she went down *that* rabbit-hole, she'd still be researching when the gangs came to finish her off.

She picked up half a grilled cheese sandwich and turned the pages with her clean hand as she snacked.

The author of this book focused on a general overview and the historical background of magical scholarship, rather than the nitty-gritty of magical activity. They also mentioned enough topics and keywords that Kera had a starting point from which to conduct further research.

An hour and two grilled-cheese sandwiches later, the book lay face-down beside her on the bed and her laptop sat open on her knees. She'd spent the last hour reading up on the properties of iron and silver, both of which had been mentioned in *The True Nature of Magic*.

So far, the problem was that both metals inhibited magic instead of shielding it. She wanted to hide her magic, but it sounded like those metals might block it instead.

Essentially, she would be left shooting blanks.

A pair of notions occurred to her simultaneously. One, she might be able to add small amounts of iron or silver to her wardrobe. Not enough to shut down her power altogether, but enough to dampen her magical signature and prevent prying eyes from noticing it. Two, she could try using spells to detect spells on herself. The grimoire contained a spell for scrying. She had used a modified form of it when she was seeking information on the terrorist incident she'd resolved not long ago.

"Yeah, that's potentially doable." She looked at Zee, who crouched in his place, silent but looking slick, as usual. "Hear that, my man? We could, say, cast a charm that sustains itself in one particular location, then go somewhere else, try to locate it by scrying, and see how well it turns up with given amounts of anti-magical substances in the way."

Or perhaps the Kims could help. This book conceptualized some of the principles of magic differently, so it stood to reason that there might also be different *spells*—either ones the author of this grimoire was unaware of or that they had chosen not to include.

"Fuckers," Kera muttered under her breath.

Her language had gone downhill since she'd started using magic, or more accurately since she'd started seeing more of how the worst people in the world behaved. Some of that could only be properly described with expletives.

She opened the second book, this one on Eastern mysticism, and began poking around for things that looked useful. Some of what she read reminded her of stuff she'd seen in old kung fu films when she was a kid—lots of references to chi, which modern science scoffed at.

A few weeks ago, she would have scoffed as well, but now she knew better.

"Okay," she mumbled, "but before we plunge into all that stuff, how about we start by looking at clothes that could be comple-mented by iron studs or silver fringes? Hell, I could sew thin strips of the stuff into the lining if I have to. Just have to make sure it doesn't constrain movement....or throw off my balance, come to think of it."

The idea appealed to her. Metal studs in her clothing had a medieval vibe to it, not to mention she was a biker.

"You like that idea, Zee?"

He didn't respond, but she suspected he approved.

"Now," Kera said, "on to Subject Number Two." She nodded gravely at Zee. "Namely, how to track down the motherfuckers who are sending people after me."

She had considered the possibility that the ones tracking her might be behind all this, but she didn't think so. So far, they didn't seem smart enough, and she hadn't seen any indication of them using magic against her.

She wanted to be done with them soon, though, so she had only one focus: whoever was coming to find her.

CHAPTER NINE

Ben crouched and put the final touches on the trap.

He felt like a James Bond supervillain, to be honest. This trap was way over the top—or to be more accurate, the *multiple* traps he'd set up were way over the top. He wasn't sure what was going to work, so he'd made a few different ones, each with multiple restraint mechanisms.

Motorcycle Man was fast, so they all involved a slowing element. One had a cloud of pepper spray, while a second had a bucket of honey, some to go on the floor and some to coat the guy. Ben figured you could slow someone down by restraining them or by distracting them.

So far, it didn't seem like anyone had tried to take down Motorcycle Man with any tactics other than brute force.

Clearly, that hadn't worked.

Once the slowing mechanism was in place, it was time to address Motorcycle Man's second major strength, which was his physical strength. Or *her* strength. Ben couldn't believe they were dealing with a woman, but this whole thing was weird. He figured it didn't much matter either way.

In either case, they needed something stronger and more

durable than another human to hold Motorcycle Man in place. Ben was going with wire nets and metal bars, the second of which he'd had to buy from a very dubious private club at an exorbitant rate.

He'd made sure not to touch it.

Then, the finale: something that would kill Motorcycle Man automatically unless one of the team members stepped in. That had been Ben's idea. It seemed like people just gave up on fighting Motorcycle Man after he'd talked to Xavi's group about it. They couldn't remember most of it. In fact, the only thing they *did* remember was that they didn't know why they were there or what had happened to make them hurt so much.

The rest of Ben's team thought Xavi was a lying little bitch who just didn't want to admit he'd gotten beaten to a pulp.

Ben wasn't so sure. He didn't know how Motorcycle Man would have pulled that off, but he knew it had happened more than once, and he didn't want his plan to go to hell even if he lost his mind.

Speaking of which, he was planning to stay in the shadows tonight. Ostensibly, it was to work the spring-loaded-knife mechanism if it malfunctioned, but actually to see if he could figure out what Motorcycle Man did to people.

Was it a drug? It had to be a drug.

He dusted off his hands and stood. His choice of location was risky—the same warehouse where Motorcycle Man had beaten up almost two dozen assorted gang members last week. Whoever this bastard was, they probably knew the inside of this place pretty well.

On the other hand, it didn't look like they'd been back since then, and after the police and rescue workers had come through, it was pretty torn up. Motorcycle Man would expect some differences, and it would be difficult to see the traps in the rubble.

Ben gave a last nod and headed for the exit, where two of his team members waited.

If he could pull this off, he was going to be set for life.

<hr>

Alone in her apartment, Kera rolled her neck and started a series of stretches. She had spent a good portion of the previous evening carefully testing her range of motion in her leathers, and despite a few ungraceful moments, she was doing well and didn't anticipate any surprises similar to the one she'd had two nights ago.

She was, however, glad she didn't have any extra equipment hanging between her legs. The leather pants didn't leave much in the way of room.

"I hope no dudes get the idea to emulate Motorcycle Man," she murmured and smiled slightly.

She had gone out after her practice but had found nothing too worrisome.

She was fairly sure that meant her opponents were regrouping, and she didn't like that. Whatever they came up with next could hurt more people, and if they realized that was her weak point...

She didn't like to think about that.

It was frustrating in the extreme that she hadn't been able to get any names out of the gang members who had attacked her. If she were honest with herself, she had gone into that fight unprepared. She hadn't known how to interrogate someone; she had just figured she'd *do* it, and that would be that.

That strategy—which wasn't a strategy at all—hadn't worked. It was also starting to catch up with her during the fights. Sure, right *now,* they couldn't do any meaningful damage to her, but what if they found a way? She hadn't understood how their world worked when she attacked the man with the Mustang.

She needed to take them out, and her window for doing so

was shorter than she'd like. The next time she ran into some hired underlings, she *had* to figure out who had hired them.

That need had led her down a rabbit hole of unpleasant research related to interrogations. Fortunately, she didn't have time for most of the *really* nasty techniques, so she didn't have to decide if she would use those.

It looked like her best bet was to intimidate them into believing she would know if they lied to her. She wanted names. Failing that, she wanted locations. She would have to get that and get out.

Once her stretches were done, she fixed herself a snack. A few weeks ago, she would have considered the amount of food an unbearably heavy meal, but things had changed radically since then. She didn't know if she was going to run into anyone tonight, but if she did, she wanted to have plenty of energy to work with.

Accordingly, she wolfed down a can of macadamia nuts, a plain avocado, and a bagel with cream cheese. Then she put on her leathers and her helmet and wheeled Zee out the door of her warehouse.

Riding around calmed her, at least at first. It was easier to let her mind settle when she had to pay attention to the road and the feel of the bike beneath her.

As had become normal at this point, she found more people than usual looking at her. People tended to look at motorcycles because the engine sounded different, and they caught the eye more than a car. Plus, in Kera's experience, most people secretly wanted a motorcycle.

Now, however, people's eyes lingered, and they perked up when they heard a motorcycle. After all, anyone in all black on a black bike might be Motorcycle Man.

It was funny to watch their eyes go out of focus and flick away. Her spells made it difficult to see or notice Zee or her. So far, they also seemed to work well on cameras, but Kera knew she couldn't count on that continuing. Sooner or later, she'd need a more comprehensive strategy.

One problem at a time, MacDonagh.

She had been riding around for nearly an hour and was beginning to think there wouldn't be any activity tonight after all when the scanner crackled to life. They were reporting a break-in…at the textile factory where Kera had begun the fight several days before.

Alarm bells went off in her head.

After the last spate of activity there, the police were going to be quick to respond, and the people she was fighting didn't want police involvement any more than she did. That meant this was either copycat kids wreaking havoc…

Or the real break-in was somewhere else.

Kera pulled over to spend a moment thinking. The last thing she wanted was to crash while wrapped up in thought or not think the problem through because she couldn't focus.

Everything told her this was a trap. They had regrouped and they were trying again, which meant there was a possibility, however unlikely, that they had found a way to take her down.

And if it *was* a trap, and they *didn't* want any interference…

She knew exactly where they would go. She pulled back out into traffic at the first opportunity and hung a U-turn soon after, heading back toward the warehouse where she had set her traps.

She doubted any of hers were still active, but she had *no* doubt that there were new ones. As she drove, she prepared herself with luck spells and others to help her remain unnoticed. She decided to stack the deck by showing up from an angle they wouldn't expect.

Driving this route again made her think of Christian, and she tried to squash the emotions. It had not been a good thing that he had been involved in the event several days back, and it was good that he was not here now.

As she drove, she tried to mask the sound of her motorcycle, though she had to be extra careful of other drivers once she had done that. It was difficult to tell if it was working, but no heads were turning.

She drove past on a nearby street, one with a good view of the warehouse. She couldn't see movement, but she had a sudden memory of a bullet tearing through one of the windows as she left the last time.

This was where the shooter would have been. She looked around but didn't see anyone there...yet.

Time to go in. She wanted to leave Zee somewhere he would help her make a quick escape, but not somewhere they'd have advance warning that she was here.

Of course, that was assuming she was correct about the trap, but her hunches had been good so far.

She parked Zee on a side street and crept back to the warehouse, moving as quietly as she could in the dark. The warehouse had been damaged internally by the fight, and emergency services must have done some damage of their own. Kera wasn't sure if it had been amusing to them to play demolition crew or if they had hoped to keep other people from doing something dangerous.

Either way, it was worth expecting that the floor wouldn't be stable under her feet and that none of her spells were in effect anymore.

She amplified her hearing magically, not only compensating for the motorcycle helmet but also giving her a keener sense of everything around her. There were people inside, but she didn't know how many or where they were.

Shit, what's the magical version of night-vision goggles?

Stealth hadn't been her forte so far, mainly because she had charged into situations with guns and explosions. She hadn't needed to be stealthy. This time, she wanted to think things through.

There were two main places she could picture people hiding in the warehouse: in the alcove underneath the stairs, which were metal and thus not entirely demolished, and in the shadows along the far wall, where a tumbled-down section of wall allowed someone to hide without sticking out.

She amplified her vision as well and leaned slightly into the room, just enough to examine the area under the stairs. Yes, there were people there. If she was careful, she might be able to jump them before they realized she was in the building.

Kera readied herself and began her slow movement into the warehouse. If they were smart, which she should assume they were, they would be watching all of the potential entrances. Still, with a combination of effects, she might be able to keep them from paying attention to her.

With a flick of one wrist, she cast her first spell. It was modeled on one taught in the book, a sound of animal noises that seemed perpetually to come from around the corner. This time, Kera made it sound like a motorcycle.

There was a flurry of movement, but she kept moving, creeping closer.

Soon she'd be close enough. A few steps more, a few—

An aerosol went off near her face, making her jerk back with a hiss. A moment later, iron bars snapped up around her: a cage of some sort, something that wouldn't look out of place in a certain type of dungeon.

There was laughter and a few whoops, and a light went on, shining directly into her eyes. The light bounced as the person holding it stepped forward.

"Hello, *Motorcycle Man.*"

Her eyes were stinging faintly. The aerosol must have had an irritant in it.

Whatever the case, she knew she didn't want to stick around

in this cage. Kera came up with a plan and executed it within a split second. The bars in front of her began to glow red-hot, then white-hot. Even inside the helmet and the leathers, she could feel the heat radiating from them. She initiated a magical poke to push them out of place and cooled them as they landed.

She had only meant to keep them from catching anything on fire, but the rapid heating and cooling had the bonus effect of shattering the metal.

Kera stepped out of the cage and stared the man down.

"Do you have *any idea*," she asked him, "what a gigantic fucking mistake you just made?"

CHAPTER TEN

Ben had thought he more or less knew what he was getting into. Motorcycle Man was strong and fast. There were drugs involved, and also weird light effects or something. The trap had worked exactly as intended. They had all been distracted by the sound of the motorcycle, but the trap hadn't.

Then the plan had gone off the rails. Ben had not expected to see the bastard straight-up melt the metal bars.

Fuck. He paused for a second.

Wait. All he had to do was keep Motorcycle Man there. Then the trap would take care of the problem for him.

He crossed his arms and stared. "You think your little magic tricks are really working, man?"

"I saw you flinch." There was a laugh from inside the motorcycle helmet. Motorcycle Man—who, it had to be said, was shorter than the average dude—stepped forward.

Determined to keep him within range of the knife, Ben stepped up to meet him.

His team sucked in their breath.

Thanks for the confidence, everyone. Ben made a mental note to take a bigger share of the payout than he'd planned.

He opened his mouth to speak, and Motorcycle Man cut him off with a spinning kick. Ben went staggering sideways, and Motorcycle Man grabbed him by the jacket. The next thing he knew, he was on his knees with something jabbing into the back of his head.

A gun? Fuck, fuck, fuck. The payout from the Startup was good, good enough that some of his own team would probably screw him over to get it.

"All right," Motorcycle Man called. "All you have to do is answer a couple of very simple questions, and your friend here gets to go home with his life. Maybe not his dignity, but his life."

There was a pause.

"Who hired you?" Motorcycle Man asked. The hand on Ben's collar tightened. "You wanna answer, smartass?"

"Fuck you." He wouldn't take a bullet for the Startup, but he also wasn't going to look like a weak little bitch in front of his team. He wasn't a huge name in LA yet, but he'd done all right for himself, and he'd managed *that* by grinding tirelessly.

Not by giving up at the first sign of trouble.

"Anyone else?" Motorcycle Man asked.

A second later, there was the twang of the knife coming up, and Ben had just enough time to fear that *he* was now in the way of it before Motorcycle Man threw himself sideways, dragging Ben with him.

The knife came out of nowhere, and it was only a combination of a hunch and good reflexes that let Kera get out of the way in time. She dove sideways, dropping the piece of metal she'd been using to make the jerk think she had a gun.

She *really* needed to get one.

"All right, motherfuckers," she called as she rolled to her feet. "That's how you want to play? Then let's play."

She went for the leader first, taking him down with another spinning kick. He slumped in a heap. Kera wrenched the knife off the spring-loaded rod before ducking away and throwing herself toward the exit.

She had to be careful about where she moved in this place. There was no way they could have anticipated which way she'd come in, which meant there were probably multiple traps.

Traps that apparently had death timers on them. It was clever, she had to admit, but it also made her furious.

She hadn't done anything to the people here. They had signed on to take her down because they didn't like the idea that someone might stand up to them when they hurt others. That, or because they didn't care that a bunch of the people in power in LA were douches who hurt people for fun and profit.

A group of three rushed her. Kera dodged to the far left and grabbed a man's arm, twisting it as she ducked. Once his arm was behind his back, she pulled him toward her, then pushed him away with all her magically-augmented might, plus a kick for good measure. He staggered into his two friends, howling about the pain in his arm.

While his friends were trying to deal with him, Kera was moving. She slid around the side of the group and landed a hard, precise jab on one man's thigh and the other man's ribs. Both hits were intended to inflict pain rather than damage, and the men yelled.

The second one shut up after she followed up the rib jab with a kick to the head. He went down in a heap, setting the middle man even further off-balance, and Kera caught *him* on the way down with an axe kick.

She was really getting into the Tae Kwon Do Mrs. Kim was teaching her. Punches were great, but kicks had incredible power behind them.

Kera stared at the group, panting. "Anyone want to answer

now? Or do you just want me to keep kicking my way through your damned group?"

They rushed her.

"Well, I guess that's one answer," Kera muttered. Not wanting to introduce more weapons into the fight than necessary, she muttered a spell to heat the metal of the knife and flung it at the wall before jumping into the air to take down her first attacker with a kick.

After landing, she planted her feet and slid into a side stance, elbow shooting out to catch one of the others in the solar plexus. As that woman doubled over with the signature gasp-and-choke of someone who'd had the wind knocked out of them, Kera sank further into the stance to avoid a chokehold, then grabbed her next attacker's arm and hinged at the hips, throwing him over her shoulder.

It wasn't as smooth as it had been in the makeshift gym. The floor wasn't stable, and her attacker wasn't positioned correctly. It worked well enough, however, and the attacker—a lanky man with black hair and a loose jacket, tumbled headfirst into the winded woman. Both of them went down.

Kera straightened and went into motion again. A couple more, she figured, before she asked again.

Then came the sound of a gun cocking.

Nope. She wasn't going to mess with guns. No matter her luck or speed, that was not a fight she wanted to get into. Kera ducked, whipped around, and streaked for the exit.

One person lay in her way: the head of this gang, still moaning in pain—and that gave her an idea. Kera skidded to her knees beside him, grabbed his coat, and gave a flick of her wrist with her free hand while muttering a spell under her breath.

A tracking spell. If she couldn't get him to answer here with his team around him and his traps set, maybe she'd be able to get to him later when he was on his own. To follow up, she threw a confusion spell over everyone there, then pushed off the floor and kept running.

The fight had been short by her standards, and she had gotten more judicious with her use of magic, so she wasn't as exhausted as she had been the last time she left this place. Kera sprinted out of the warehouse and made for Zee, swinging one leg over the seat and slipping the key into the ignition.

Thank goodness for luck spells. Not only had she gotten the key out of her pocket on the first try, but it also slid into place perfectly. She grinned as she revved the bike and burned rubber. She was congratulating herself on her good preparation when the sound of squealing tires came from behind her and the glare of high-beams hit her mirrors.

Bastards. They'd been waiting for her. The traps hadn't all been in the warehouse.

Her good mood evaporated when she looked over her shoulder and thought she made out the shape of a Mustang.

That bastard *would* fucking be involved. Suddenly, the grudge made a lot more sense.

"Should've poisoned his beer when I had the chance," Kera muttered.

She focused her attention on driving. She knew this area fairly well, and she didn't want to bring this chase into a residential neighborhood. On the other hand, those smaller streets would give her a chance to get away.

With a grimace, she called on the powers of the universe and tried to give Zee a burst of speed. It wasn't a perfect solution since she was pushing him faster than was safe on these streets, but it helped her pull away from the people chasing her.

She looped around, trying to lose her pursuers by heading in a large circle. Surely, they wouldn't think she was going back to the warehouse. Between that, her distance, and her don't-notice-me spells, she might be able to slip away.

She wove through the streets, zig-zagging but never quite losing her pursuers. They'd had the good sense to split up, which meant she could never be sure she'd turn the correct way to lose them.

Still, she was slowly but surely getting away.

Patience, she told herself and grinned behind the motorcycle helmet. Patience wasn't her strong suit.

She was nearly back at the warehouse when things went sideways again. She came up fast on an SUV, which swerved out of the way. Kera shot past it, barely taking in the equipment on the top of the vehicle: satellite dishes.

A news vehicle.

"Of all the rotten luck." Kera put on another burst of speed. "Zee, I promise you get to rest soon."

She was close to getting away from her pursuers now, very close. They were falling behind, and the news vehicle would slow them down further.

What she hadn't counted on was that the gang members weren't going to want a news truck filming them.

"That's him!" Mia called excitedly.

She had insisted they go to the warehouse instead of the textile factory, and Doug had called her crazy. But she had been *right,* she thought triumphantly. She had been absolutely right.

"Doug—"

"Yeah, I see him, but do *you* see what's behind us?" He sounded worried.

Mia looked over her shoulder and swore. Motorcycle Man hadn't been alone. He had been evading a whole set of cars. Some of them were old, rusted bangers, but some were sleek and well-maintained, easily a match for the horsepower of the loaded-down SUV.

As Mia watched, one of the cars streaked up alongside and swerved sideways.

"Are you fucking kidding me?" she yelled. "What the hell, Doug?"

"We're the people who can identify them later, and they've lost Motorcycle Man," Doug said grimly. "I think *we're* now the priority 1. I just need to get us out of here..." Another car swerved in front of them, and Doug braked hard. "Fuck! Should I have turned?"

"I don't know!" Mia grabbed the oh-shit handle to stay stable as Doug swerved. "Fuck, fuck, fuck."

"I'm doing the best I can," he gritted out.

"I know," she said, heartfelt. "This is...you're doing really well."

Doug shot her a thankful look. "I always thought I wanted to be a war reporter. Turns out I was wrong. I hope I survive realizing that."

Another car pulled up beside them, and the window rolled down. Someone was staring out at them. Mia took a quick look behind them.

"Doug, *BRAKE!*"

Doug, thankfully, complied. The SUV screeched to a halt in the middle of the road, and the other cars shot past. The gunshots that had been meant for Mia and Doug streaked past into thin air.

Mia gaped. Her heart was pounding, and she wanted to throw up. Doug, thankfully, was already moving again. He whipped the SUV into a U-turn and took off in the other direction. Lights hit them as the other cars followed suit.

The motorcycle came out of nowhere, whipping past them the other way. Mia thought she saw the helmet nod once, then the motorcycle sped toward the oncoming cars and wove between them, lightning-quick.

With Motorcycle Man as a target, the cars broke off their

chase of Doug and Mia. They whipped around again and began chasing their main target as Doug laid on the gas and sped away.

"Holy shit," he was muttering as they came to their first stoplight. The road behind them was empty. "Holy shit, Mia. Holy *shit.*"

"That was Motorcycle Man," Mia said. She had folded her hands in her lap. "It was, wasn't it? You saw the nod, right?"

"Yeah." He shook his head. "Am I crazy, or did he just run interference for us on *purpose?*"

"I don't think you're crazy," Mia assured him quietly. She was cold, now that the adrenaline had left her body. Her teeth were chattering. "I think he came back for us." She looked at Doug. "That's…"

They stared at each other until a honk made them jump out of their skin. Someone at the cross street leaned out their window and waved at the green light.

"Right," Doug muttered. He got the SUV into motion with a lurch and breathed out as they continued down the street. "God, I need…I don't know. I don't know if I need coffee or a drink."

"Straight bourbon," Mia said at once.

"Never took you for a bourbon person."

"Yeah, well, you learn something new every day." Her phone buzzed, and she pulled it out of her pocket. "Work email. Says we need to come in tomorrow for…" Her voice trailed off.

"For…" Doug prompted.

"For a meet with law enforcement," Mia told him. "Shit. I wonder what that's about?"

Several miles away, Kera was pulling into her little warehouse apartment, her heart still pounding.

Tonight had been equal parts good and terrifying. She had evaded the traps the gangs had set for her, but those traps indicated that they were adapting to her. They'd known human strength wasn't enough to restrain her. They'd decided to make her square off against steel bars, and they were only going to escalate from here.

Plus, they had almost taken out a news van.

Kera couldn't stop picturing the passenger's face. The woman's eyes had been wide and terrified. The man driving had looked grim. She hadn't wanted them to see her. Frankly, she had wanted to get away from them almost as much as she'd wanted to get away from her pursuers.

But she couldn't leave them to be picked off by the gang-bangers.

She sighed as she turned Zee off and went to close the door. She was going to have to do some serious diagnostics on him tomorrow to make sure she hadn't done permanent damage, and then she was going to need to do some more planning.

If she didn't take those people out at the source, innocent civilians were going to get hurt.

She was just slumping onto her bed when her phone buzzed twice. Frowning, she turned it over—and groaned.

The first text was from Cevin, letting her know he'd changed the schedule to give her a shift the next day. He was apologetic about all the shifts she'd missed, and Kera knew he had gone to some trouble to move things around. This was a kindness she couldn't refuse.

"Guess I'm taking a night off from saving the world, Zee," she told her motorcycle. "Probably best for *your* health, and maybe I'll come up with some good ideas in the meantime."

Then she looked at her second text, only to groan again. It was Jennifer, asking her how the project for Cevin's new wardrobe was going.

I'll be working tomorrow night, Kera texted back. *Schedule change. I'll show you some options then.*

She looked at Zee and shook her head. "And apparently, I'm

getting up early to research shirts for Cevin. What a life, huh, Zee?"

CHAPTER ELEVEN

Los Angeles, it turned out, was filled with motorcycle enthusiasts. There were bars. There were districts. There were social media groups. James and LeBlanc researched them and decided to reach out the next morning.

"Motorcycle Man is out and about at night," James explained to Mother LeBlanc. "This way, we're less likely to wind up talking to him by accident. Or her."

"Mmm." She wrapped her shawl around her and waited for him to get his shoes on.

There were strict rules about staying at and leaving the safe house, so they had cleared their departure with MacDonald and Richardson. James disliked the necessity since it made him feel rather more controlled than he would like. On the other hand, he had to admit that having access to the agents' contacts was useful.

And he could hardly ask them to bring informants to someplace that wasn't safe.

The agents had set up a meeting with two local reporters and had asked James and LeBlanc to observe, so the two groups would meet up again in about two hours. That didn't leave James and LeBlanc much time, but perhaps they had enough to get a solid lead.

The two of them had zeroed in on the neighborhoods of Little Tokyo and Chinatown, the sites of the recent surge in gang violence—and the epicenter of where the LA Witches tags had been seen. Someone in the area, James reasoned, might have noticed a particular motorcycle time and again.

The man at the motorcycle repair shop nearby, however, seemed to take an immediate dislike to them.

"Can I help you?" he asked as they walked in.

"Yes," James said. He smiled. "We're visiting professors at UCLA, and we've gotten interested in the sociological implications of the Motorcycle Man phenomenon."

He didn't expect anyone to share his interest, but he had learned long ago that people tended to think of academics as fundamentally unmoored from the realities of the world, and therefore, not very threatening. While a motorcycle enthusiast might not be keen to tell a reporter about the masked vigilante, they might be willing to tell a professor.

Also, people expected and thus ignored eccentricity from academics, which meant that the details of James and LeBlanc's mode of dress, speech, or interest would not be as noteworthy.

The proprietor, however, did not open up easily. He raised an eyebrow at James, who tried again.

"We've seen positive reactions from the motorcycle community," James said. "The idea that Motorcycle Man is showing a quality of the community that *riders* knew existed but other people did not see—that motorcycle riders are inherently helpful, community-minded people."

The proprietor's mood softened. "That's true," he admitted. "People are coming in, saying they want to pay some tribute to him. A lot of them are asking for their bikes to be repainted all black. I've run out of leather sets twice." He opened his mouth to say more, then closed it.

"What is it?" Mother LeBlanc asked him. "Is something wrong?"

"You said you're…college professors? Researchers?"

Both James and LeBlanc nodded.

"Not, like, cops or anything?"

"Not cops," LeBlanc said with a smile. Behind her customary pleasantness lurked a wealth of feeling, however.

It seemed to convince the man behind the counter, who nodded. "Right. So, a lot of the people who come in here are thinking, maybe the cops aren't going to like this guy for very long, right? Like, *they* want to be the ones taking down gangs and all that. They don't want this guy showing them up."

James nodded. The man was more correct than he knew, though his reasoning was off.

"A lot of people are trying to make themselves look like the guy, so the cops can't figure out which one of us he is," the proprietor explained. "And some of them are starting to do shit like he is. Stopping to help at car crashes, stuff like that."

James felt LeBlanc's sudden tension. This was the sort of thing they had worried about—that vigilante justice would spread, wreaking havoc and drawing more attention to Motorcycle Man.

He knew he had to be low-key, however, or this man might clam up. "So, you think it's one guy," he clarified, "but people are imitating him? I want to make sure I have that correct. You're not saying it was multiple people to start with."

"I don't think so," the man said at once. "I thought about it. Some people have been taking pictures of guys they *think* are Motorcycle Man, but it's never the same bike. Like, one'll be a Honda, another'll be a Kawasaki, and the riders are different. Hell, someone told me they'd seen him recently, and it was a chick I know who works at a bar near here. I think people are trying to hide him, sure, but they're also trying to show that the whole community is like that. Helpful, you know?"

James nodded. "Thank you for your help." His mind was racing. "You said there were a lot of pictures?"

"Oh, yeah. Lots of clear pictures of different bikes, helmets, all of that. But the really big stuff, like that hostage situation or the fire? None of those pictures are in focus. No one can see the bike or get a good bead on the guy." The man shrugged. "Not like I'd take a good picture inside a burning building, but it's just…weird, you know?"

The two thaumaturgists *did* know. They nodded.

"Well, thank you for your time." James slid a card across the counter. "Like I said, we're fascinated by the changed perceptions of the public toward motorcycle riders and the accompanying shifts in behavior you've seen within the community." The more jargon he could throw out in a single sentence, the more the man would be bored and write him off as an eccentric genius instead of a threat.

But he might call if he thought James was going to produce work that flattered the motorcycle community.

"I'll, uh…I'll save this," the man said. He held out a hand. "Mike, by the way."

"Dr. Lovecraft," James told him.

"Dr. LeBlanc," his companion added with a smile.

As they walked out into the sunshine, she looked at him. "Well, this may be difficult. The community has embraced him as one of their own. There will be multiple clones on the street."

"Only one doing magic, though," James said. He considered. "Actually, this is perfect if you think about it. A bunch of people dress up as him and keep doing good works. We take the *actual* Motorcycle Man out of the equation, and things peter out very slowly. Eventually, people realize there hasn't been a major event in a while, and the whole thing dies."

"You're forgetting the meeting we have soon," LeBlanc told him. She checked a pocket watch that she had pulled out of the folds of her dress. "The smear campaign our compatriots are determined to wage."

"They'll piss off the motorcycle community," James said. "Though I suppose that's not their top concern. Anyway, an *I am Spartacus* thing will just help us cover our tracks."

"Perhaps you're right." LeBlanc sniffed. "In the meantime, we have an hour before we have to meet them, and I smell something delicious. Shall we eat?"

"You can't cook whatever it is in your dress?"

"Cooking is an *art*, James." She smiled at him and swished off, her skirts swirling around her in a rainbow. "I could pull a painting out, but it wouldn't be a Van Gogh."

James shook his head as he followed her. "Someday," he mumbled, "I am going to figure out how that spell works."

<hr>

Ted clapped his friend on the back with unnecessary and excessive force, causing Christian to spill his iced tea on his plate. He moved his sandwich out of the way and stared at the plate, no more or less interested in eating it than he had been a few minutes ago.

"Dude, cheer up!" Ted urged, settling back into his half of the booth. "You got a chick—temporarily rather than permanently, but still—who was *way* out of your league. If you can score two dates with *her*, the sky's the limit. If you ask me, the best thing you can do next is try to up your game and go for an honest-to-god supermodel next time. Maybe Heidi Klum? I mean, start with the classics, right?"

Chris picked up his sandwich and took a dutiful bite. Chewing was a surprisingly energy-intensive process when one had no interest in eating. He gave thanks that the bread wasn't drenched with tea.

He should probably also be grateful to Ted for getting him out of the house, but he wasn't quite feeling that yet.

His friend went on. "I'm serious. Like, is she still with that Seal guy? I haven't been following the whole thing, but I still have special memories of her from when I was pubertal. Or maybe… wait, who's that chick in the *Transformers* movies?"

Someone at a table across from them shot Ted a weird look but returned to his platter of spaghetti without comment.

Chris swallowed. "Right. Yeah, but I don't *want* any of them. I want *Kera*. I fell for *her*, not her face or her body, Ted. Those help, sure, but it was the whole package. Everything. And I turned her down. She might feel as shitty as I do, but there's no way I can take back whatever I told her."

It was more painful now that he had accepted what had happened. He'd said something that had fucked it up for all time. He had rejected her, apparently while he was drunk. Kera had seemed confident in her understanding of the event and was merely abiding by his wishes.

Allowing *him* to reap the agonizing, despondent harvest of his actions.

He just wished he could remember what he'd said. It was all a hazy blur in his mind. He didn't even know what to be angry at himself about.

Ted was silent for a couple minutes after that, gazing into the distance with a rare philosophical expression as he munched on his cheeseburger. "Hey," he said, at length, "I'm sorry, buddy. I want you to feel better. That's all."

Christian managed a wan smile. "I know, man. Thank you." He sighed. "So, when are we going back to the Mermaid?"

Ted blinked at him. His mouth hung open, full of mostly-chewed food. "*What?*"

"Well," Chris clarified, "aren't you still trying to get that brunette's phone number?"

Ted gulped down his mouthful. "Oh, uh, yeah. Actually, it was

Stephanie, the black girl. Jenn was the brunette, and she declined. And I wouldn't mind talking to her, but I'm not going to make you go back to that place. Not after what happened."

Christian wasn't sure what to make of his friend's response. He had expected Ted to leap at the opportunity to flirt with an attractive young woman.

"Ted," he pointed out, "you helped me get a date with Kera, so I should help you in return."

Ted shook his head. "No way, man. There are tons of bars and tons of hot girls in the world, especially in LA. We don't need to go back to the Mermaid. You look like shit right now, but you seem *better* than you did yesterday, so, you know, I don't want to screw that up."

Chris was nearly embarrassed by his gratitude, and he blushed. In his current emotional state, knowing that someone gave a shit...

"Thanks, Ted. You're a pretty decent human being after all."

"Shit, don't tell anyone." Ted shuddered. "I have a reputation to maintain."

"Who *wants* to be known as a jerk?" Christian demanded.

Ted laughed, and they cheered up a little as they finished their lunch and left the diner behind to head back to work.

As they strode out, neither of them noticed a trim, average-sized man with black hair and a dark suit who had been sitting at the booth behind Chris, listening to their every word.

"Isn't that precious?" Johnny Torrez smirked into his coffee. "The great and glorious *reina de las ángeles rubias* got herself turned down by a nerdy-ass office worker."

He had put a few moves of his own on Kera a couple weeks back, but for some reason, she'd been standoffish and unresponsive. As the current situation clearly demonstrated, her taste in men was terrible. At least he had shot up her oh-so-slick motorbike later that same night.

And since the Mermaid was still on Pauline's list of places

they needed to penetrate, any information about it or its employees or patrons that he happened to collect might come in handy. Sure, right now, she was more interested in Motorcycle Man than anything else, but that would eventually change.

After all, despite last night's failure, Johnny was fairly sure they were getting closer. From a distance, he had seen how the trap worked. Ben might have a concussion, and his group had more than a few broken bones between them, but they were getting closer to taking Motorcycle Man out.

Then they'd return to their original plans.

His waitress came by. "Hey. Do you need anything else?"

"No," Johnny told her. "What're *you* doing later tonight, though?"

After another afternoon of Pauline yelling at all of them, he might as well have some fun.

Kera was going to be early to work, so she figured she would have plenty of time to research shirts. It wasn't something she would normally look forward to, but she was excited about doing something boring for a change.

Huh. That was a paradox.

She was drifting through the outskirts of the area, looking for a likely-looking coffee shop, when a car caught her eye.

That Mustang. She would know *that* Mustang anywhere.

She didn't pause to think. She followed the Mustang, keeping a few car-lengths back. She always had her don't-notice-me spells up these days, but those only went so far. They didn't work if you made yourself obvious.

To her surprise, the Mustang headed downtown, and to her further surprise, turned into the parking lot of an office building. Kera continued past the parking structure and looped around to the front, where she snagged a street parking space. The beauty of motorcycles was that they could fit anywhere.

She trotted up to the front door of the building and slipped into the lobby, her helmet under her arm, to look for one of the boards that would show every company in the building. The parking structure, after all, had said EMPLOYEES ONLY.

She looked through the names, all of them vague and tech-sounding.

"Huh." Maybe their nighttime mugger had a day job.

That was odd but not impossible. She filed the piece of information for further thought later and headed back to her bike before anyone could notice her on the security cameras.

CHAPTER TWELVE

Doug flicked a crumpled-up straw wrapper into the trash can. It was weird being back in the office after how much time he and Mia had spent in the field lately. He was already bored.

He was also antsy. He and Mia had received their summons to be here for a meeting with "law enforcement," a term that was non-specific enough to be worrisome. Between that and their close call with the gangs, Doug hadn't slept well last night.

Mia either *had* slept well, or she had hopped herself up on coffee. He couldn't tell which. She was sitting at her desktop PC, alternating between periods of brief but furious typing and long stretches of silence when she read things over.

He saw her frown before she spoke up. "Frank says it's the FBI."

Doug raised his eyebrows. Frank Tranh was their boss, and he was much more mild-mannered than the stereotype of the news-paper editor yelling about pictures of Spiderman. Frank gener-ally looked out for them, and this heads-up was another way of showing that.

"So, we're still thinking this is about Motorcycle Man?" Doug asked.

"Who else?" Mia asked with a shrug.

Doug nodded. He was impressed, though not surprised, that the FBI had concerns about how the media was reporting on the issue. Given the overall level of unsubstantiated information out on the streets, not to mention the public's perception of what the LEOs seemed to consider a potential threat, it made sense.

He went to peer over Mia's shoulder, scanning the email Frank had forwarded. It was long-winded in the extreme and concluded with a vague request for cooperation.

It was difficult to tease out what was meant, though.

"Christ," Doug complained. "This is why I hate working with law enforcement. Seventy bajillion pages of legalese and bullshit government jargon and evasion. If they want us to do something, why the hell can't they ask in plain English?"

Mia frowned the way she did when thinking hard and crossed her arms over her chest. "That's the feds for you."

"Maybe we should talk to Boss Man before the meeting," Doug suggested. "He might have more context, or there might be an obscure rule about working with the FBI that we haven't had to deal with before."

They walked down the hall, Doug looking around for unfamiliar faces. There weren't any yet, and the office was fairly quiet since it was lunchtime.

When they stepped into Frank's office, he was lounging in his chair and looking at them evenly. He'd clearly expected them and was prepared, if not enthusiastic, about the discussion.

"Hi," Doug said. "So, we're here for the meeting in a few, but we wanted to ask about that email you forwarded us. We only have a general idea of what the hell they mean. Something about cooperating with them on the Motorcycle Man story is our guess?"

"We don't want them, of all people, mad at us," Mia added. "We'd just like some clarification before we do anything further."

Frank nodded and sighed, rubbing his eyes. "Yes, I read the

damn thing four times. The gist of the message, as near as I can tell, is that they want us to stop puffing this mysterious guy up with good publicity. They are going to ask us to hang back and suggest that the situation is more complicated. Specifically, to sow the idea that Motorcycle Man might be the bad guy after all."

Doug's eyebrows snapped together in a frown. "Why?"

Frank shifted in his seat. "Requests like this from the government are rare. I don't think either one of you has gotten one before, right?"

Doug and Mia shook their heads.

"Right. They're usually about international news or political reporting. The thing is, we try to take them seriously and really consider whether we want to go along with it. They have their reasons and we have ours, but they can't always tell us theirs."

"How do we know theirs are on the level, then?" Doug asked.

Frank tried to soften the blow. "Consider this." He held up his hands, palms outward. "They have access to classified information about ongoing investigations. They often know things we do not. There might be a whole other side to the story we have not uncovered yet. If we make someone out to be a hero and they turn out to be a total asshole, it could interfere with what law enforcement is trying to achieve, get innocent people hurt, *and* make us look stupid. Then we lose viewers, readers, and the public trust."

Doug bit his tongue, trying to mediate his words as a tremor of rage went through him. Everything in him wanted to walk out and not go to the meeting now.

"But Motorcycle Man *is* a hero," he countered when his voice was steady. "He's been doing all kinds of dangerous stuff and going out of his way to save people's lives at great personal risk. Of *course*, the public wants to hear about that, and since he's taken measures to protect his identity, it's not like we're libeling anyone."

Frank pointed a finger and raised his eyebrows. "Yes, and *why* doesn't he want to be identified?"

Mia jumped in. "There could be multiple reasons. Law enforcement has a tendency to throw the book at vigilantes as hard—or harder—than they do at regular criminals. Media exposure means the friends of people he's beaten up might show up at his home. Stuff like that. Or maybe he—or she—doesn't want to compromise their employer. There are plenty of reasons his actions might not be nefarious."

The supervisor inhaled deeply and let the air out in a long, ragged breath of exasperation. "Look, I'm sorry, but you two are going to need to go into that meeting and be *polite*. The traditional news business has more competition than ever from random websites and social media influencers, and the last thing we need is to end up on the FBI's shit list."

When Doug and Mia said nothing, just glowered back, Frank leaned forward. "Understand? I'm not saying you need to promise anything, but I *am* telling you not to just run your mouth in there. I'm *also* suggesting that maybe our owners won't want to run interference on your behalf, so be clear with yourselves about whether you're willing to lose your jobs over this."

Mia's hands clenched.

"I am *trying* to keep you two safe," Frank said. "Please, do me a single goddamned favor, okay?"

"*What?*" Doug ground out.

"Go into this meeting *acknowledging* the possibility that they know something you don't," Frank said. "Just *think* about their request. Evaluate it on its own merits, okay?"

Doug glowered but nodded, not trusting his voice.

After a moment, Mia nodded too.

"Okay," Frank said. "They're in Room 204. They asked to meet with just the two of you."

"Great," Doug muttered. "So, can I ask a single goddamned favor of *you*? If we're not back in an hour, send a search party."

"You got it," Frank agreed.

"The answer I was looking for was, 'You're being paranoid,' but okay." Doug sighed and held the door for Mia. "Come on, let's go see what those bastards want."

In room 205, James and LeBlanc sat at a table and kept their eyes fixed on the monitor in front of them.

They had agreed to join the FBI agents at the news station but had opted not to be in the meeting. MacDonald and Richardson had agreed it was best not to give the press anything more to work with than necessary, and that it was *also* not a good idea to have James and LeBlanc do anything unpredictable.

James did not mention that he and LeBlanc felt much the same about the FBI.

They watched the video feed from MacDonald's lapel pin as the two reporters came into the room. Mia Angel was surprisingly short, whereas her partner was tall, big-boned, and looked very unhappy to be there.

"Ms. Angel," Agent MacDonald said. "Mr. Lopez. Good to meet you. I'm Agent MacDonald, and this is Agent Richardson. Thank you for meeting with us."

The reporters made noncommittal noises.

"We understand that what we're about to ask of you seems strange," Richardson broke in. "You have a commitment to reporting the unbiased truth, and we respect that. In fact, we've been very impressed by your reporting on Motorcycle Man so far."

Neither of the reporters spoke, though Doug Lopez was openly glowering now.

"You will perhaps have noticed," Richardson went on, "that there has been a rise in gang violence within the greater Los Angeles area, as well as several clashes between gang members and Motorcycle Man. Allegedly, of course, since we're unable to get either the gang members or Motorcycle Man to confirm their identities." He tried a smile.

The reporters moved their mouths into the appropriate shape, but the smiles did not reach their eyes.

"They're not receptive," LeBlanc remarked.

"Reporters in the United States have a very strong belief in freedom of the press," James pointed out.

"Yes, James, I know. I've lived here for quite some time." She shot him a look. "I think we should arrange our own meeting with those two."

"Why?"

"Because they aren't receptive to the FBI so far, but neither were we. It's one of the reasons I didn't want to be part of this meeting. I wanted them to see working with us as separate from working with the feds."

"Hmmm." James considered. "Well, let's see if they make any headway first."

On the video stream, Doug and Mia were strenuously objecting to the agents' assertions about Motorcycle Man.

"You're *seriously* expecting us to put out there as if we know it to be true that the rise in gang violence is the result of Motorcycle Man, not the other way around?" Doug Lopez looked like he was going to have an aneurysm. "You realize that would be conjecture."

"I'm not asking you for conjecture," Richardson said simply. "I'm asking you to research it. We have seen this cycle before. A vigilante attempts to bypass law enforcement, and the streets get more dangerous for *everyone*. We're asking you to consider that possibility here. We're asking you to introduce that *question* into your reporting."

"No, you're not," Doug argued. "You came here with the goal of smearing Motorcycle Man in the press. Us 'introducing that question' would slant our coverage. We've been focused on facts.

Motorcycle Man *has* saved hostages the police weren't able to get to. He got people out of a burning building. He saved three siblings from a car crash. None of that tells us he's a bad person."

"We didn't say he's a bad person," Agent MacDonald interjected softly. "Those things you mentioned are good. Likewise, we can understand the impetus behind the various fights he's been in with gang members. With an increase in cartel activity, we understand why a reasonable, ethical citizen might feel the need to take the law into their own hands."

"Then what's the problem?" Doug shot back.

"The problem is that things are escalating beyond what he seems to have planned for," Agent Richardson said equally bluntly. "Do you understand that? Having people play judge, jury, and executioner is a dangerous game."

That got through to them. The reporters sighed and looked away.

"Just think about it," Agent MacDonald told them and handed them a card. "We're available if you have questions. We are, of course, available if you have leads as well. We're trying to make sure the city functions well for *everyone*. Again, we don't think Motorcycle Man is a bad person. We're just saying he might be causing problems when he's trying to solve them."

The two agents left, and LeBlanc and James exchanged glances.

"They did better than I expected," LeBlanc admitted.

"Me as well." James shook his head. "God, this is a cluster, isn't it? We came here to do the same thing they're trying to do. It doesn't paint us in a flattering light, does it?"

"The goal isn't to look good for posterity, James," she told him. "It's to do the right thing. It's to keep the world calm. *That* is our goal."

CHAPTER THIRTEEN

Kera had been dreading her shift at the Mermaid, but she realized quite quickly that a dose of normalcy was exactly what she had wanted. Not only did it feel good to be someone other than Motorcycle Man, but she also had the added distraction of focusing on her Cevin project.

After Kera had shown Jennifer and Stephanie her picks for Cevin's wardrobe, the two of them debated at length—easy, given the nearly empty bar.

Jennifer currently had the proverbial mic. "If you ask me, the problem is that he hasn't picked a direction for his look. All his shirts look too formal but also kind of cheap? He either needs to go for the bad-boy look, which he probably can't pull off, or he needs to dress, y'know, *snazzier.*"

No one had mentioned who they were talking about. That way, in case Cevin wandered out of his office and overheard, they could plausibly claim it was some other guy they knew outside of work.

Stephanie, leaning against the outside of the bar while she kept an eye on her tables, acceded. "Uh-huh. He falls between the cracks. It's his attitude too, but a man has to believe that what he's wearing looks good on him or the attitude will fail."

Kera nodded. What her friend was describing had some overlap with glamour magic.

"It's true," she chimed in. "Internal and external can reinforce each other. As above, so below, and like that."

Jennifer laughed, "Where'd you hear that?"

Stephanie, meanwhile, closed her eyes as though trying to think of something.

"I dunno," Kera shrugged. "Read it online. Can't remember where it was from. Oh, hey, I'll be right back. I think I have something Jennifer would like."

A customer farther down the bar raised an empty glass in her line of sight. She rushed over and refilled it for him before returning to the brainstorming session.

She pulled out her phone as she approached and scrolled to a particular picture. "Here. Take a look."

The other women leaned in, curious. It was a tailored maroon shirt, button-down but meant to be worn open, designed for men of Cevin's height. Its shoulders were stiff and slightly built up, which ought to resolve his slouching problem. Recommended to go with it were a plain white undershirt and a black vest.

"That," Stephanie opined, pointing at the screen, "would look good on him."

As the words left her mouth, footsteps approached. Cevin trudged up behind the bar from his office, doing one of his sporadic checkups to ensure everything was running smoothly.

Kera gave him a minute to scan the counter and the floor, then she called, "Hey, Cevin. Come look at this. It involves you."

The man sighed and wandered over. "Okay, but let's not waste too much time, huh?"

They showed him the screen, mentioning how nice it would look on him. They couldn't help thinking it would be a good thing to wear to a club or on a first date, and they could send him the link if he wanted.

To their surprise, Cevin looked not so much dubious as horrified. "I could never wear that," he said bluntly. "It's so…ugh, I don't know. Guido-y? That's not a California thing, but it's the best way I can put it."

"What?" Jenn scoffed. "How do you figure? It's classy!"

"It's *purple*," Cevin protested.

Kera pinched her nose. "No, it's *maroon*, or maybe burgundy, depending on the light. More of a deep red. A very masculine color."

He rolled his shoulders and scratched his side. "If you say so. The vest doesn't work, though. It's like something a lawyer would wear."

Stephanie pointed out, "Lawyers usually make good money. That's not a bad thing, especially if you're trying to make a good impression."

The man squinted. "Are you trying to tell me something?"

Kera exchanged glances with her friends. When they responded with subtle tilts of their heads, she realized that the time to spring the plan on him was upon them.

"Yes," she confirmed. "Sorry, Cevin, but there's no more getting out of it. You need a date, and we're going to help you get one. This is non-negotiable. You have no say in the matter. We'll all quit or something if you try to resist."

Their boss groaned and put a hand over his eyes, and Jenn couldn't help cracking up. "Seriously," she clarified, "we want you to do well."

Stephanie added, "There's a single lady at one of my tables you should talk to. I think you might be her type. As the manager, you have an excuse to go over and check to make sure she's enjoying her meal. I'll supervise. You can do this."

Kera glanced at the table in question. She recognized the woman sitting there as a sometime bar patron to whom she'd mentioned Cevin. The woman had been vague and equivocal, though, so Kera had no idea what her boss' chances with her might be.

Cevin squirmed. "Uh, well, I, um, well…"

Jenn gave him a gentle shove. "Go on. Do your manager duty by making the customers feel welcome."

Kera echoed, "Yeah, what she said."

Stephanie and Cevin walked across the floor to the table. Kera, leaning over the bar, could hear only snippets of the ensuing conversation. She made out Cevin offering the lady a standardized We Care-type public relations spiel, followed by further talk in a lower voice. The woman's eyes flicked left and right, and she visibly bit her lip. Finally, she blurted something, then burst into laughter.

Cevin's cheeks turned tomato-red and he stammered something else, then hurried away. Stephanie moved in to cover his escape.

Kera cleared her throat as Cevin approached. "Uh-oh. What happened, man?"

He ducked behind the bar and positioned himself near the corner so he'd be out of the woman's line of sight. He scowled and looked ready to sprint back to his office, but then he relented and spoke.

"Well, um, I said the usual stuff, then I asked if she wanted to go out and have dinner and a drink sometime."

He paused; there was total silence.

"And," he went on, his breath coming out in a sigh, "she cracked up and pointed out that she was *already* having dinner and a drink. I couldn't think of anything to say after that. Like, I was going to suggest, I don't know, playing video games? Ugh, this isn't my thing."

Kera's teeth clamped down on her tongue as she nodded, attempting to look sympathetic. Jenn's resolve was not as great as hers, and she broke into helpless snickers.

"That's great!" Jenn finally gasped.

Kera and Stephanie gave her confused looks.

"Excuse me?" Cevin asked.

"Well, no, actually, it sucks." Jenn waved a hand.

Kera groaned and put her head in her hands.

"But you know what I *mean*," Jenn continued. "At least you tried, right?"

Cevin looked like he wanted to melt into the floor. "Yeah. Great." He slouched back to his office, turning to call to Kera, "When you get a moment, stop by. I put some new security measures in place for closing."

"Will do," Kera called. When Cevin was gone, she stared at Jenn. "I don't think you made him feel better."

"He's going to get turned down a lot," Jenn said defensively. "Everyone does. He's getting used to it, and that's good."

"Yeah, I…" Kera motioned for the three of them to huddle. "I don't think he gets that yet," she pointed out. "If he gets turned down too much, he might just tap out. We may need to rethink our strategy here. Like, is there any way we can pass him off as someone who can't talk? As in, he has a speech disorder or something? It might help."

Jenn nodded. "Probably. We'd need to research that stuff to sound like we know what we're talking about, though."

They chattered for another minute about the new tactics they would be pursuing to set Cevin up with someone without reaching a conclusion. Kera noticed Stephanie staring at her arm and shoulder.

"Kera," Stephanie said slowly, "where'd you get those bruises?" Her eyes were bright with concern.

Crap, I forgot to hide them, Kera cursed herself. *Should have worn a long-sleeve shirt or used a healing spell.*

"Oh, I…well, I've been getting back into martial arts. I did karate in high school, and lately I have been sparring with some people who mostly do Korean arts. They're reasonably similar."

Jennifer raised an eyebrow. "Damn, girl. Remind me not to piss you off. And I'll stay three feet behind you next time I have to walk out after closing time."

"I thought about taking self-defense classes," Stephanie mused, "especially with all the dangerous stuff going on lately. Do you have room for one more at your class?"

"Uh," Kera stammered, "I mean, maybe? It's kind of a private thing, though, not a commercial school. Like, I'm more of an apprentice than a student, if that makes sense?"

Jenn couldn't resist quipping, "Wax on, wax off," but the other two ignored her.

"If you two can take the room for a bit, I'll go talk to Cevin," Kera said.

"Sure." Jenn waved a hand. "We'll deal with the huge crowds of people, don't worry. Leave your phone, though. We want to look at those shirts."

"It's going to take more than a shirt," Kera said, but she tossed her phone to Stephanie and headed back.

Stephanie watched Kera go, feeling a cloud over her thoughts. It wasn't like the woman to be so evasive, especially after her sad moment a couple of days before. A bad breakup, and now bruises? Not to mention, *as above, so below.* Was Kera getting religious?

In most towns, that wouldn't be a worry, but LA was notoriously full of cults. While they mostly preyed on celebrities, it wasn't uncommon for normal people to get sucked in as well.

Stephanie wavered, then raised the phone and navigated out of the photo album.

"Shouldn't be doing this," she muttered, "but girl, I can tell something's wrong with you."

One of the recently-used apps on Kera's phone was an ereader. Stephanie opened it and saw what looked like an instruction manual of some sort. There were bullet points and highlighted pieces, with notes from Kera.

The book was called *How to Be a Badass Witch*. Authors unknown. A crazy title, but from the level of note-taking, it seemed like something Kera was taking seriously.

"*What?*" Stephanie muttered. When a customer gestured for her, she switched the phone back to the photo app and put it in her pocket before hurrying over to get the customer more water.

As soon as she was done, however, she searched for the book on her phone. She couldn't find it on any of the major retailers, but the search engine did return a few results—copies that had been ripped off and uploaded to other sites.

She sent the link to herself to download later. "Sorry, not trying to get this without paying for it," she told the authors. "Just trying to figure out why my friend lost a ton of weight, is showing up with bruises all over, and always looks like she's going to either pass out or cry."

CHAPTER FOURTEEN

As Doug Lopez typed on his office desktop, a curiously steely resolve set in—the determination to forge ahead, knowing damn well he probably wouldn't like the consequences of his actions.

At least he would not be alone. Mia agreed with him. They had gone beyond co-workers and were now, in a manner of speaking, partners in crime.

"This," she'd raged last night after they were far away from Frank's office, "is utter, absolute *bullshit*. The American press is not subject to censorship by elite institutions. Save that shit for China. We're here to report the facts."

For once, Doug hadn't had any clever remarks to follow up with. She'd said what he was thinking.

"We're not in the business of changing people's opinions," he had affirmed. "There *has* been a plague of crime lately, and someone has to stand up to it, regardless of whether the goddamn FBI wants them smeared as dangerous vigilantes or whatever. It's not like we're encouraging anything one way or another. If an incredible story happens, people should be able to hear about it."

Mia had been trembling with anger. He had never seen her like that.

"Fuck it. I say we do what we're supposed to do—tell people what happened. That's all." The woman clenched her fists. "What can they really do to us? Wasn't it phrased as a suggestion? That was how Frank had put it. Dammit. Can we head to a bar? I need a drink."

They were on the same page about that, too.

Today, he decided they'd probably both had one too many, but not enough to impair their ability to do their job. After all, they had spent weeks gathering information—in some cases, firsthand—on Motorcycle Man and his various exploits. At present, it was simply a matter of putting it into a cohesive story.

Mia wandered over, swigging coffee from a paper cup and placing a second on his desk. "How are you doing?"

"Pretty well." He finished the sentence he was on, then gave himself a break to refuel. Mia had read his mind about the need for caffeine. He took a sip, then clarified, "I'm about two-thirds done with my section. Did you start yours yet?"

She nodded. "Only the first paragraph, but the outline is the hard part. I'm about to get going on the rest."

The project was a significant one—a detailed rundown of Motorcycle Man's brawl at the textile factory and the ripples it had sent throughout the proverbial pond. They had statements from witnesses as well as anonymous comments from the police, photographs, expert reconstructions of what might have gone down, and interviews from some of the gang members who had been arrested at the scene.

Doug raised his cup. "To the facts, and only the facts."

Ms. Angel joined him in the toast, and the journalists drank their coffee in unison before returning to work.

They had agreed one minor concession to the feds—that they would avoid glorifying Motorcycle Man and stay as neutral and objective as possible. But as Doug typed, the task grew increasingly tough, thanks to his burgeoning emotions.

It was well-established that their vigilante had rescued people from crashed cars and burning buildings. As for the gang brawls, those could conceivably be smeared as criminal-on-criminal violence, but even then, the sheer badassery on display made it tough for him to think of Motorcycle Man as the villain of the story.

He briefly considered that someone else might have usurped Motorcycle Man's identity to pursue a private gang war—an impostor with their own goals, motives which were perhaps separate from the altruistic ones Motorcycle Man had originally displayed. It might explain the mysterious "LA Witches" connection, too.

But if that were the case, the imitation had been perfect. And, there was no evidence beyond mere conjecture.

Doug stopped writing and turned his head to where his partner was working separately on the laptop she'd brought in.

"Mia," he called, "I have a question."

"Yeah?" she responded, the keys still clacking beneath her fingers.

He coughed. "We've discussed this before, but humor me. Do you believe Motorcycle Man is a good guy? As in, has it occurred to you that someone else might be doing copycat stuff, or he—or she, whoever—might be a total bastard and is doing this to redeem themselves? It occurred to me a minute ago."

She didn't answer right away, though she stopped typing. "Yes, I thought of that too, but I don't think that's the case." She turned in her chair to face him across the office. "There aren't a lot of reasons someone would want to hide their identity that are bad enough to negate what they're doing. I mean, yeah, we have to hope they aren't a serial killer or something, but I doubt it. Even if those reasons are bad, what they're currently doing is good. Saving people doesn't magically become an act of evil simply because the person doing the saving has a history of other shit, does it?"

Doug breathed in through his nose. Posing the question and hearing his partner's answer had made him feel better instantly. "Yeah, I'd say you're right. Thanks. Of course, this means that if we change our minds and cave to the feds, we get to live out our days knowing we're lying SOBs who aren't fit to be reporters."

Mia chuckled, a soft, dry, sardonic sound. "Yep. We might lose our jobs over this one. I'm guessing that has occurred to you too."

"Of course," he replied. "But hey, I used to change oil. People's cars always need maintenance. It's a stable industry."

"And I waited tables in college," she added. "We will survive, and we'll know we did the right thing."

An hour later, the piece was finished. Doug combined the two sections and did a once-over to correct any inconsistencies, then sent his revision to Mia so she could do the same, and the story was finished.

Ms. Angel asked Mr. Lopez, "Turn it in? No turning back once I hit Send."

"Do it," said Doug.

Her finger descended on the Enter key, and the click seemed to echo in the room. She took a deep breath. "Just the facts, and some basic analysis. We tell people what happened, try to elucidate likely possibilities for why Motorcycle Man is hiding his or her identity, and that's it. Not a smear or a puff piece. That is the opposite of what we're supposed to do."

Doug nodded. "We'll toast to that again later, preferably over something alcoholic instead of caffeinated."

They sat waiting for confirmation that the story had been received, and a jittery tension rose in both of them and in the air between them until it became palpable. Lopez imagined a SWAT team breaking down the door of their office at any minute, shining lights in their eyes despite the room being bright, pointing guns, and ordering them to assume undignified positions on the floor.

But nothing happened.

"Huh," Mia quipped. "I'm a little disappointed that nobody launched a tear gas canister in here yet."

Doug laughed. "Same. It turns out that losing your job for standing up to the FBI is actually pretty boring and time-consuming. Maybe we should do a story about *that*."

Mia shut down her laptop and stood. "You might be on to something, but later. I think it's about time for us to go home. After we get steaks and overpriced margaritas, that is. If we get fired, who knows when we'll be able to splurge on dinner again, so we might as well do it this one last time."

Doug powered down his desktop and offered her his arm. "Your logic is impeccable. Let's go."

Since Kera had opened on her shift, she wasn't closing that night. She stuck her head into Cevin's office on the way out.

"Bye, Cevin, see you soon."

He gave a wave but didn't turn around.

Kera considered him. "By the way…"

Cevin sighed and turned around. "What?" Kera could tell he was trying to make himself look less embarrassed after his failed pickup attempt.

"You *are* going to wear that shirt," Kera told him.

Cevin sighed again. "Look, you're all very nice girls, and I appreciate that you want to help, but getting turned into a punching bag isn't my idea of a good time."

"Uh-huh. So, you're telling me you *never* want a relationship?"

"When did I say that?" Cevin protested.

"You said you don't want to get turned into a punching bag." Kera shrugged. "Dating *sucks*, man. You're going to get shot down a lot. You'll also shoot down some people, and it'll suck for them. Like, that's just how it goes. If you want to go out with someone, you're going to have to go through this bit."

Cevin glowered at her.

"You're also going to have to do something about your wardrobe," Kera said. "Try a new look! I'm doing it. Join me."

"I don't think the eye makeup would look as good on me," Cevin quipped.

"Then you'd better try the shirt, hadn't you? Or so help me, we'll put makeup *all* over you." She gave him a mock glare and headed out. "I'll have the shirt soon!"

Cevin didn't respond, but she could picture him glowering.

The night was young by her standards, and Kera knew just how she wanted to spend it, especially now that her shift had put her in a better mood. She revved Zee and headed to one of her favorite twenty-four-hour drive-throughs, then sat in the parking lot and demolished her burrito while she got ready to do the scrying spell.

The man she had tagged last night with a tracker had clearly believed it was better not to go against her one-on-one—which, to be fair, he was correct about. If Kera could get him alone when his team wasn't there and the police weren't coming, she figured she had a pretty good shot of getting information out of him.

Plus, if she could scare him into believing she was going to take out whoever had hired him, he might spread the word and get some of their contractors to drop the job.

Once she had dealt with whoever her nemesis was, she could deal with the long-term plan of being Motorcycle Man without being assassinated or unmasked.

She wiped her hands, threw the napkin into the nearby trash can, and took a deep breath before slipping into a scrying trance. This time, perhaps because she was scrying for a specific person with a specific magical tag, it was much easier to locate him. He was north of her, perhaps in Chinatown, perhaps beyond.

Kera looked around to see if anyone was watching, then made a quick change to Zee's appearance, giving him blue accents and changing the look of her coat. The best way to sneak up on this person was to make them think she *wasn't* Motorcycle Man, and everyone knew Motorcycle Man wore all black and drove an all-black bike.

She started the bike and headed off. As she drove, she kept checking her spells, making sure her engine's sound was dampened and her glamours were in place.

There was a way to maintain an active scrying trance while moving, but Kera didn't have the hang of it. She kept having to stop to see if she was going in the correct direction. At the very least, she was able to determine as she got closer, and finally she found herself outside an apartment building on the eastern side of Chinatown.

She found an out-of-the-way nook to stash Zee in, then set off to find an alley that would lead her to the back door of the building. Once she found it, getting the door open wasn't difficult—a deadbolt she could nudge with magic—and she was able to slip up the stairs.

It didn't take her long to figure out which apartment was his, after which she lingered in the hall to see if there were any sounds within.

She could hear a TV, but otherwise, nothing—no shifting around, no talking. Most people, after all, would be asleep.

Kera readied herself, unlocked the door, and pushed it open to see the man passed out on the couch, some action movie playing on the TV. She closed the door behind her and locked it, then took the time to check if anyone else was in the apartment.

No one was.

Perfect. She took a moment to pick her angle of approach. As quickly as she could, she rolled him onto his stomach on the couch and got his hands behind him, securing them with a zip-tie. As he woke up with a yell, she secured his feet.

Then, moving into his line of sight, she made a gesture with one hand and undid the glamour, allowing him to see her as she was—a figure in all black, not the camel-colored riding coat she had appeared to be wearing.

His yell died in his throat.

Kera studied him. He was Vietnamese, of middling height, and slim.

"You know who I am," Kera said. She kept her voice pitched low as she crouched. "You also know there's no one here for backup, so let's chat, shall we?"

He glared at her, but he was smart enough not to spit threats he couldn't back up.

"You and I both know we don't have a quarrel with each other," Kera told him. "You got hired to take me out. I get it. A job's a job, right? Good money."

He looked at her warily.

"All I want is to know who hired you," she told him. "That's it; that's all. I want to have a chat with them on my own instead of them sending dozens of you guys at me as cannon fodder. That's in both our interests, right?"

He looked away for a moment.

"You have something to say?" Kera asked. She took a moment to listen and make sure no one was sneaking up on her, but there weren't any sounds.

"How the hell did you find me?" he muttered finally.

"All *you* need to know is that it worked." She was getting annoyed. "Help me out here. I don't want random people getting hurt or worse, just because some bastards decided to assassinate me. I want to go talk to them and ask them what their fucking problem with me is."

"You're interfering in all sorts of shit you don't understand," the man spat at her. "What do you *not* get about them coming after you? You don't get to just come in and tell people how to run their lives."

"No?" Kera tilted her head. "So, you all get to mug people and shake down businesses and that's just fine, but no one gets to interfere with *you*?"

"You sure as hell don't get to complain about what happens when people take exception to you getting involved."

She leaned close. "Neither. Do. You."

He said nothing, just gritted his teeth and looked away.

"I'll ask again," Kera said. "Who hired you?" She wasn't going to say an *or else* since she wasn't sure she had it in her to kill someone who couldn't fight back. She was still having nightmares about Deke Anastidis. This guy might be a jerk, but she didn't want to get into the escalated conversation of "What are you going to do to me if I don't cooperate?"

Finally, the man said, "The Startup."

"The startup what?"

"The group is called the Startup," he said. He rolled his eyes. "Not one of the big names yet, but they're coming up."

"Tell me about them." There was a memory trying to make its way to the surface, but she couldn't figure out what it was.

"No one knows much. The leader is some chick, might be Russian. There's a big ginger dude and a *Chicano*."

"That's *all* you know about them?"

"They don't make a big deal of themselves." He shrugged as well as he could with the zip-ties on his hands. "I mean, they moved in quick. They were getting the other gangs to piss each other off, but those guys weren't doing much. The Startup has some distribution, and they pay well."

"I see." Kera considered. She couldn't remember pissing off anyone she would have identified as Russian, but she supposed she must have, without researching it. "Tell me about the ginger and the *Chicano*."

"Ginger has one of those stupid names, all Swedish or whatever. *Chicano*..." He shrugged again. "He's got a pretty sweet Mustang. That's all I know."

Kera went still. Now she understood what was going on and got back the memory she'd been trying to uncover. It had been a sign on the wall of a nondescript office building, pointing to a series of vague startup-sounding names in a building where the Mustang-driver had parked. "I see," she said finally. "Any idea where I could find those two?"

"We met them in Little Tokyo. If they've got headquarters, no one knows where they are."

Kera gauged that he was telling the truth. "Thank you. So, here's how things are going to go. I'm going to untie you, and I'm going to leave you here. You're going to think about what I said: when you fuck with people, you don't get to complain if someone fights back. You spread the word that I don't really want to hurt anyone. That the Startup is a bunch of cowardly little bitches who are sending people to take me out because I've wiped the floor with them a few times now. They're trying to pay their way out of some shit they started and can't finish."

The man frowned but nodded. "And?"

"And, if people make it so I have no choice but to kill them, I'm going to kill them," Kera said. "Goes for you, goes for anyone else the Startup hires, goes for the Startup. Got it?" She saw he was getting ready to argue. "This isn't a negotiation. The decision is made. *Do not fuck with me.* You won't win."

She cut off both zip-ties and headed across the room.

"Who *are* you?" the man asked finally. He had sat up, although slowly, and was rubbing his wrists. "How do you do the shit you do?"

Kera didn't answer. She just closed the door behind her and headed down the corridor, changing her appearance with another glamour.

The Startup. Those were the people who had shaken down the Mermaid, and they were the ones trying to take her out now. Did they know she was Motorcycle Man? She wasn't sure, but she knew the man with the Mustang knew about her motorcycle.

The truth was, he'd probably shit himself if he knew the blonde waitress he'd been hitting on was his arch-nemesis.

She grinned. Now she had a name and someone to go after. Although...

"It'd be easier to feel badass," Kera muttered to herself, "if my fucking pants didn't keep falling down."

It was time for another burrito.

"Fucking *what?*" Pauline hissed. She slammed her hands on the table.

Sven, who'd had the honor of delivering the bad news, grimaced and cracked his neck. He settled back in his chair.

"Yeah," he confirmed. "Word came in this morning. None of the gangs want to ally with us. It's not personal. With a couple minor and obvious exceptions, they have no specific reason to hate us or be at war with us. It's just that—"

Pauline cut him off. "That *what?* What, Sven? Get to the point." She knew he'd been on the verge of doing so, but she didn't care. She was *angry.*

He faked a cough. "They're saying we used them to go after Motorcycle Man and the LA Witches, and they're getting slaughtered. That we started this shit, and we're trying to use them to finish it. Nobody wants to deal with them. They're acquiring a semi-mythical boogeyman-type reputation on the streets. The biggest fish aren't scared of them, but they're taking serious notice. And the medium-sized fish, aka the ones we're trying to recruit, want nothing to do with them."

Lia chimed in. "I have heard similar things and can confirm

what Sven said. No one wants to risk incurring the Witches' wrath, at least until the city knows more about who they are and what they're capable of."

Pauline turned away to keep from wasting valuable company time by screaming incoherently in unhinged fury. She practiced a couple of relaxation and mental clarity exercises she had learned from various TED Talks and motivational speakers and turned back once she was functional again.

"All right," she murmured. "We have established that our potential allies are all cowards who don't understand that calculated risk is an essential component of any successful business. All of them are apparently content to let the Witches and Motorcycle Man walk all over all of us."

"They knew what they were getting into," Johnny said. "They don't get to cry about it now. They took on the job and got paid."

"Yes," Pauline said softly. Her nostrils widened and her eyes narrowed, but she wasn't looking at Johnny. Oddly enough, she seemed *less* furious than she had been a couple of minutes ago.

Lia started to say something about the progress she had made on her dossier, regardless of the failure of their primary objective, but Pauline motioned for her to shut up. She did, reluctantly.

"This," their leader went on, her voice calmer, "is ridiculous." Her tone was still icy. "No one can tell me who those wannabe bitches are, where they're based, how many of them there are, nothing. And all the other gangs are bending over for them on the basis of *rumors* and a couple of stupid brawls? It's absurd."

She unfolded an arm and pointed it at Johnny. "So far, he's the only one who has stood up to them. I need more people like Johnny, who are not simply going to roll over and play dead the instant they encounter actual opposition. We were the first people to stand up to them, weren't we? Therefore, if we *finish* what we started, it will make us look that much more effective to our competitors and potential partners."

Johnny's mouth went slack in amazement, but he closed it, and it began to twist itself into a broad but subdued grin.

Lia raised a finger, and when Pauline didn't object, she spoke. "If no one can figure out where the LA Witches are headquartered or who else might be working for them, it makes sense to be cautious."

"Yes, yes, *cautious*." Pauline's voice was like acid. "Or—and hear me out—what if we weren't cowardly little bitches about this?"

She glared around the room. Lia sat frozen, and Sven was looking away.

"We're going to continue with the main plan," Pauline said. "And by that, I mean *annihilating* Motorcycle Man and his little harem of uppity gangster chicks, or whatever they are."

"We already tried annihilating him, and it didn't work," Sven pointed out. "The usual methods don't seem to be effective."

"Well," Pauline snapped, her temper flaring up again, "you need to figure out a way to *make* them work or pursue new and improved methods. Johnny will take point in planning the operation since apparently he's the only one of you who isn't a little bitch."

Lia's face flushed with hurt, and Sven's took on a curdled expression as though he had indigestion.

Johnny, on the other hand, grinned even wider.

* * *

Mrs. Kim pointed at the dummy's left leg. "You must kick it just so. When he kicks toward your head *high*, you kick his leg *low*. Make him fall."

Kera inhaled. The concept wasn't hard to grasp, thanks to her training in Shotokan karate, and her opponent was a dummy rather than a living, breathing, potentially dangerous human being.

Mrs. Kim was proving to be an extremely strict and demanding teacher, putting Kera through a gauntlet of tests and demanding vast numbers of repetitions until Kera's form was perfect. The woman's somewhat limited English made it difficult for her to explain things in detail.

In some ways, she was the best instructor Kera had ever had.

Kera ducked and pivoted in one motion, her mind in four or five places at once, trying to pull the many factors at play into a single cohesive action: the successful execution of a difficult move. She imagined that the dummy *was* in motion and wanted to kill or maim her. Then she swung her leg around behind the figure, and the upper front junction of her foot and ankle crashed into its leg near the bottom of the calf.

The dummy toppled violently to the floor. Kera, in the same motion, rolled aside and clear, then sprang back up into a fighting stance. She stared at the fallen mannequin.

Mrs. Kim nodded. "Good. Now, again."

Kera frowned but set the dummy on its feet and obeyed.

As she continued to drill kicks and punches, throws and take-downs, clinches and submission holds, blocks and evasions and general exercises in stance, movement, and mindset, she found herself doing better despite her growing fatigue. It was as though her short lifetime's worth of frustration and anger were finding an outlet through her actions.

She had been a cheerleader, and then a computer science major, a stereotypical rich girl and then a bartender. Wrath and discontent at the crimes perpetrated on innocent people around her had always bothered her conscience. At the same time, she had always felt useless, as though she was supposed to sit back and do stupid rich-girl things rather than helping anyone or accomplishing anything constructive.

These days, at long last, she was taking on both of those issues at once.

Kera knew the day's training session was nearly over. They

had been going at it for over two hours, with Mrs. Kim some-times demonstrating, though her illness made it hard for her to do much and almost impossible to spar with the girl. The older lady was getting tired.

For all her strictness and perfectionism, though, there was a foundation of gentleness and care in everything she said and did. When Kera stole a glance at her, she saw the woman's eyes glowing with pride.

Near the end of the session, Mrs. Kim demonstrated a low-effort throw, instructing her how to move with the takedown and fall correctly to avoid injury.

Kera moved toward the older woman, jabbing toward her face, and found her arm and wrist seized. She was spun around, and the moment she felt the pressure on her joints, she jumped into the movement and was briefly airborne before striking the mat and rolling.

She got to her feet, huffing and blinking, surprised that such a frail person could toss her with so little effort.

Mrs. Kim's eyes were fixed on her. "Kera. You okay?"

"Yes," she replied, brushing herself off. "Would have messed my arm up badly if I'd gotten the timing wrong, but I'm fine. The mat absorbed most of the fall."

The woman's mouth puckered in frustration. "I know. What I mean is..." She seemed to scan her brain for the right words. "Are you okay with...your life? That nice boy who was at dinner. How are things with him."

Kera's face flushed. The Kims had danced circles around the question earlier, and she had dodged them, not wanting to talk about it. It would be rude and ungracious to try and evade a direct inquiry.

"I...well, we had another date, and it was, um, okay, I guess." She swallowed, feeling like a fool.

Mrs. Kim's expression didn't change. "My husband was talking about him," she went on. "'What happened with that boy,' he asked. We both liked him, and now we are...curiosity. Curious."

Kera's shoulders slumped in defeat. There would be no getting out of it.

"I dumped him," she confessed. "Not because I don't like him or anything went wrong. I memory-wiped him; used magic to make him forget what happened. Then I told him he'd said he didn't want to see me anymore. I figured if he thought it was his decision, he wouldn't come to my place or keep calling me. I don't want him to get hurt. My life is a lot more dangerous now than it used to be."

The words had rushed out of her faster and louder than she'd intended, and having said them, she felt the skin on the back of her neck crawling with shame, yet there was also a sense of having offloaded a great weight from her shoulders. She was relieved at having just come out and said it finally.

Mrs. Kim's face was drawn in thought, and she made a low throaty sound. "I understand. Maybe you should think about it. This is about you as well, not only him. Think about that."

Kera stepped off the mat and removed her gi, partly as an excuse to turn her face away from the woman's keen gaze.

What the hell does that mean? she wondered. *She clearly doesn't think I made the right choice, at least not entirely. I know it's about me, in part. I've got all these conflicting stupid emotions, and now I feel like everything became more complicated than it was to begin with.*

Mrs. Kim beckoned. "Come into the house and eat."

Nodding, the girl followed her. Once she was seated at the Kims' dinner table, the lady brought out two trays heaped with food, some of it fresh, much of it left over. Kera suspected her host was now cooking extra with every meal with the intent of giving it to her later.

Mrs. Kim pointed to a bookcase visible through the doorway that led from the dining room to the living room. "More books in there. Study while you eat. I must go and do an...errand."

She nodded and walked out.

Kera shrugged. "Okay, then. I just hope she isn't worried about grease stains on the pages." She helped herself to a wad of extra napkins before she went to the case and examined the spines of the tomes therein.

Most of the books dealt with magic, religion, the occult, and mystical traditions, as well as related or overlapping topics such as herbology, yoga, and obscure aspects of nature and science. There was a wealth of information among them, and there was no way Kera could read and absorb all of it in the course of a single meal.

She decided she'd need to make room to open the books and read properly, so she dug into the food. Her mouth was watering; the calories she'd burned during martial arts practice seemed to have depleted her energy almost as much as casting spells did.

She started by tearing into a big slab of grilled pork belly and supplemented it with spoonfuls from a bowl of spicy *budae jjigae* stew, along with some fried rice. Additionally, there was a bulging manicotti, a turkey club sandwich, a bag of potato chips, and half a tray of brownies. Kera sampled everything, making a huge dent in the enormous mass of food in only five minutes.

After wiping her hands off carefully, she opened one of the books and began to read the introduction. The author said much that was carefully vague but mostly accurate. She explained that magic was, to some extent, a kind of contract between the magician and the greater forces within the universe.

She also mentioned that much of what was called "magic" had turned out to be aspects of the natural reality humans didn't understand well. Kera nodded and finished the turkey club, then forged ahead to the more confusing nuts and bolts of the book.

As her eyes moved over a particularly obtuse passage, one which would have required intense concentration to understand, the young woman's mind glazed over. She couldn't think about this stuff as hard as she wanted to; she was distracted.

It was because of Mrs. Kim's cryptically disapproving comment earlier. Her obvious disagreement with Kera's decision to cut Chris out of her life.

She tightened the muscles along her jaw. "I love that woman," she muttered, "but she doesn't understand the nuances of my situation. She isn't thinking clearly. She's falling back on what she knows, which is how things turned out for *her* decades ago and in another country. There's no way things can work out as smoothly between Chris and me as they did between her and Mr. Kim."

She sighed as the emotions flowed out and away again, leaving her feeling marginally better. She returned to her reading with a clear mind.

At first, anyway. Ten minutes later, the thoughts began to turn back to the subjects of love and companionship, which now seemed distant and foreclosed-upon. It was like when her great aunt had been moved to a care facility in a different state; she was still alive, but Kera had doubted she'd see her again.

Her heart ached. She was in no condition for serious research, after all.

"Maybe," she posited, "just maybe, there are, like, cute guys who are also witches. Or, uh, sorcerers? Whatever the term is. It would help. If that hypothetical guy is out there, please let us meet."

She spent a moment enjoying the notion until something else occurred to her. "Ugh, with my luck, those bitches who've been going around the country are going to find him and snuff out his powers. Maybe his life, too."

Shoveling another mass of rice and meat into her mouth, Kera searched for a way to make something positive out of *that,* difficult though it was.

"If they kill him, I could go on an everlasting rampage of vengeance. Shit, that sounds kind of *fun.*"

After all the anxiety she had been suffering over what would happen when the people behind the book finally found her, if indeed they could, she needed to take her aggression out on *someone.*

Minutes later, Mrs. Kim returned, and she had brought a friend.

"Kera," she began, "this is Richard. He is a family friend."

Kera stood up to introduce herself properly. The man before her was in his early thirties, in excellent physical conditions, and might have been *hapa*, but was probably full Korean. He wore a blue t-shirt and loose-fitting athletic pants.

"Hi," he said, extending his hand. "You can call me Rick."

Kera took the hand, shook it, and smiled. "I'm Kera, but Mrs. Kim probably told you that. What, uh, brings you to their residence? Sorry, you've probably been here more than I have."

The older woman stated, "Sparring partner. He will help you."

Kera raised an eyebrow as the man nodded.

"Yeah," he confirmed. "Due to her illness, she asked me to help you get in more practice with someone who can, you know, fight for longer and take a few good hits. Not that she's helpless." He gestured at the small lady beside him. "But you know what I mean."

He seemed vaguely embarrassed, and Mrs. Kim leaned in to tell him, "Kera is stronger than she looks." Then she added a couple of comments in her native language.

Nodding, Rick looked at Kera again and said, "Okay, then. We can wait half an hour or so since it looks like you just got done eating. Cramps tend to ruin things."

Kera shrugged. "Nah, give me five minutes to clean up and we'll be good. I have a *really* high metabolism."

All three contributed to clearing the table and filling the sink with soapy water. While they worked, Kera asked Rick about his background in martial arts.

"Tang Soo Do," he explained, "which has some overlap with both Tae Kwon Do and Shotokan karate, so it will seem familiar.

Mrs. Kim told me about your background. I've been practicing since I was eleven. Twenty-three years. Currently a fourth-degree black belt. I also studied some judo and Brazilian jiu-jitsu, but only for about a year each, and I'm rusty in those."

Kera gave a slow nod as she slipped her dishes into the sink. He was trying not to sound boastful, but his record was impressive as all hell.

She replied, "Nice. I'm, uh, less advanced than that by a considerable margin. I mean, I'm not bad, but try not to kill me, hey?"

He laughed. "Deal."

The trio headed out to the small *dojang*. Mrs. Kim asked Kera to take her shoes and socks back off but didn't make her put her gi back on since Rick hadn't brought his. Both of them were dressed in sportswear that would serve well enough.

He announced, "Light to medium contact. Is that okay?"

"Sure," Kera said.

They took up positions on opposite sides of the mat, stretching and warming up before facing each other and settling into fighting stances. Kera paid close attention to her opponent and the way he moved and held himself. It all spoke of great skill and easy confidence.

Not using magic against him, she decided. *That would defeat the purpose. Well, maybe a slight boost to speed and strength, but otherwise, we're doing this* au natural. *I need to find out how good I am against someone who lacks supernatural abilities but is extremely good.*

While Mrs. Kim watched, Rick asked, "You ready?"

"Yes, sir," Kera told him. She raised her fists.

They advanced at counterintuitive angles, feinting and changing direction with rapid movements. Each tried to throw the other off by tricking them into an incorrect guess as to what would come next. As they closed the distance, Kera saw her opening.

He was about to overstretch himself by trying for a kick at her legs. She went low and punched at his lower torso, only for him to suddenly be behind her, slamming his forearm into her back while knocking her legs out from under her with his foot. As she fell, he grabbed her arm and pinned it behind her once she was on the mat.

"Oof. Smooth. I guess you win this exchange?"

He let her get up, and they went at it again. This time, it wasn't over so quickly. Kera stayed on her feet and they dodged around each other, trading fast blows amid serpentine movements, trying to wear each other down. Rick was possibly the most skilled martial artist she had ever fought.

Over the course of twenty minutes, she landed two or three decent blows on him, but mostly she got her ass handed to her. He refrained from hurting her, but she would probably have some good bruises to remember the occasion by.

Finally, they parted, and Mrs. Kim announced, "Good for now. Rest."

Panting, Kera approached her sparring partner and shook his hand. "You're good," she observed.

"Thanks." Despite being a decade older than she was, he was only sweating minimally. "You're not too bad either. Room for improvement, but for someone of middling rank and experience, I would say you're doing great. You're *really* fast and strong, more so than most people I've fought. You're not on PCP or something, are you?" He laughed.

"Oh, ha," she replied, making herself grin stupidly, "I'm afraid not. Thanks, though."

Does he know? Is he in on the whole secret of thaumaturgy, gatha, or whatever you call it the way the Kims are? Or is he in the dark about my ability to augment myself?

They spent a minute or two catching their breath and gulping from a water bottle Mrs. Kim had brought out. When they were done, she said, "You should fight again."

Kera tried not to wince. "Honestly, he might kill me after that, plus all the training I did earlier." She hoped it sounded like a joke. "I mean, maybe some other time?"

Mrs. Kim frowned. "No. You need more practice. Come. We talk."

Rick waited while the women walked outside and stepped closer to the house. Once they were alone, the older lady turned to the girl. "There. You see?"

Kera blinked, waiting for clarification.

"You see that speed and strength are not enough. Not by themselves. You must have technique. Need more practice! Less feeling bad for yourself. You spar again."

Kera sighed. "Okay, but I have to leave and get ready for work soon."

Mrs. Kim led her back to the *dojang* by the shoulder. "Ten minutes."

She repeated her instructions to Rick, who gave an awkward shrug before resuming his combat stance. "Sorry, Kera," he quipped, "but I'm not going to talk back to her. After all, she could kick my ass if she wanted to."

CHAPTER SIXTEEN

Stephanie sat alone in her bedroom, a single dim lamp in the corner leaving the room relatively dark aside from the white glow of her tablet.

She had hurried through her closing tasks tonight, desperate to get home and download the book she'd found on Kera's phone. With all the strange things that had happened lately, she was worried that Kera had somehow gotten in over her head.

She still couldn't find the book on Amazon, but it *did* have a presence, including multiple reviews on GoodReads. One of the more recent ones commented that it had been pulled from publication sometime in the last couple of weeks.

Stephanie idly chewed her nails, a bad habit she thought she'd nixed years ago, as she read what the various users had to say. Their reviews and comments were a mixed bag. That was how it always was on the Internet; reading people's thoughts about a movie she regarded as "pretty good," Stephanie always found some folks who thought it was an abject turd and others who considered it the best film in the history of cinema.

For this book, even by Internet standards, different individuals' results varied to a ridiculous degree.

The majority, probably three-quarters, insisted that the book was nonsense. That none of it was real and its authors were frauds or charlatans, and that any other reviews to the contrary were the work of shills, lunatics, and the intellectually disabled.

There were also some who regarded the book as an "entertaining reference." They didn't take it seriously as an instructional manual and had picked it up to learn about magic—or as the book called it, thaumaturgy—as an idea, for academic reasons, or just for fun.

But in addition to these, there were several that claimed magic was real and functional and amazing. Persons who had gained the strength of six men, charmed others into doing their bidding, cured themselves of influenza, or learned to light fires remotely and extinguish them at will.

"Boys and girls," Stephanie whispered to the screen, "either you are all crazy as hell, or Kera is into something more people need to know about. For real."

Two reviews, among the longer and more detailed ones, made reference to miscellaneous crap that had been in the news. Incidents in South Carolina, Florida, Texas, New Mexico, and elsewhere that involved people who claimed to have strange powers or had been implicated in weird happenings, only for everything to vanish a short time later without conclusive proof. They went on to suggest that what might have been going on was low-level mass hysteria or a bizarre hoax.

Stephanie leaned back, and her eyes went distant.

Why, she wondered, would her co-worker be interested in this stuff? Kera MacDonagh wasn't credulous, New Age-y, or the superstitious type. She'd always struck Stephanie as a grounded, sensible, rational woman. After all, she had majored in computer science. Those folks weren't known for dabbling in witchcraft.

Then again...

Kera had recently come in late on one or two occasions, previously unheard of for her. She had also lost a lot of weight in a short period of time, gained mysterious markings on her body, been out of work for multiple days for reasons she'd glossed over —which Cevin had refused to talk about, too—and had suddenly dyed her hair black for no appreciable reason.

Kera, who rode a black motorbike with a matching helmet.

Stephanie sat bolt upright. "Nah," she insisted to herself, "she is *not* Motorcycle Man. That's ridiculous. Stephanie, you need to go to bed and get some rest."

But as she brushed her teeth, the notion refused to leave her mind. She was buzzing with hypotheses and implications and questions she didn't know how to either answer or ignore.

Upon returning to her room, Stephanie woke her tablet back up and did one last thing. She went back to the site where she'd found a pirated PDF copy of the book.

"Shouldn't be doing this shit," she muttered as she hit the button and downloaded a copy. But she wasn't going to figure out if this was for real unless she did her damned research.

For the first time in what seemed like far too long, Johnny found he didn't actively dread showing up at Pauline's office when summoned. He had a spring in his step as he approached and knocked on the door.

"Come in," Pauline called.

When Johnny walked in, he did a double-take. Pauline looked…different.

She didn't appear ready to discuss that, however.

She got right down to business, folding her arms and running her tongue over the tips of her teeth. "All right, since I cannot rely on any of you to ultimately figure out what the hell is going on, *I'll* make the plan, and you will do as you're told."

Johnny frowned. He might have been wrong about this being a good meeting. "With all due respect, Boss Lady, we *know* what's going on. It's only a matter of hunting down our enemies and dealing with them."

She replied in a voice that was sharp but not angry, "You are essentially right, and I appreciate your attitude. No one else has demonstrated the level of commitment you have, Johnny. However, you're glossing over the specifics, which are complicated."

Johnny frowned but said nothing. He wasn't quite sure where this was going.

Pauline looked at him. "I will conduct a reconnaissance operation designed to draw Motorcycle Man and the LA Witches out of the woodwork so we can learn more about them. We will then use that information to eliminate them once and for all. Brute force has proven ineffective. We should have been using espionage and subterfuge from the beginning."

Johnny nodded. He couldn't think of what to say.

"You will be joining me on this job since you're the only one who has shown an acceptable level of enthusiasm for hunting down our enemies and stomping them into the goddamn dirt where they belong. Now is not the time for excessive caution or prudence."

"Hey, I try." He leaned against the wall, grinning. "So, what's the gist of your plan?"

"I was getting to that," Pauline reprimanded. "First, I'll be coming along in person, though in disguise. Probably in the role of, say, the vapid, dull-witted girlfriend of a stupid rich playboy."

"Oh, that explains…" Johnny gestured at her outfit. She was wearing very different makeup and clothing, as well as a reddish-brown wig. She also had thigh-high boots over her jeans that showed off how nice her legs were.

Johnny narrowed his eyes, though his mouth was twisted with amusement. "So, does that mean I'll be playing the rich playboy?"

"Most likely, yes," she confirmed. "Unless I can find someone better on short notice, in which case you would be our bodyguard. Either way, we'll find a good use for you. As for when we're doing this, it's tonight. I hate wasting time. And as to *where* we'll be going, I would say the most sensible option is to stake out the place where our woes began, which has been a thorn in our collective side this entire time."

Her hands had rolled into tight, bony fists, and her red nails were making equally red marks on her palms.

Johnny nodded, understanding at once what she meant. The prospect filled him with vague low-level dread, but also a certain vicious excitement.

"The Mermaid," he surmised.

Doug Lopez's mouth went through a series of sputtering motions before actual words came out. "What the shit?"

Mia rushed over from her desk. "What is it? It's not something related to *our* story, is it? Ugh, wait, don't answer that. Of course it is."

She looked over his shoulder at his laptop's screen. He was viewing their most recent report on Motorcycle Man and his exploits, or rather, the final draft of their report.

It had been altered. *Substantially.*

Mia's mouth imitated Doug's, twisting in odd shapes as her eyes bulged in wrathful disbelief. Random weird sounds came out eventually.

Someone had reworded sentences here and there, deleted others, and added a couple of new paragraphs, all of them bent toward a particular goal: pandering to the feds. The report now fulfilled the Bureau's "suggestion" that Motorcycle Man be smeared, vetoing the public's honest opinions.

There were cryptic suggestions that Motorcycle Man was the alter ego of a mentally imbalanced career criminal, and his stunts had been no more than distractions from his illegal activities.

Not to mention, the article threw shade on the vigilante's heroic rescue efforts, positing that he had been reckless and stupid and had unnecessarily endangered the populace by refusing to let the professionals deal with things.

And at the end of the story was an advertisement for a live report the station was doing on their TV channel, which would begin in three minutes.

Doug asked, "Do we even want to watch it? I'm not sure I do. It's going to be a total crapfest. I mean, look at *this*." He waved his hand at the screen. "And we had zero involvement in the live show, so whatever nuances might have remained in our text story will go out the window."

Mia rubbed her eyes, once again feeling like she could use a stiff drink. "Oh, man. Yeah, it's going to suck, but we have to. We have to know what they're doing with our work so we can calibrate our anger to the appropriate level."

Nodding, Doug agreed, "You're probably right. I'm guessing it will be somewhere between 'really pissed' and 'nuclear explosion.'"

"Most likely. It's your turn to refill our coffee, though."

Mia sat down and switched to the station's live stream as her partner hurried to the coffee machine. He returned with both cups full and steaming as the report began.

The journalist running the stream was a newer girl named Sandy whom Doug and Mia had only worked with a couple of times. She mostly ran with other departments, and as far as the two of them were aware, she'd had no involvement in the Motorcycle Man case before now.

"Hello," she began, posing in front of a lush and prosperous suburban neighborhood, "and welcome to *Motorcycle Man: Friend or Foe? A Special Live Report*. We're here near Los Feliz to speak to several residents who have gathered to discuss the mysterious vigilante everyone has been talking about, but whose true identity and motivations have remained shadowy."

Doug groaned. "Motorcycle Man hasn't operated in that neighborhood. They deliberately avoided the downtown area where people would be more likely to have firsthand information."

"Yeah," Mia grumbled, "and they're already setting the stage for character assassination by using the word 'shadowy' when they could have said something more neutral like 'obscure.' Goddammit."

She had a terrible sinking feeling that her anger level was going to trend toward the "nuclear" end of the spectrum Doug had described.

Sandy went on to give a brief, rough, half-assed overview of the situation before pausing to interview a couple of residents from the crowd of local observers. Doug and Mia wondered if they were legit or if they had been planted in the crowd.

She asked a cantankerous-looking fat guy in a nice button-down shirt, "How do you feel about Motorcycle Man's complete flaunting of local laws and customs? New facts about the case suggest he may have a criminal background and may have crossed county lines as part of his vigilante activities."

Doug's fingertips clawed the desk.

The man gave a relatively noncommittal and elliptical response in which he blathered about how he didn't support anyone breaking the law and figured that most people were better off calling the cops if they had a problem.

Sandy quickly interviewed two more people, both women, one of whom said she wanted to like Motorcycle Man but she wasn't sure what to think, and another who huffily questioned why Motorcycle Man felt the need to hide his face and identity if he was so good and virtuous.

"Moving on," Sandy elaborated as she looked into the camera, "new information has, as I mentioned, recently come out. We received word from an agent of the Federal Bureau of Investigation, speaking on condition of anonymity, that the so-called

Motorcycle Man might be an individual who was previously committed to a state mental health facility, or possibly a soldier for a local organized crime syndicate..."

She went on to touch upon a half dozen different conspiracy theories harvested from the Internet, carefully avoiding committing to any of them but implying that they might be true. Not a single one cast Motorcycle Man in a positive light.

There was a brief cut to some infographics on LA crime statistics and past instances of supposed vigilantes causing problems while trying to protect themselves or others from looters, rioters, and muggers. Then the camera returned to the live feed of Sandy, who had moved into the foothills not too far from Griffith Observatory, the better to get a wider shot of the city below.

"And so," she concluded, "Los Angeles struggles with indecision in what are already uncertain times. The FBI has assured us that they are on the case and that all guilty parties will be brought to justice for any and all crimes committed. This is Sandy Satkowiak, signing off."

Doug closed the screen of his laptop and took six or seven deep breaths, struggling to resist the urge to fling the device at the wall. "What a shitshow," he muttered.

Mia was less restrained. "Oh, fuck this! They stopped just short of outright lying but still spent the whole fucking broadcast massaging the facts and seeding their bullshit agenda in the minds of viewers. As though public trust in the American news media isn't abysmal enough! Fuck! We're *real* journalists with integrity, and these shills keep hamstringing us every step of the way. And a hero is going to take a fall because of it. Ugh!"

She kicked the trash can, spilling its contents across the floor, then spent a moment calming herself down before she grabbed a couple of leftover napkins and cleaned up the mess.

Doug, meanwhile, could do little more than sit and stare into space. He was as furious as his partner, but his rage was tempered by a cold, sick feeling of depression and futility. After all their work on the Motorcycle Man story, *this* was the final result.

In a feeble effort to take his mind off things, he checked his email.

"Oh, look," he mumbled. "The boss sent us a couple of emails. Want to read them?"

"*No*," Mia snapped. "Definitely not. Thanks for asking."

Doug nodded. "Same. I can't put up with the bastard right now. I wonder if he wrote the emails himself, or if it's just crap from the FBI that he has politely forwarded to our inboxes."

Mia stood and tossed the last of the napkins in the trash, which had been restored to its rightful place. "Who cares?" she growled. Then she lowered herself back into her chair and ran her fingers through her hair many more times than was necessary.

To break the awkward silence as much as anything else, Doug quipped, "It's effective, I'll give them that—the sneaky, under-handed techniques they used. They never said any of this stuff was confirmed or offered evidence. They simply threw the ideas out there and are letting the people fill in the blanks on their own. When someone gets to do the last part of the mental work themselves, they feel more sure of their false, incorrect conclusions. Brilliant."

A shudder went through Mia as she forced herself to stay seated. Another tantrum wouldn't solve anything. "That's one word for it. They won't get away with this. We have to do something."

Doug breathed in through his nose and out through his mouth. "Once again, we are in agreement, but what the hell *can* we do?"

"I don't know," Mia admitted, "but we're smart. We'll figure it out. And soon."

Mr. and Mrs. Kim sat down to dinner. Though the electric lights were on in the next room to provide extra illumination, they had a single candle burning in the center of the table.

Sam was at a friend's house for the evening, so it was just the two of them. They did not eat meals together with no one else present as often as they once had and enjoyed it immensely when the occasion presented itself.

"I am much better lately," Mrs. Kim told her husband in Korean. "Nothing has grown worse since Kera started her healing sessions, and getting up and training in martial arts again is making me feel stronger and healthier like I'm fifteen years younger again."

Her husband gave her a small yet warm smile. "Good, very good. I always knew my flower would find a way to live through the frosts. You have always been strong. Sam is almost an adult, but he still needs his mother around. You will improve still more, I think."

"I think so too," she told him.

They clasped hands for a moment, then dug into their meal, a basic but tasty and nourishing chicken stir fry, along with strong green tea. At first, they chatted about daily life and how Sam was doing, but Mr. Kim's mood grew distant and pensive. His wife kept trying to strike up further conversation, only for him to drift off into his own thoughts.

When both had finished off the majority of their food and drink, she looked across the table and asked, "My dear, what is wrong? I can tell you're occupied with something. It would be better to state it outright than let it simmer."

He frowned and settled back in his chair, letting out a sigh of resignation. She recognized the half-annoyed, half-relieved expression on his face. It meant he'd acknowledged that she was right.

"I am worried about Kera," he said finally. "She is taking on too much too quickly, and I fear she won't be able to handle it all. Things have grown complicated of late."

His hardened hands flexed on the table as he rolled them into and out of fists and then rubbed his knuckles. Since Kera had used her abilities to channel healing energy into his hands, his arthritis had all but vanished, but old habits died hard.

His wife made a low sound in her throat as she reflected on his words. "She has good sense," she pointed out. "Again and again, Kera has surprised me with her understanding, especially for one so young. She does not want to learn everything or do everything associated with magic. There is prudence and caution underneath her seeming recklessness." She hesitated. "But she is cutting people off. I am worried about her decision to memory-wipe the boy. It was a big choice to make for him."

"Yes," Mr. Kim said. "And I fear for her. I wish she had a better teacher than me. She has a good one in you, of course, but that's for martial arts. When it comes to magic, I am no great master, and it goes beyond that. She could use a good mentor for life in general. Someone who could protect her better and talk sense into her. As you say, she refuses to be convinced that she does not have to face all this strife alone."

Mrs. Kim put her hand on his shoulder and rubbed the back of his neck. "My dear, you are far better than nothing, even if we did not remain in Korea long enough for you to attain full mastery of your abilities. Besides, nowadays the kids have the Internet, don't they? That might help her learn things. She could get in contact with other people who have had similar experiences."

The man grunted. "Thank you, Ye-Jin. But there's also the matter of these people who are going around the country and seeking out individuals who have the gift. I still remember when people came to find me after it became clear what I was. We were both terrified for our lives. You recall that, don't you? We had to run. It was part of why we came to America. I don't want the same thing to happen to Kera. She might do something stupid or have to flee to Mexico. Who knows?"

"We cannot know what will happen," Mrs. Kim pointed out. "It may be that her experience is different, better than ours. It has been many years, and this is a different country. We will help her however we can, but it's no use worrying about things that haven't yet occurred."

She stood and began to gather the dishes.

As her husband handed over his plates and utensils, he added, "She should have tried to make things work with that boy. He probably would have been good for her. Maybe not, but things could have succeeded or failed on their own merits rather than being based on her hiding and sabotaging the whole thing. She'll do nothing but make herself miserable with this. Sad and lonely and scared."

His wife took the dishes to the kitchen, then walked back toward the table. "We can give her advice, but no more than that. It's not our place to make decisions *for* her. In the meantime, I think we should take Sam somewhere. Do something fun. Quality time, I think they call it in America. It's been too long, and we've been very focused on Kera."

Mr. Kim smiled at her. "Yes, I think you're right. We all love Kera, but the three of us need to get away, if only for a day or so. I'll think of something and talk to Sam when he gets back."

"Good." Mrs. Kim kissed her husband on the top of his head, and he stood and followed her to the kitchen, where they washed the dishes together.

CHAPTER SEVENTEEN

James was glad they'd started setting things up early since it took a good half-hour to get all the necessary technology running. They then had to smooth it over with a couple of infusions of magic, not to mention the obligatory cloaking spells to stop the FBI from listening in.

Anyone outside the room or watching surveillance inside it would hear a quietly-murmured conversation about very boring things. James hoped it drove them crazy. After all, he'd wanted to be in a hotel, not here. He and LeBlanc had pointed out that they had ways of remaining incognito, but the agents had insisted they remain here.

Since their contacts were useful, James and LeBlanc had decided to accept the terms, though he was not best pleased to be sleeping in an old full bed instead of a new, luxurious, king-sized one.

Finally, the video conference was ready to go.

James and Mother LeBlanc sat close together by a small desk in one of the safe house's bedrooms. On the screen of his laptop, the picture came into focus and divulged the other ten members of the Council of Thaumaturgy sitting in their usual arrangement, although they had congregated at Lauren Jones' house rather than headquarters.

Lauren was the most well-rounded thaumaturgist among them in terms of her aptitude for different types of magic. She was also the best teacher, so it was fitting that she was hosting a roundtable on whether they should take on a new student. She was a thoroughly average but pleasant-looking woman and often had to remind people to call her "Lauren" instead of "Miss Jones" or her personal non-favorite, "Hey, lady."

James waved at the camera and watched the motion in the lower corner of the screen. "Hello, ladies and gentlemen. Thank you for joining us."

LeBlanc waved too and gave them a nice smile and nod. "We appreciate your convening on such short notice."

James noticed something, though. Despite Lauren providing the venue, the arrangement of the members at their table suggested Lady Mitchell was in charge.

Of course, he lamented, but he was fairly sure he managed to prevent his consternation from showing on his face. *She had better not keep going off on nitpicky tangents like she did last time.*

"Good evening," Mitchell began. "Assuming that this is indeed as important as you told us it was, we are willing to consider it worth our time. Of course, please do not *waste* time, either. Let's hear it."

The other members nodded.

James didn't want to be doing this any more than they did. He had no complaints about getting it over with quickly and efficiently.

"Of course. To summarize the agenda, we have a new plan concerning the final prospective witch, the one in Los Angeles who has been causing us so many headaches."

Four or five of the people on the other side of the screen started in their seats. They hadn't expected such an announcement. They had probably figured their two wayward colleagues were going to announce that they'd dealt with the problem and were coming home.

Everyone except Hugh Buchanan, who was always taciturn, tried to talk at once. Amidst the general clamor, James made out a handful of iterations of "What plan?" and at least one person used the word "ridiculous."

Mother LeBlanc raised a hand to convince them to shut up, and Mitchell did the same thing on her end. Silence set back in.

Mitchell took the lead again. "A new plan, you say? Why, did the old one not cause enough problems for everyone?"

James cleared his throat loudly and folded his hands together. Rather than answer her bad-faith question, he dodged it to continue explaining his purpose.

"The individual we have locked onto possesses power the likes of which we haven't seen for many years. This is a channeler of once-in-a-generation abilities, my friends, and their actions suggest greater wisdom and self-control than we had expected at first. There is a degree of potential here that would be downright tragic to waste."

Lady Mitchell made a clucking sound while covering her eyes and remarked, "You refer, of course, to the person who is pretending to be a superhero and has attracted the attention of the FBI, yes?"

Grave rumblings of discontent circulated among the ten.

James went on, attempting to make his point as clearly as possible before Mitchell could sabotage him further.

"Our nascent thaumaturge has managed not to burn out, despite being active for a greater period of time than the others. They've kept their identity hidden, and we suspect they may have learned some rudimentary techniques for disguising the use of their magic. Whoever they are, this is a level of resourcefulness that demands respect. They keep doing needlessly flashy and bombastic things, yes, but they don't seem to be seeking personal celebrity. It's not as though they've come forth and started a self-aggrandizing cult or anything like that."

The other thaumaturges were silent. Damian Diaz asked, "Mother, what do you think? You haven't said a word."

LeBlanc stated, "James and I have slight differences of opinion on this topic, but I will confirm that everything he has said is true. I question his conclusions, but I am forced to agree that we are dealing with an...*exceptional* individual."

"Very well," said Mitchell. "What are those conclusions, Mr. Patterson?"

James narrowly stopped himself from wincing. She had used his obnoxious nickname; someone had tossed it around at a party years ago in reference to the fact that both he and the famous author had started out in advertising.

"I propose that we bring this person into the fold. Under heavy supervision, of course. Lay down the law, but also offer them the opportunity to advance far beyond what they could teach themself. Offer our guidance, but if they prove to be hopeless and unreachable, then, well, we'll follow the standard operating procedure for loose cannons, but not before we *try* to make the best of such talent. Not before we try to accomplish what we originally agreed to do, which is pass on our ways to a deserving disciple."

He sat up straighter as he spoke and put all the passion he could into his voice, playing on the Council's usually subdued fear of passing into irrelevance.

The looks on their faces made him think that maybe, just maybe, it was working.

Lady Mitchell would not be so easily deterred. "James, you speak of preserving our tradition, yet this person flaunts it. They are behaving like a human wrecking ball. Thaumaturgists are supposed to enjoy a quieter life than that since the work we do affects more people than the residents of a single city, yet on a milder scale. Hence, less unwanted attention."

Amanda Moore, monikered "the Dark One" due to her all-black wardrobe—mostly she found it to be a slimming color, but she also enjoyed the mysterious reputation it gave her—butted in. "And animals. We do not only serve humankind."

"Indeed," Zacharia confirmed. "Our discipline exists for the benefit of all creatures that live under the sky, or even under the earth."

Rufus Mayer added, "They're connected anyway. One can readily become another, given a little nudge." He was a transmutation specialist, after all. "Of course, as Mitchell pointed out, it's best to avoid doing anything too *publicly*."

James simmered with annoyance. They raised good points, but all of them seemed to be missing the main thrust of his argument. They were dragging the debate out with tangents related to their personal agendas while seeming to half-heartedly support Mitchell.

LeBlanc kept quiet. She had agreed to hear the rest of the council's opinion of James' proposal and saw no point in speaking until something resembling a consensus began to emerge.

Frustrated, James brought his fist down on the desk. The screen rattled and the bang passed through the microphone, startling the other council members on the video call.

"If the traditional method of keeping our heads down is so foolproof," he demanded to know, "why are we dying out? Answer me that. We *must* adapt. We need to reform how we approach these things and have the open minds necessary to accept an infusion of new people. Yes, we can ensure they follow most of the rules, but are we really so all-knowing as to think that no one else can teach *us* anything? This person may have found ways of working with power that our order has forgotten, which might serve us well as we forge ahead into the twenty-first century."

A few mutters greeted him, but James could tell he was

getting to them. Zacharia of all people echoed his words, and Rufus, Amanda, Damian, and Samantha conceded that he probably had a point.

Quiet set in again as the stalemate lingered.

"Well," Mitchell quipped, "that is six for and six against so far. Mother LeBlanc? Hugh? Have you anything to add?"

Hugh Buchanan coughed and leaned forward, his grim but somehow kindly face drawn with intense thought. "I prefer not to speak up unless I'm certain about what needs to be said since those who talk before they know are seldom worth listening to. But within the flood of rhetoric that tends to issue from Mr. Lovecraft's mouth, I'd say there is at least a small stone of truth. I say we allow him to proceed with his plan. With, of course, the understanding that he is to abort it if things go south."

James felt as if wings had sprouted from his back. "Thanks, Hugh."

Mitchell frowned. "I see. Well, then. The other five of us might not like it, but it would appear that you have the bare minimum support necessary to proceed, James."

LeBlanc raised her hand. "Consider me neutral, though I will continue to participate in the plan. I believe that James' plan, since it contains a failsafe option, is fundamentally sound."

After another two minutes of vagaries and formalities, the conference ended.

James told them, "Thank you again for your time, ladies and gentlemen. I strongly suspect this council has decided on the right course of action."

"We will see," Mitchell replied. "Good luck to both of you."

James leaned forward and shut off the video and audio feeds. Then he leaned back on the couch, blowing his breath toward the ceiling and ruffling his hair.

LeBlanc smiled. "Good performance. I agreed to abide by the council's judgment, and so I will. You may indeed have a point, but everything depends on what we discover when we meet

Motorcycle Man in the flesh. I have a feeling we'll be able to make our final decision quickly once that is accomplished."

"Right." James nodded. "So that's that. Let's find him."

Half an hour later, he sat on a couch in the safe house, waiting for his partner to finish dressing.

They'd had a short debriefing session with Richardson and MacDonald, then they had made their plans for the evening.

They would be going out for a drink at a bar called the Mermaid. It had been mentioned on the news in conjunction with a story about growing rowdiness and gang activity in the Little Tokyo area. As such, it seemed as good a place as any they could think of to begin the hunt for their prospective student.

James sighed and glanced at his phone, which told him it was 8:23 p.m. They were on the verge of missing out on the earlier portion of the prime drinking hours, but he supposed that even a positively ancient woman with all the wisdom and miraculous power of multiple lifetimes could not be rushed when it came to getting herself ready for a night on the town.

He had changed into a nice suit and tie. They were perhaps a tad outdated but fit his purposes. He wondered if LeBlanc was refurbishing her dress into something modern like a pair of yoga pants.

At 8:25, footsteps moved on the second floor, then descended the staircase. Nodding with grim satisfaction, James stood up and went to meet his "date."

He stopped in his tracks. Mother LeBlanc looked…different.

"How do you like it?" she asked.

For once, she had put aside her flowing rainbow-hued dress. Instead, she wore tight black leggings that shimmered in the light, resembling an oil slick, and an oversize indigo sweater she had belted at the waist, with the hem coming halfway down her thighs. Though it flattered her figure, it seemed to have nearly as many folds and hidden pockets as her usual dress did.

"Well," James commented, "it's different. In a good way.

Damn. You know, honestly, if I seem flabbergasted here, I think it's mainly that in all these years, I've *never* seen you wear anything else."

LeBlanc shrugged. "I am not going to attract undue attention by going to the bar in my usual attire. This is more conservative, wouldn't you say?"

"In a manner of speaking, yes," he conceded. "Less unusual, though a tad provocative."

She came down the rest of the stairs and put her shoes on. "That's to be expected, isn't it? I understand that young people these days go to bars to flaunt themselves by looks or other social signifiers. That's common throughout most of history in one way or another."

James turned his mind to practical matters. "Okay, whatever. Let's review the plan. We park somewhere in the vicinity of the Mermaid and walk a short way so we have an excuse to survey the area. Get a feel for who and what is around."

"Yes, of course," said LeBlanc. "And while observing the clientele, we should do some rudimentary mind-reading and aura-sensing. That is a simple way to detect excessive concealment, which might point us in the right direction. Motorcycle Man might not be there, but someone might have information that can lead us to him. Or her."

They stepped out of the house and into the Rolls Royce, which James had to hope wouldn't be too tempting a target for car thieves. Granted, he had ways of protecting it from such people, but still.

As James fired up the engine and pulled onto the road, something buzzed in his brain—an overwhelming curiosity that demanded satisfaction.

He couldn't control himself any longer.

"LeBlanc," he began in a low voice, running his tongue over his lips. "I have to ask. With you in the new outfit and all, can you still do, y'know, the trick?"

She turned her head to him, then, without a word, reached into her sweater and pulled out a live chicken. It clucked at them and tried to flap its wings, and a single white feather wafted to the floor.

"Yes." LeBlanc put the bird back where she'd found it.

Doug and Mia parked the SUV and climbed out.

"Well," said Doug, "here we are, riding the coattails of someone else's story. No career of our own anymore."

If he'd thought they drank too much a few nights ago, he had a feeling that *tonight* was going to be even worse. Both of them were in a bitch of a mood—well-earned, in his opinion.

Mia checked her makeup in a pocket mirror. "Trey Mancuso is good, and he wasn't the one who changed our article. If this is all connected like those agents are claiming, this is a good place to start researching. I still want to figure out what the hell *is* going on." She sighed. "Even if we're not employed as reporters anymore. You can take the reporter out of the newsroom, but…"

"Whatever." Doug sighed. "Anyway, even if we can't find a scoop, they have alcohol."

They walked past the crowd of early-twenty-somethings who had gathered outside and who eyed the pair before returning to their loud, boisterous conversations. Doug pushed open the front door, and they seated themselves at a corner table with a good view of the rest of the establishment.

The place was busy, and it looked like it would take a minute before one of the servers could be with them. They sat in glum silence, pretending to read the menu. The place was reasonably busy but hardly rowdy or violent.

"Hey," Doug quipped, "hotbed of gang activity, right? Gang stuff is our specialty. We'll have a great story in no time flat. Get a new job."

"Mm, yeah, I guess." Mia's voice was barely audible. "Better than nothing."

A young woman came by and introduced herself as Stephanie, their waitress for the evening. The two journalists said hello and declined food, moving straight to drinks. Doug ordered a whiskey and Coke, Mia a vodka grasshopper. Both asked for the beverages to be made stronger than normal.

Stephanie jotted down the orders. "No problem. I'll be right back with those."

"Thanks," Doug told her.

Ten minutes later, both had polished off the first half of their drinks and were starting to feel buzzed. They glanced around the bar, reflexively noting the characters who seemed troublesome or interesting but not truly focusing on any of them.

"Fuck," said Mia. "It isn't the same. *Nothing* is going to be the same for a while, is it?"

Doug stirred his whiskey-spiked Coke with a fork. "Probably not. If we took their offer, we'd be breaking our own rules. If we didn't, we were as good as fired; we knew that. Nothing we find tonight is going to change that, so let's get drunk and hope something falls into our laps. We can do real investigating another night when the world doesn't seem so terrible and ridiculous."

Mia slugged down the rest of her grasshopper. "Whatever. Are we on a blacklist now? We *did* get sold the fuck out, after all. Frank shipped us down the river to Shit Creek, paddle-less. Dropped this 'choice'—which was not a choice, not a fucking choice at all— in our laps. We were finally starting to get somewhere, and…" She shook her head. "Yeah, we're definitely on a blacklist."

Her partner shrugged. "Who knows?" Then something occurred to him—a fight-fire-with-fire notion.

"Mia," he said in a low voice, practically a whisper, "I have an idea about how we can pay them back and have our fiendish revenge and stuff."

She faced him, bug-eyed and skeptical. "What? How? You're not talking about going postal, are you?"

"Tempting, but no." He glanced around to ensure no one was listening. "You know how government employees are always leaking information to journalists? Well, nothing says we can't do a certain amount of leaking ourselves."

Her interest piqued, Mia sat up straighter and banished the fuzz of inebriation from her mind. "Huh. You mean, quit and keep surreptitiously putting out the real stories?"

"Yup." He grinned. "If they're going to report conjectures and conspiracy theories as if they were facts, it's only fitting that we do the exact opposite."

His partner ran a finger over her lips, and her eyes glazed over in thought. "I like it. Well, wait. There is one problem. We still have to observe the baseline journalistic ethics. We need to make sure we just keep reporting facts. We don't want to look like huge suckers if it turns out Motorcycle Man *is* a total douche." She sighed. "After all, what if they're right?"

"If they were right," Doug said, "they'd have proof that the gang violence was a response to Motorcycle Man, but how *could* it be? The dude started off his 'career,' so to speak, by saving people from a car crash. That wasn't poking at gangs."

"Right." She shook her head. "Being stupid, I guess. You know how you get when you realize you've lost your job and no one will admit it's for a bullshit reason? That's how I feel."

Doug frowned and drained the rest of his drink. "Yeah. Turns out I *do* know how that feels."

He looked over as two people, a slight man and an exotic-looking woman, appeared more or less out of nowhere and sat down next to the journalists at their table, which was, after all, only half-occupied.

"Hello," said the man, who was looking dapper in a spotless gray suit and tie, though something about him was off in a scarcely perceptible, unsettling way. He spoke with a faint New England upper-crust accent.

"Hello," said the woman, who cut a striking figure in a large indigo sweater that served as a short dress. Something about her was a bit odd and disturbing too. Her accent suggested the Louisiana bayou country.

While Doug's mouth twisted in irritation, Mia accepted the interruption and responded, "Hi there. We were just finishing our drinks, so if you're expecting company, we'll be leaving soon."

"Oh, no, quite all right." The woman reached into the folds of her sweater as though checking for something, then laid her slim dark hands on the table. "We've only just arrived in town, and no one else is with us."

The man added, "We're out for a quick drink ourselves. Heard about this place from some of the locals and figured we'd stop by since it's getting too late to bother driving around Beverly Hills looking for all the celebrity mansions. But, well, we couldn't help overhearing you mention that Motorcycle Man."

"Indeed," the woman confirmed. "It seems as though everyone is talking about him. I must confess, I'm curious."

The man smiled. "Same."

Doug was going to give them a bare-bones summary of what everyone knew before pleading the Fifth on the rest, but for some reason he could not identify, he felt the urge to say more. The couple, whoever they were, seemed like people he could trust. The obscure strangeness about them only enhanced the feeling.

"Yeah," Doug began, wondering in the back of his mind if he was about to make a mistake. "Lots of talk, but most of it is BS. The government is not very happy with him, but so far, it looks like he's doing good things, right?"

Mia shifted her hips and shoulders. She felt uncomfortably torn between wanting to join Doug in telling their whole story and being cautious and reticent. To stall while she thought it over, she said, "Nice to meet you. I'm Mia, and he's Doug. And you are?"

Their guests were not fazed by the question.

"Jay," stated the man.

"You may call me Em," the woman chimed in.

Doug echoed the greeting and continued to ramble. "So yeah, we're reporters, and we have a certain amount of involvement in that whole goddamn fiasco. Or we were involved until the higher-ups yanked it away from us and put their bullshit spin on it. That's part of why we're drunk. Right, Mia?"

Carried away by her co-worker's enthusiasm and unable to resist the unexplained urge to spill the beans to their new friends, Mia relented. "Yeah, that's right. It was a crock of shit. Unless we're severely mistaken, Motorcycle Man is a straight-up *hero*. We never uncovered his identity, but we were on the scene when he rescued a building full of people, for one thing. And then..."

She went on, any doubt leaving her mind that perhaps she shouldn't be talking so much while Em and Jay listened, rapt.

When all of the story had been told save the boring technical details, the two journalists shared a glass of water to help prepare them for the drive home and the next day.

"Oh, one other thing," Doug added. "We were thinking about slipping the real story to the public via the Internet or something, but Mia suggested, smart girl that she is, that we ought to wait for more information. In case it turns out that Motorcycle Man is a bad guy after all."

"Right," his partner confirmed. "We still have *some* standards as journalists, goddammit."

Jay and Em exchanged quick glances.

"That," said the woman, "is an excellent idea, and I encourage you not to trouble yourselves further. The truth will reveal itself in time, as it always does, and you've been through a lot. You will need to recover from your emotional exhaustion before you're fit to move on to the next stage."

"Absolutely," the man affirmed. "Don't string yourselves out and risk making a mistake by chasing down factoids at a time like this. Take a few days off and go to a spa or something. After you're refreshed, you can review what-all info is available and go from there."

Doug and Mia nodded. The strange couple was so friendly and reasonable that they found it virtually impossible to disagree.

"In fact," Jay concluded, "I'd say you both ought to go home and get some sleep."

"Yeah," Doug responded. "Shit, I'm sleepy."

Mia rubbed her eyes. "Me too. We should go. Hey, it was really nice meeting you two. Enjoy your time in LA.!"

"Oh," said Em, "we will."

"Oh," Mother LeBlanc said, "we will."

She and James watched as the journalists shuffled out the front entrance and were gone.

Lovecraft nodded after them. "That was enlightening. I find myself charmed by their reluctance to go along with the spooks. In any event, they'll be safely out of the way for the rest of the weekend. Probably into next week, too."

LeBlanc sipped her water. "Indeed. The spa suggestion was a good one; they could use a break. We, on the other hand, have work to do. I don't suppose you have noticed anyone who might...qualify? I, so far, have not."

Their waitress Stephanie stopped by. "Did those two leave without paying?"

James waved a hand. "We'll pick up their tab. We offered to do so, and they forgot to tell you."

"Oh," Stephanie said. "Thanks."

Once she was gone, Lovecraft answered his friend's inquiry. "I haven't sensed anyone, either. It's wall to wall normies in here tonight, it would seem."

"Disappointing," LeBlanc stated.

She noticed a three-pack of young men eyeing her across the floor, a group of shady-looking individuals starting to raise their voices and wave their fists, and a small party of mostly girls who had downed two or three drinks too many and were cackling wildly, to the point of disturbing everyone around them.

"And," she added, "it's terribly rowdy in here, isn't it? It would be nice if they all calmed down enough for me to hear myself think."

James chuckled into his glass. "Wouldn't it, though?"

With no further words, they collaborated on a lightweight calming spell, layering it across most of the bar. As experienced as they were, they got the amount of channeling exactly right, and the patrons settled into either happy relaxation or mellow neutrality, depending on what their mood had been before.

LeBlanc smiled. "Yes, that's better."

After a moment of peaceful contemplation, she noticed something, and upon identifying it, she had a suggestion worth talking about.

"James. There is a faint signature here, but it's faded to the point that I only noticed it a moment ago. A residual signature. Do you sense it?"

He furrowed his brow. "Barely? I'm not as fine-tuned as you are. After all, *I'm* the age I look. Practically a toddler by comparison."

Ignoring the remark, LeBlanc went on, "Someone has performed thaumaturgy here, and it was not all that long ago. Motorcycle Man might not be present tonight, but I suspect this is one of their regular haunts."

James moved his head slowly up and down. "Yeah, that could well be. Shall we leave him a message?"

"Absolutely." LeBlanc seemed hyper-aware though calm. She was taking in the information delivered by everything going on around her while also thinking about the subject at hand. "But it must not be a warning. We gain nothing by scaring them off. Motorcycle Man must want to come to us and have good reason to seek our help."

James finished what little remained of Doug's whiskey and Coke, then ordered one of his own, though light on the whiskey since he refused to let LeBlanc drive his car.

"Yes," he declared once they were alone again. "Motorcycle Man is doing unambiguously good and helpful things and at least *attempting* to stay quiet about it, albeit he's pretty fucking incompetent about that part, given that the whole city is talking about him. In any event, there is an altruistic motive at work here. We want him to realize that with our assistance, he can help *more* people."

Using their shared and private language of subtle hand gestures and incantations disguised as low-volume nonverbal sounds, the two thaumaturges wove their spell, beseeching the divine powers to open the channels of power, which they then imbued into a random brick in the west wall. It lay near the junction of the main floor and the employees' area and was adjacent to the sidewalk outside so it covered the property.

On approaching it, a person with the gift would hear the intended message in their mind.

Unbeknownst to them, when they heard it, Lovecraft and LeBlanc would know. Traces of the message would cling to that person for a week or more, and they'd probably be none the wiser.

"Good," James mumbled after the casting was finished. "Ought to get the job done. We can be persuasive when we want to be."

LeBlanc raised her water glass, and they shared a low-key toast. "Of course, if that fails, we can always track them. Your idea to put the book out led us to this individual, which will perhaps prove to be a good thing. But we must not make the same mistakes twice."

"True," James admitted. "Okay, I'm hungry. I think they serve food here, but I'd like to see more of the town. What do you say we hit up the nearest five-star restaurant?"

LeBlanc stroked her chin. "A late supper does sound nice, but not at a five-star establishment. Really, James, you don't have to splurge to eat well. Los Angeles has some of the best street food in the *world*. Almost as good as New Orleans."

"Fine." He sighed. "We'll do it your way."

CHAPTER EIGHTEEN

Another night at the Mermaid, Kera thought, glancing across the darkened floor. *It's weird, though, how much the vibe has changed in the last few days. Did this suddenly become the shitty part of town? Did word get out that this was the place to be for all the local douchebags?*

Increasingly, it seemed that their patrons were less likely to be there for fun or relaxation and more likely to be there to drink off a shitty mood, look for trouble, posture obnoxiously in front of others, or scout for "marks" to whom they might sell drugs or other illegal goods and services. There had been a fight in the street outside the other day, albeit not when Kera was working. If she had been there, she probably would have broken it up, despite it technically being none of her employer's business.

She refilled the whiskey and Coke of the laid-back, unspeaking middle-aged guy who had sidled in a half-hour earlier, and he nodded his thanks. Everyone else seemed okay for the time being despite the vague air of tension that hung cloud-like over the place. Kera turned to her drink counter to check her stock.

Cevin wandered out of his office to scan the dining floor as well as check on Jenn and Kera.

"You girls okay?" he asked. It had a double meaning, which they both picked up on; he wanted to make sure they weren't overworked or falling behind, but also to determine if any trouble was brewing.

Jenn nodded. "Yeah, fine." She wasn't as sensitive or observant as her co-bartender and seemed less bothered by the shift in demographics.

The manager moved toward the other young woman.

Kera, who'd heard the question, turned to him. "I'm good. I heard about that fight a couple of nights ago. Good thing nobody was too badly hurt, and it happened off the Mermaid's property. Still, wasn't at least one of those guys in here before he got into that mess?"

Her boss's mouth drooped. "Yeah, unfortunately. It only takes one or two people to spread the word that this isn't a safe or classy place. I mean, yes, it was only one incident, but there was also some girl getting harassed by the entrance and another prick dealing drugs in the lot next door. It adds up. In all honesty, it worries the hell out of me that this place might be turning into the type of bar I really, really don't want to run."

She put a hand on his arm. "It won't, boss-man. A few rotten apples have drifted by is all. The cops showed up in all those cases, right? They'll pick out the bad actors, then other assholes will know they can't get away with stuff, and things will go back to normal."

Kera wasn't sure that was true but saying it seemed to comfort her boss a little. He gave her a thin smile, nodded, and went into the kitchen to check on everyone and help with food orders.

Once he had left, Kera turned to examine the patrons lining the bar, as well as the others at tables and booths on the dining floor. She studied them and felt and sensed the residues of their attitudes and intentions.

She couldn't be certain how, but in the last week or so, things like that were growing more apparent to her. *Passively*. It wasn't required that she cast a spell; her mind somehow picked up on what other people were thinking with greater ease now.

It must be a side effect of learning magic, she concluded. *Like, once you open your consciousness to the divine powers of the universe, you can't help perceiving things you might not have noticed before the mind's eye was opened.*

Or perhaps it was something else. The important thing was that it worked.

The new people, the patrons contributing to the negative vibe despite their facade of partying enjoyment, were here for *research*, she concluded. She couldn't pin it down in any greater detail than that, but they were studying something and trying to find things out. Being unable to determine what disturbed her.

Hopefully they haven't come to research me. She kept her concern off her face. If they were watching her, they might notice a shift in her mood.

There was another thing, too: interlocking lines of tension and enmity, some of which crossed between different groups at different tables. Gang feuds, possibly, or maybe one of the people in Group A had stolen the significant other of a person in Group B. It was tough to say.

Whatever it was, it smelled like trouble brewing.

Kera checked up on her drinkers, then asked Jenn to watch the bar for a couple of minutes while she excused herself to the break room. There, she opened her locker and pulled out her grimoire.

"Let's see," she murmured under her breath. "I know there was a calming spell in here somewhere."

She located it seconds later. The incantation and hand gestures were simple and not much different from the ones for the healing spell and the charm of forgetting, though the mental work of channeling differed substantially. She double-checked the formula, then headed back to work.

Once she was back in her place, Kera targeted the groups who had begun to worry her and cast the spell four times in quick succession, scattering the effects around the bar. No one seemed to notice what she was doing.

The effects were instantaneous. Conversations that had been growing raucous and full of hard-edged laughter became muted and halfhearted. Guys and girls who had seemed animated and antsy and ready to jump out of their seats slumped and sighed as if hopped up on relaxants. Most importantly, the electrical currents of hostility all but vanished.

Jenn's head turned toward the floor, and she blinked. "Did something happen that I missed?"

Kera's abdominal muscles tightened. "Nah, I think everyone's just getting tired. It's kinda late, and they've all been drinking."

Shit, I might have overdone it, she chastised herself. *Ought to have spent an extra minute or so limiting the amount of energy I channeled into it.*

Cevin reappeared from the kitchen. He too noticed the sea change, compared to when he'd been there five or ten minutes previously.

"Huh," he commented, "that's weird. Came out to see why it got so quiet all of a sudden. Did something happen?"

Kera repeated the lame excuse she's suggested to Jennifer since it was good to be consistent. It occurred to her that she felt tired and lightheaded, probably from a combination of work and the strain of casting.

Yup. Put too much power into the spell, so now I get to pay the price physically. And what about them? Are there going to be any lingering side effects? That certainly wasn't what I wanted to happen.

"Well," she added to her boss, "it's good that, um, things aren't going as badly as you were worried about, right? We dodged a bullet."

He shrugged. "I guess so."

Kera scanned the floor again and noticed for the first time

that the attractive woman Cevin had failed with the other evening was present. This time she was with another chick, probably a friend or co-worker. Mercifully, she wasn't with any of the groups of dickheads Kera had neutralized.

Mental note, she told herself. *If that woman is back, maybe Cevin didn't strike out as hard as we thought.*

"Hey, Kera," a guy at the far corner of the bar piped up. "Running dry here." He waved his glass at her. His mood was mellow, but his choice of words was aggravating.

She wanted to snap at him to be patient and have faith, but her will reasserted itself. She only said, "Okay, coming."

The drain on her energy had damaged her mood. She felt as though she'd woken up five minutes ago after four hours of sleep and hadn't had a cup of coffee yet, and it got worse as the night dragged on. Increasingly she found it hard to be nice to people.

Thanks to the calming spell, no one in the bar seemed inclined to complain or start a fight with her, but then again, the spell was the source of her fatigue.

Magic truly is a double-edged sword, isn't it? She shook her head and contemplated sneaking a drink behind the corner. *It solves one problem and creates another. Next time I feel this strung out, I can't rely on the thaumaturgic equivalent of Valium to save me, especially when I'm supposed to be hiding my abilities. Whoops.*

She calmed down by checking her stock of items, then stood up to look at the groups and see if anyone needed a refill. Everything was good as she scanned the room...until her gaze locked onto one particular individual. Her stomach muscles tightened, and her nostrils flared.

It was *him*—Mustang Man, the bastard who'd shot up Zee while trying to extort something from Cevin. And who'd hit on her before that, and if she recalled, had shown up at least once since then, despite what she had done to his car in retaliation.

The man who was one of the known members of the Startup.

He was with a woman, and Kera wasn't sure if that was a good or bad thing. At least it meant he probably wouldn't flirt with her.

His partner was around Kera's age or perhaps slightly older. She was attractive in a basic ditzy way, with long auburn hair, heavy bluish eye shadow, and a pair of boots that came halfway up her thighs even though she was wearing tight blue jeans beneath them. The two of them chatted sporadically, but they seemed to spend a lot of time looking at the other patrons.

And the staff. The woman caught Kera's eye, and she gave a short, curt nod before returning to work.

Ten minutes later, Kera had caught up with her half of the bar, which included another couple who seemed harmless as well as a pair of rough-looking guys who had been sedate so far but might be trouble later. Cevin walked by again. He was checking on things more often than usual.

Kera had an idea.

"Hey, Cevin," she called, and he hurried over to the bar. In a lower voice, "Check out that chick over there—the one who's bimboed all the way up. I've, uh, seen her before, and I hereby nominate her as your next attempted conquest. Seriously, go talk to her."

Blinking, her boss turned toward the table. "Her? She's with a guy!"

"Hey," Kera assured him, "I didn't tell you to blatantly ask her out or say anything risqué. Just strike up a brief conversation and see how it goes. With that one, if you strike out, it's *good*. So, like, let's try reverse psychology. With the other lady a couple of nights ago, you were trying too hard. If you're *not* really trying, you might do better. It makes perfect sense when you think about it."

Cevin visibly squirmed as he considered it. It was obvious he disliked the idea.

"The last thing I want is to start a fight in my own bar. Christ.

And I don't like the look of that guy she's with. He seems like trouble."

Part of Kera's experiment had been to see if Cevin would remember Mustang Man, and it seemed that he did not.

That was probably good. The man was more dangerous than either of them had thought.

"Okay," she replied, "maybe you're right, and he's the overly protective or jealous type. Although, um, you could always send me in to soften them up and be sure. Has anyone waited on their table yet?"

Cevin pursed his lips. "Stephanie had them under control, but the floor is getting busy. Maybe you could go check and see if they need a drink refill. Tell me if I should try it, huh? I trust female intuition more than my own when it comes to this sort of thing."

She laughed, though part of her was nervous. *I have more intuition than the average female, that's for certain.* "Sure thing. One second."

Kera finished making a drink for another patron, then walked toward the couple. Both noticed her and stared as she approached.

"Hi," she said, waving to them, "your server will be right back, but in the meantime, can I get either of you another drink?"

The woman flicked her eyes away, then said, "Yes, please." The voice was sharp and crisp; somehow, it didn't go with her appearance. She handed Kera a glass that was a quarter full of whiskey sour, the orange slice leaning against the residual ice.

The man said nothing but handed her an empty beer glass.

Kera smiled. "No problem." She took the containers, and her consciousness reached toward them, trying to sense the character of their thoughts and feelings—another part of the strange, passively-active abilities she'd gained since first dabbling in thaumaturgy.

She was struck by what she felt and not in a good way.

Neither of the pair gave off vibes that could be called good or pleasant, and the nature of them was similar from both.

In the woman's case, it was far stronger. Constant, seething anger mixed with loneliness and a desperate desire to prove herself, regardless of the consequences. Souls in more or less continuous pain, who probably wanted to extend the pain to others.

As she turned to head back to the bar, Kera paused, not wanting her feelings to be too obvious. Something about the couple scared her, especially the girl, despite knowing that Mustang Man was an unpleasant and dangerous individual. This, she sensed, might be the woman who ran the Startup. That would make her dangerous too, but Kera now knew where the danger came from.

She pitied them. Before she knew what she did, she was speaking an incantation under her breath and drawing down the power of the universe.

Casting spells on random schmucks. Is that the right thing to do? Sometimes I wonder, but I think these two need a little magic to keep their evening from going to shit, not to mention to keep them from shitting on everyone else's evening.

The calming spell engaged and soothing energy flowed over the man and the woman, numbing their tensions and directing their thoughts toward more peaceful matters. She added a small dose of memory-wipe for good measure.

They blinked and relaxed.

Kera strode to the bar, reassured the two slightly thuggish guys that she'd be with them in a moment, and refilled the two drinks from the table. When she brought them back out, she noticed that the vibe was gentler than it had been.

"Oh," the woman with the thigh-high boots said. "Um, thank you."

"Yeah," Mustang Man agreed. "That was...nice."

Kera smiled, told them not to mention it, and hurried back to the bar. With any luck, the pair would have a better evening now. She suspected that both of them needed a lot more than a single temporary spell in much the same way that a volcano needed more than a bucket of ice water.

Kera took a step or two down the bar to check on everyone and everything else and noticed Cevin trudging toward her. Again, his mood did not appear to be good, and she could guess why.

"Hi, Cevin," she greeted him. "Need help with anything?"

He scowled, though not at her. "That's my line, isn't it? But no, unless you can go back in time and stop that broadcast from going out. Our clientele took a turn for the worse, and…fuck. Can I sue them for defamation?"

Kera nodded at a double table packed with reporters. "Well, there they are if you want to serve them some legal papers along with, uh, whatever else they ordered. God, I suck at jokes."

That brought a light chuckle from him, so she supposed his spirits hadn't been *too* blackened by recent events. "Maybe later. Still, you know they're scouting for their next story. I bet they *want* there to be another fight or drug deal. They don't care what it does to our reputation."

Kera pointed out, "We do have more customers now, including them. They say any publicity is good publicity, right? More people buying food and drinks."

He considered it but shook his head. "The kitchen isn't staffed for such large parties. In fact, I'm going to have to help out back there any minute now. We're attracting a clientele I never wanted, regardless of whether they pay the same as everyone else. What happens when the novelty goes away and we're just that shitty bar everyone thinks of as being full of gang members and general assholes?"

Before Kera could think of another way to cheer him up, he darted off with surprising speed toward the kitchen, making good on his promise.

Twenty minutes later, once the cooks were caught up, he was back out front, taking off an apron and double-checking for signs of trouble.

Kera had come to another lull in business at the bar and flagged him down.

"Cevin, I think what we need to get your mind off this stuff is another attempt at Operation Get You a Date. What do you say, boss?"

His reaction reminded her of a cat drawing back to puff up and hiss. "Ugh, no. Last time was enough of a horrible, embarrassing failure, wasn't it?"

"It wasn't *that* bad," she protested. "And the road to success is paved with failures. If you watch the bar for a few minutes, I'll do touch-up waiting on the tables and see if I can find you a prospect. Come on, it'll be fun." She poked him in the side with her elbow.

Jenn appeared behind them. "I second that notion. Sorry, Cevin, but there's no getting out of it."

Sighing, he agreed to let Kera do a scouting run if nothing else.

While he and Jenn kept an eye on the drinkers, Kera strode across the floor, nominally to check if anyone needed a refill, but also to filter through the customers for single ladies.

She found one.

Holy living crap, Kera marveled. *That chick has to be a supermodel. Or a trophy wife, but I don't think she has a ring on. Does she? Damn. Poor Cevin. His road to success is going to be paved with a bunch more stones, isn't it?*

The woman resembled a young Monica Bellucci, Kera thought. When she asked her if she needed anything, she seemed polite, though a tad aloof.

"Okay," Kera said, "let your server know if you need anything else. Also, our manager will be out to talk to everyone shortly. Enjoy the rest of your night!"

The attractive woman nodded and waved her off.

Kera went to fetch Cevin. "Found one, and you're in luck. She's hot. Well, I can never be certain what the hell men think is hot, but I'd be shocked if you disagree. I'll put it that way."

Cevin visibly trembled and adjusted his collar. "*That* hot? No point. Have some mercy, Kera. The hotter she is, the more humiliating it will be when she shoots me down."

Kera locked eyes with Jenn, who nodded and leaned over the bar to push Cevin forward with both hands. As he stumbled into a walk, Kera took him by the arm and guided him halfway toward Ms. Not-Bellucci before he realized what was happening.

"Don't worry," she whispered. *He's probably doomed*, she thought.

The woman looked up as the two approached. Cevin stared at her, so Kera took the initiative. "Hello, again. This is Cevin, the head honcho here. He, uh, is also in charge of security for the place. You might have heard some of that crap on the news. Well, with him running things, we want all our customers to know that they're safe. Right?"

Cevin swallowed. "Um, yeah. I installed extra cameras and floodlights out back. And, uh, I have past experience dealing with assholes who come around to this place. We, y'know, have our ways of taking care of that kind of thing. The Mermaid is still a respectable establishment."

The supermodel's eyes opened a notch wider. "Oh, really?" She was intrigued.

"Yep," Kera confirmed. "I gotta get back to the bar. Have fun!"

She departed, but Cevin stayed where he was, and though the noise of the rest of the bar blotted things out, the two kept conversing. Not to mention, Kera could sense a warm, faintly electrochemical vibe rising between them.

Damn. Who would have thought? I mean, he is tall, even though he slouches.

Jenn caught her eye as she returned to the bar. "Ooh! How'd it go? He isn't back, so that's probably a good sign."

"Amazingly," Kera reported. "Well, so far. He might still screw it up with a dumbass remark, but he's off to a good start. I'm as shocked as he was. That chick looks like Monica Bellucci, doesn't she?"

"Umm..." Jenn squinted. "Kinda? But yeah, it's about time he made progress with someone."

Ten minutes later, Cevin returned, looking sweaty but happy.

Kera checked on her customers, then sidled up. "Did you get a date?"

"Well," he began, "not exactly, but we talked all that time without me making a fool of myself. She said she'd stop in again sometime! I figured that was enough and not to push my luck. I can ask her out next time, right?"

Kera fought a sudden schoolgirl-esque urge to swoon and say, "Awww." Instead, she smiled.

"Yeah, good plan. And congrats!"

"Thanks." His sheepish grin broadened, and it looked like he was standing straighter than usual. "After the fucking week I've had, I'll take the win. *Any* win."

Kera's mood soared on his behalf, but perhaps an hour later, she *felt* something before she saw it, and it concerned her. Stephanie was tired, and something was clearly bothering her.

"Hey, Steph," she called. "You all right? You've been working hard. Let me know if you want to take a five-minute break. I can cover your tables."

The waitress responded, "Oh, thank you. I think I'll be fine, though. And yes, all is well. Just tired, like you say."

There was more; Kera could sense it. The other woman was avoiding something. Avoiding *her*, maybe.

Kera decided not to push it. It might be a personal problem that was none of her business, and if Stephanie wanted to discuss it later, she knew Kera would listen.

A moment later, Steph changed the subject. "I haven't seen Chris or Ted lately. Was hoping they'd be back in some time, to be honest. Chris is nice, and Ted is, you know, entertaining."

Kera's face fell. "Uh. Yeah. That's weird, isn't it?" She felt as though she'd broken a priceless vase of her mom's and been caught in the act. Her stomach swam, and her face flushed. "Whatever, though. If they want to come back, they will."

"I hope so," Stephanie agreed, then walked off to check on a table.

Kera bit her tongue as she refilled someone's tequila, then retreated to the most well-shadowed corner of the bar.

Goddammit, Steph. I know you didn't mean anything by that, but couldn't you have said anything *else? They're never coming back, and it's because of me.*

CHAPTER NINETEEN

Lia sat alone in the Startup's rented office. She checked the time on her watch. It was 10:14 a.m., and the meeting was supposed to start at 10. It was unusual for Pauline to be late, and she began to wonder if they'd been in a car accident or something.

About a minute later, two pairs of footsteps approached, and the door opened. In strode Pauline, followed by Johnny.

Lia sensed at once that something was wrong, but it was nothing like the *kind* of wrongness she had expected.

Both of them seemed relaxed and unbothered. Less tense than usual, let alone the seething wrath Lia would have assumed, given whatever had happened to delay them. She wondered if they had smoked some weed or taken pills before they came in. Pauline didn't use drugs much anymore, but the recent stresses might have caused her to relapse.

They'd both been out of touch the night before, something Lia worried meant there was a relationship developing. With two such famously quick-tempered people, she couldn't see that ending well.

There wasn't any tension or shared energy between them today. No quick looks or secret smiles.

Strange.

It was Lia's nature to carefully consider and calculate everything before she spoke or acted. She remained silent as the pair took their places and thought the situation over. The biggest thing to discuss, as far as Lia was concerned, was the recent news report on Motorcycle Man, which cast him in a bad light and suggested that his public support was far weaker than they'd guessed.

She had no idea how Pauline would react to it. If she was mellow, she might well take the news better, or it could mean that she already knew and had finally succumbed to a total mental breakdown.

Then again, Johnny appeared equally chill. Lia found herself wishing that Sven was present to balance things out. He was busy hunting down another possible gang alliance.

Pauline took her place at the head of the room, but unusually, she slouched against the podium. "Good morning. How are things?"

Lia blinked. "I'm fine, Pauline, thank you. I hope nothing happened on your way to work. Did you see the, ah, story?"

Johnny leaned back in his seat and laughed in a calm, pleasant way that was quite unlike him. "Nah. What story?"

"Yes," Pauline echoed, "what do you mean?" She sounded mildly curious but mostly bored.

Clearing her throat and hoping she wasn't about to walk into a minefield, Lia related the "special report" on the news and all it had contained, as well as what was in the accompanying print story and the high points of the public commentary she'd seen on both. The gist was that out of the blue, the press and some of the common people were turning against their nemesis.

Pauline's attention wavered once or twice during Lia's account, as though she didn't much care. She said at the end, "Oh, I guess that's good. It might make things simpler. It seems like all has been well lately, though, hasn't it?"

"Yup," Johnny agreed.

Lia squirmed, briefly entertaining the thought that her co-workers had been replaced by alien replicants.

"Uh, things are not terrible," she pointed out, "but I thought it might concern you. It changes how we approach this from a PR perspective and could affect both our potential alliances and our product flow, though probably in a positive way. Also, may I ask how things went last night?"

Pauline stared at her blankly. "What happened last night?"

Lia was growing irritated. If she and Johnny had gone on a drug binge, half the organization's upper echelon was effectively paralyzed. She explained how Pauline had hinted at a plan to flush out Motorcycle Man with Johnny's aid, which seemed to involve going undercover to a nearby hangout spot or something.

As she spoke, Pauline still seemed bored but was irritated by all the "new" information she had apparently forgotten.

"What?" Ms. Testrevosky snapped. "When did I say that? Wait, I think I remember something. Not much. Johnny, nothing happened, did it?"

"I dunno," he answered her. "Yeah, nothing much. It was okay."

Then they lost track of the conversation and began discussing what to have for lunch.

Lia's hand trembled. She wanted to break the pen she was holding and fling the pieces at her boss. She'd never seen this level of irresponsibility in her friend before.

"*God*dammit, Pauline! What the hell is wrong with you?" she exploded. "This is an important crossroads for our outfit, as you yourself emphasized yesterday, and you're acting like you're out of your head! If there's a problem, can you at least tell me what it is? Please, I want to help, but I have no idea what's going on." She took a deep breath, wondering if she'd made a severe error.

Johnny fidgeted and looked at her with a "What's her problem?" expression like a teenage boy preparing to make fun of an outspoken classmate. Then he settled back in his seat and appeared to lose interest in the proceedings.

At the same time, Pauline's face contorted as conflicting thoughts and emotions rippled through her. Traces of her old strident self began to show through.

"Lia," she began in a sharper voice, "who do you think you…" She paused. "Wait. *Wait.* I'm starting to remember. Fuck. I think my drink was spiked. Yes. We were at the Mermaid, and we had a drink. That's all I can recall. Someone must have tampered with my fucking drink!"

Well, Lia thought, *at least she's getting back to normal.*

Johnny chimed in but didn't have much to add. "Yeah, maybe," he murmured. "Everyone was, umm, hanging out. It was…there wasn't much to talk about?" He shrugged.

At the front of the room, Pauline had turned away from her employees. Her fists were shaking, and her bleached-blonde ponytail, which was abnormally disheveled, swayed behind her.

"Why can't I remember what happened?" she raged. "This is *bullshit.* I don't want to be here. I need a goddamn shower and a comfortable change of clothes. Someone is going to pay for this. If I am unhappy, *they* deserve to be unhappy too. Period."

She spun on her heel and stormed out of the office, slamming the door behind her. Johnny and Lia sat in silence.

Johnny laughed in the odd, lazy tone of a contemptuous teenager, then started puttering with his phone.

Under her breath, Lia said to no one in particular, "I liked her better as a pseudo-stoner."

<hr>

"This is so frickin' bizarre," Doug Lopez quipped as he flipped through his notebook. He was lounging in a glorified lawn chair at the spa, a towel around his waist and a non-alcoholic vitamin-fortified cocktail resting beside him. "We must have cared a ton about this, but now it's like we don't? Why was this important to us? I don't know. I miss having that kind of motivation."

Mia Angel sat next to him in a similar chair, sipping a brown glass bottle of raspberry-flavored kombucha. "I seem to vaguely recall it. We must have burnt out worse than I thought. It's been nice to relax, but yeah. That stuff was getting boring."

Doug nodded to indicate he had heard her, but he was engrossed in the pages in front of him.

"Man, look at this stuff. As chilled out as things have been lately, this sounds exciting, doesn't it? We were there when Motorcycle Man took down that terrorist, and right at the end of the brawl, we chased him through the streets behind those gangsters. Shit. Is it wrong to feel nostalgic for stuff that happened within the last two or three weeks?"

An employee came by and offered them hot towels. Mia accepted one, thanked the man, and wiped her face with it. "Part of me wants to enjoy the rest of my vacation. We *were* working harder than was good for our health, but you have a point. We were so close to a breakthrough."

An idea had come to her, and she wasn't sure if she dared to say it out loud. Doug would probably be amenable to it, but she worried that she might regret it anyway. There would be no turning back once the proverbial cat was out of the bag. If she spoke, their little holiday decompression session would be over and done with forever.

Fuck it, she thought and inhaled.

"Hey, Doug. We should go back to the Mermaid and check things out, just to see if anything interesting is going on. We might get our mojo back, right?"

Her partner perked up, his eyebrows rising and his eyes darting around as thoughts and emotions sparked in his brain.

"That is an excellent idea. When?"

"Eh." She sipped her drink. "Soon. No need to do it right

away. Maybe tomorrow. Or tonight, if we can't find anything else to do. I'm cool either way."

Secretly, though, she was hoping he would insist on leaving ASAP.

Doug sat up straighter. "Let's do it tonight. I mean, I'm feeling pretty relaxed, so no need to rush, but we might as well."

Mia smiled. "Sure, whatever." She pulled out her phone and checked the time. "It's only a quarter after two. We have plenty of time."

Doug drained his cocktail and began stretching as though he were ready to get up any moment now.

"Hey," he observed, "making things nice and simple, we're on vacation! We won't need to take hours out of our work schedule to do this or have to account for or justify our whereabouts. Frank can get stuffed. We're doing this for *fun*."

Mia finished her kombucha and set the bottle on the table. "Good point. And if something weird happens, we can always say we enjoyed the place when we were there, and going back was a matter of nostalgia."

"Right." Doug stood. "Granted, I suppose we have to consider the place's growing reputation as a hotbed of petty crime and douchebaggery, but it doesn't seem that bad. And we're *reporters*. We have experience knowing what's up and steering clear of danger."

Mia stood as well, turning the various possibilities over in her head. Something still felt weird and wrong, like her being able to remember so little of their previous visit and the oddly sudden nature of their compulsion to abandon the case and take a break when things in LA were tense in general.

She shrugged. "Meh. What's the worst that could happen? We drink too much beer and eat some underwhelming onion rings?"

Doug was gathering his things with increased energy, though he still seemed listless compared to his usual self.

"That's the spirit. We've survived way worse than that. I bet *nothing* will happen."

"Ha-*ha!*" Kera laughed, hoisting the package in a triumphant motion. Cevin's shirt had arrived on her day off, but she was willing to bring it in. "Cevin will have it available when Monica Bellucci's doppelganger comes back." She frowned and set the package on her kitchen table. "Unless she came back yesterday. Or is coming tonight. Shit."

Twenty-five minutes later, she and Zee were buzzing toward the Mermaid. Though it was a warm day, bringing Cevin his new shirt reminded her that she and the Kims had planned to assemble a magic-blocking outfit soon. Might as well be today. She had gathered the iron and silver and tossed them into her pack before slipping on her leather jacket.

Kera barged through the front door, package in hand. The bar was open, but it was still early, and only two customers lounged about.

Stephanie and Jenn noticed her at once and crowded around. They had instantly figured out why Kera was there.

"Yup," she confirmed. "That day has arrived. Hey, Cevin! Special delivery."

The manager wandered out, perplexed but not displeased to see Kera. Then his eyes drifted down to the package, which the girls had started to open on his behalf.

"Oh, no," he moaned. "You didn't actually order that thing, did you? The purple one?"

Kera raised a finger. "Burgundy, not purple. Here, you should try it on. It's probably going to be rumpled from shipping, but still." She pulled it free and unfolded it, and all three women oohed and ahhed, speculating about how it would look.

Cevin's face blanched. "God, it's so *fancy*. I refuse to wear that.

I'm sorry. Like, I appreciate that you spent money on me, but you'd be better off donating it to a needy French aristocrat or something."

Jenn pretended to be shocked and offended. "He's refusing our gift! I never. What kind of ingratitude is that?"

"Yeah," Stephanie chimed in. "This was our early Bosses Appreciation Day present. If you don't accept it, we ain't getting you anything for Christmas. Only fair."

"Come on," Kera coaxed, "try it on for one hour today, then if you absolutely hate it, you don't have to wear it again."

He continued to resist, but eventually, their bullying wore him down. He threw up his hands. "Fine. Should have known better than to argue with three women at once. Here, hand it over. I accept my fate, but I'm trying it on in the office before I come out."

Cevin took the shirt. Stephanie had to stay behind to watch a table, but Kera and Jenn followed him back to his office, where he pulled it on over the nondescript tan t-shirt he was wearing. He examined himself in the mirror with a mixture of confusion and disapproval, folding down the collar and fiddling with the sleeves as the girls moved in to help him adjust everything.

Kera crossed her arms and tapped her foot. "Honestly, it looks great on you. That's not even a white lie."

"Ditto," said Jenn. "That model will love it. Why haven't you worn this color before, man?"

He grimaced. "It's better if I don't answer that question. Anyway, I'm not wearing this out on the floor."

"Oh, but you promised to wear it for one hour," Kera reminded him. "You never stay in your office for that long."

Unable to argue with her, he decided to get it over with and slogged out front. Stephanie noticed at once and remarked, "Ooh, that looks good. We should have bought it for you a month sooner."

"It looks ridiculous," he stated in a monotone. "So yes, if you wanted to embarrass me a month ago, that makes sense."

A gay guy sitting at the bar, one of the two customers present, jumped in. "Actually, it does look nice. Goes well with your hair and eyes."

"Seriously?" Cevin still couldn't believe it. "Thanks, I guess." He turned and looked himself over in the bar's mirror. "I mean, it's not *terrible*..."

Kera wandered in back to check her locker, then headed to the bathroom before she left, more to give herself a moment to unwind than anything else.

Then it struck.

We know who you are and what you are doing.

A pair of voices speaking in unison, but not audibly. She heard mental voices speaking straight into her brain from somewhere outside. She froze in place, more terrified than she had been when that crazed Anastidis guy had nearly killed her.

But have no fear; We are not your enemy. We want to help you. We understand what you are going through.

"Who?" Kera gasped in a tiny voice. She had no idea if the owners of the psychic voices were nearby. They might be watching her. The double voice was gentle, yet it rang with a degree of power that she was somehow certain dwarfed her own.

You seek to help people. Let us guide you and assist you. With our aid, you can do far more good deeds than you could alone. If you want to seek us out, cast Firefly into the sky, and we will find you. This is your opportunity. We look forward to meeting you.

Then it was gone.

Kera swallowed. "Shit. Shit shit *shit*." Someone had been here looking for her, or they were nearby right now. Someone with magic. Someone who knew what the Firefly spell was—one of the first enchantments mentioned in the book.

It was *them*.

"Not. Interested," she spat. She didn't know if they could hear her, but she wasn't going to stick around to find out. She left, hurrying away before she could even see how Cevin was doing.

Pauline had ordered the core team members to re-assemble at the office at 5:30 p.m., much later than was usual for them to meet. By that point, most of the other people in the building were packing up to head home, if not already gone.

She had come to a decision, and she felt there was no reason to waste time before making them aware of it.

Lia arrived at 5:25, followed by Sven and Johnny, who came in together at 5:27. Pauline nodded in satisfaction. She would not have taken it well if any of them had been late.

She cleared her throat and took all three employees in with her expansive gaze.

"Now that everyone has arrived, we might as well begin. First of all, I would like a *brief* rundown from each of you on the progress you have made today. Limit your remarks to two or three minutes. Once you have completed them, I have important news. Lia, we'll start with you."

Pauline stood and listened, a layer of well-practiced patience atop her simmering core of emotionality and impulsivity. She half-heard the things her underlings told her and filed the important parts in her mind for further use, but mostly she was having them report to her as a preamble.

Once Lia finished assuring her that their product was starting to flow again, and Sven and Johnny mentioned some promising leads with other gang alliances or potential front businesses, Pauline cut them off with a raised palm.

"Good," she declared. "You have not wasted your time. I would like to see more progress, but what you have described is adequate. All of that pales in comparison to what we must do next."

The shifting of the vibe in the room toward serious concern was palpable. Her three lieutenants leaned closer to hear.

Pauline let her thoughts drift back to last night, and once again, she found she could remember almost nothing. Rage welled up, and now was the time to vent it.

"Someone fucked with me," she rasped. Lia, Sven, and Johnny flinched at the violent, guttural shift in her voice. "I cannot recall what happened at that bar last night, which means the *zasranets* who congregate there or work there or whatever thought they could get away with drugging me like I was a typical American *dura* who doesn't even *have her own company!*"

A ball appeared in Sven's cheek from his tongue rolling there. He was the only one who understood Russian, but their boss's sudden rant was perfectly clear to all three.

Before they could ask questions, Pauline went on. "The Mermaid is going to become a *crater*. They denied our business partnership, they have harbored our enemies, and now they have insulted me. A big fucking crater. *That* is the message we need to send."

Lia frowned. Sven grimaced. Johnny appeared to be weighing the pros and cons rather than cheering, as they all should have been. It made Pauline angrier.

"What do you say to that?" she demanded.

Lia raised a hand. "Ah, Pauline, excuse me, but you might want to reconsider. There could be, if you'll pardon the unintentional pun, a great deal of fallout."

Johnny turned his head to see what Sven had to say before responding.

Sven coughed. "Yeah, I'm not sure. If we take out other gangs, the police won't be overly aggressive in pursuing it. They're usually happy if we kill each other. If we take out *civilians*, they're going to be all over us. The fucking *FBI* will show up, and maybe DHS, ATF—the works. Especially if we make a literal crater. Tell me that was a metaphor?"

The boss's eyes blazed. "It was not a goddamn metaphor. I want that place wiped out of existence."

Johnny shrugged. He was still playing it safe in his newfound state of grace.

Pauline pointed at Lia. "I want you to coordinate the necessary messages to the other outfits. Johnny and Sven will then deliver the messages and make sure our plan is abundantly clear to them."

Torrez spoke for the first time since Pauline had revealed what they would do. "What's the message?"

"*Stay away from the Mermaid*," Pauline answered. "Do not elaborate beyond that, but that way, when the place goes up in a vapor cloud, everyone will know we were responsible."

Lia inquired, "Do you mean you want to do this to increase our chances of a merger with another gang?"

"Fuck, no," Pauline snapped. "It's so people will know what happens when they piss me off. They'll be crawling to us on their knees, *begging* to join us or do business on terms favorable to our interests."

Each of her employees gave a slow, gentle nod. None spoke.

Pauline fidgeted in place. They were not demonstrating the team player attitudes or the willingness to go the extra mile she expected of people who intended to rise in the world of corporate startups.

They would obey all the same.

"Go," she told them. "I'll contact you later with the details. Make any other preparations you think might be useful, but clear them with me first."

She sat down, opened a folder, and ignored them as they shuffled out. Somehow, she got the impression that they wanted to whisper among themselves, but they didn't. They merely left the building in silence.

Lamar stared at his phone, his breathing shallow.

He hadn't liked what was going on recently. The Startup and the LA Witches had been throwing people at each other like it was a fucking battlefield, and Motorcycle Man didn't help matters. Lamar had even been approached by the Startup to take part in their campaign against whoever it was they were fighting.

He hadn't accepted. Something about that place set his teeth on edge. They showed up with deep reserves of money and started taking control of the drug market with insane efficiency, but no one knew who ran them or how many people they had?

Gang leaders liked a bit of mystery; that was expected, but complete anonymity was weird.

And now, it looked like he had been right.

The message that had gone out to all of the gangs was clear: *Stay away from the Mermaid. The LA Witches will be destroyed tonight, as will Motorcycle Man. The Startup will not tolerate any interference.*

Lamar knew the rules. You didn't snitch. The Startup would be expecting only the two gangs to be present, plus Motorcycle Man. They would expect to have things done before the police got involved.

Because gang business was gang business, and anyone willing to turn a civilian site into a crater was going to torture snitches to within an inch of their life.

You didn't tell the cops what was going on.

But this was over the line. Lamar shook his head. This was too far over the line. You didn't shoot up a restaurant. Sometimes civilians got hurt, but that wasn't the same as going guns blazing into a place that was full of them.

He knew what he had to do.

CHAPTER TWENTY

Kera had no idea what to do next or how to get away. The thought that her pursuers had been in the Mermaid and had noticed her was terrifying, so she went to the only place where she knew that someone had experience with this.

The Kims' house.

She killed the engine and left Zee parked in the half-lot around the side of the Kims' store, where it would attract little attention.

Sam was behind the register. "Oh, hi, Kera. Mom and Dad are upstairs if you want to see them."

She gave him a nod and a smile as she passed him. "Thanks, Sam."

His parents were in the living room. Mrs. Kim lying on the couch, half-conscious, and her husband was sitting in a chair by her side.

Alarms went off in Kera's brain. *Oh, no. Her cancer got worse again. It's metastasizing at a faster rate, isn't it? Shit, shit, shit!* She didn't know how to deal with this on top of everything else.

"Hi, I, uh, I had something I needed to say, but is everything okay here?" She tried to give no indication of her near-panic.

"Yes," said Mr. Kim. "We are okay. We want to speak to you, though. It's about your recent choices."

The girl drew back a step. It was a relief knowing that her guess had been wrong, but now she had other things to consider. "Okay. Whatever it is, you don't have to sugarcoat it."

Ye-Jin rolled over and opened her eyes. She didn't look good, but she did not seem to be suffering or severely ill, either. Kera put a hand on her shoulder and tried to relax.

Mr. Kim began, "We know your life has changed immeasurably since you discovered who and what you are." His words had the feel of a rehearsed speech but a heartfelt one. "It does great credit to you that your first thought was to sacrifice yourself for the good of others. You do not allow yourself to stand aside and let them be hurt when you could aid them, but I think you have begun to wonder what a long life might look like with no one close to you."

Kera's stoic façade cracked. A faint ripple went through her neck and shoulders and a lump formed in her throat, but she swallowed it at once and nodded.

The couple exchanged glances, then Mr. Kim continued, "We ask only one thing of you, which is that you respect that we are people who have seen more decades of life than you have, and we have a perspective on things that you should consider carefully. Will you agree to listen and think things over before you jump up and act in haste?"

She almost groaned but bit her lip and nodded.

"We have reason to believe that things are getting…more difficult for you," Mr. Kim said. "We have seen stories in the news, and you told Ye-Jin about the choice you made regarding Christian."

Kera waited, but Mr. Kim seemed to be struggling to find the right words. His wife murmured something in Korean and he listened to her, nodding.

She must have told him what to say because he looked at Kera again. "The young are often more willing to sacrifice themselves, you see, particularly people like us with our special talents. It is a supremely honorable thing, but we also mourn for many who could have done a great deal of good throughout their lives if they had lived. Don't we? If there comes a time soon when you face the option of throwing yourself into almost-certain death for a chance of victory, please, Kera, from both of us, *think twice.*"

Mrs. Kim put a hand over hers, and Kera closed her eyes, unable to speak. Their love and concern mingled with and tempered her reckless desire to charge into battle.

"All right," she murmured, her voice shaky. "I, um…I'll try to be smart. I won't be a martyr if I can win *and* survive."

The Kims smiled. "Good," said Ye-Jin.

"Uh, now it's my turn for bad news," Kera said. She went to get a chair and sat down, her legs suddenly wobbly. "I think…I think the people who've been searching for magic have found me."

The Kims went still.

"They left a message for me in the bathroom where I work," Kera explained. "It said they don't mean me any harm, and they know what I'm going through. I…" She tried to find words for the dread that had coiled up in her chest. "I just don't have a good feeling about it. Power is being snuffed out. The book has been removed. I…"

The Kims gazed at her.

Kera's head jerked up. "What if I led them here?" she gasped.

The couple froze. Mr. Kim swallowed and his wife put a hand on his arm, speaking rapidly in Korean. She held up a finger to Kera and seemed to be arguing, saying something he didn't want to hear.

Kera's intuition must have been good because Mr. Kim's eyebrows snapped together and he spoke back just as quickly, waving his hands.

Mrs. Kim said something gentle and wry, and Mr. Kim

sighed, then nodded and looked down. He didn't look at Kera for a moment, then he got up, headed into the house, and came back with a small silk bag.

"We have this for you." He pulled a curious object about the size and dimensions of a teacup saucer or a miniature Blu-Ray disc from it.

Kera accepted it. It was made of what looked to be jade or crystal, and shapes and letters were carved into it on both sides. A mandala pattern, she guessed, an ancient relic of Buddhist, Taoist, or folk-Korean origin.

"Thanks," she said. "What is it?"

"A device," Mr. Kim answered her, "which will block your magic from the sight of others. We had forgotten about it until earlier today. A man gave it to us shortly before we left Korea. He said it would protect us from prying eyes. We only half-believed him at the time. But before you arrived, I tested it with a spell or two. It works, and it is much easier to carry than a cloak with a bunch of iron and silver in it, isn't it?"

Kera marveled at the thing. If what Mr. Kim said was true, the relic would be very useful. Then again, they might have had a use for it themselves.

"Will you be okay without it?" She opened her coat to show them the silver she had stashed there.

Mr. Kim nodded and smiled. "Yes, we are fine. You must think about it and believe in it for it to work. It acts on the mind as much as on the energies of the universe itself. Now, then. What you do from here on is a choice that only you can make, but we do have one request."

Kera nodded. "Anything."

"I asked you to be careful with your strength," Mrs. Kim said, "but could you do just a little bit of healing for me? There is a bit of pain, just here." She pointed. "I am very much better, so I do not want you to drain yourself."

"Of course." Kera nodded. "Yes. I, uh…okay." She took off her coat and knelt by the chair.

James and LeBlanc were back at the safehouse by the time the message spell went off. Agent Richardson was relating a story about something his partner had once done, involving a remote-controlled car and a couple of very large hogs that had gotten loose from a farm while pretending that MacDonald, who was in the next room, couldn't hear him.

"And since her name is MacDonald and we were on a farm and all, I couldn't resist going up to her and—"

James had been listening with honest interest, but the agent's words blanked out as something like an alarm filled his mind. He nodded and laughed, giving no outward sign of what had happened.

"Excuse me," he muttered, standing up and heading into the kitchen, where LeBlanc and MacDonald were making tea.

LeBlanc caught his eye, and both nodded.

MacDonald noticed and asked, "You guys are trying to protect me from the harmful effects of Richardson's extremely inaccurate anecdotes? Or is this serious?"

James frowned. "Busted. It's one of those serious things where if you don't do what we say, we will refuse to cooperate and make your life a living hell. If you cooperate, it will lead to all of us succeeding in our mutual goals sooner."

While MacDonald narrowed her eyes, Richardson called, "I heard that."

LeBlanc spoke up. "Please leave the house, or at least stay in the room in the northeast corner of the second floor."

Two minutes of arguing later, the feds chose the northeast room.

Locking themselves into the living room, which lay in the

southwest corner of the first floor, James muttered, "Outside would have been better, but we'll take what we can get." He'd brought a metal bowl filled with water from the kitchen.

LeBlanc pulled the curtains shut. "Standard procedure?"

They cloaked and shielded the room and cursed the bugs the agents had set up. Once again, their tech would fail to provide them with useful info on what the thaumaturgists were doing.

James set the bowl in the center of the floor and they knelt beside it, channeling their powers into a full-strength scrying spell.

Nothing. Minutes passed.

Lovecraft broke the silence. "What the hell?"

"Something is wrong." LeBlanc rubbed her chin, and her face elongated in apprehension. "We could not possibly have failed at the spell. There must be an extra factor at work here, something we did not consider."

James leaned back, rubbing his hands. "Um, okay. Here's a proposal: We *don't* tell the Council we did everything we could to ensure we could track this person, and somehow, it didn't goddamn work."

LeBlanc ignored him and went to a nearby bookshelf, where she found a map of Southern California and placed it in the bottom of the scrying bowl. "Not as good as direct tracking," she admitted, "but we will be able to see any thaumaturgic activity in the LA area."

James huffed. "Right, though it defeats the purpose of what we did last night, doesn't it?"

"Not entirely," LeBlanc countered. "But pay attention to the bowl."

They sat staring at the map beneath the water for close to an hour. The FBI agents were probably getting antsy, but this was too important for James and LeBlanc to take their focus off this greater goal.

LeBlanc's eyes flicked upward for a split second. "James, are you twiddling your thumbs?"

"No," he snapped back. "You took your eyes off the water, but not for long enough to see that I'm merely flexing my hands. Furthermore, your blinking breaks have been taking far too long. I think I saw your eyes close for half a second at a time, maybe longer."

She snorted. "How would you be able to see that unless you were looking up as well?"

A green flare erupted beneath the water.

Both thaumaturges' eyes were on the scrying bowl in an instant, yet they had trouble processing what they saw. The ethereal flame was nothing like the ones they'd seen before; it spiraled haphazardly while also seeming far weaker than what they expected for a magic-user of Motorcycle Man's caliber.

James squinted. "I can't tell where that was, exactly. And it looks so...confused."

They were still pondering that when they heard the footsteps in the hall, then pounding on the door.

"Guys?" It was MacDonald. "We have a problem."

When they opened the door, her face was a grayish color. "Lamar just contacted us."

"On his own?" James asked skeptically.

"All of the gangs have gotten word to stay away from a bar in Little Tokyo tonight," MacDonald said. "The Startup says they're going to turn it into, and I quote, 'a giant fucking crater' unless the LA Witches stop them. We're going in."

James and LeBlanc looked at each other. The LA Witches were one person who would not have an easy time interfering on that level.

"I think we can agree that if Motorcycle Man gets involved in something like this, it's going to be a shit show," James said.

"Exactly," MacDonald snapped.

LeBlanc reached out to put a hand on her arm. Her brown

eyes were serene. "We have just found his trail," she said. "We will deal with him. You deal with the Startup."

"Okay." MacDonald nodded her head. "We'll get our resources moving. Good hunting."

"You, too," James told her.

Concentrating on healing, Kera found, took her mind off the storm of anxieties that had arisen since she'd received the bizarre psychic message, in part because it was so goddamn hard. She gave it her all until she felt the slight dizziness that told her she was approaching her limits.

"Okay," she gasped, "I'm sorry, but I think I have to stop now."

Mrs. Kim put her other hand atop Kera's. "Thank you. It is enough." They rested together, not speaking, for a couple of minutes, the older woman lying on the couch, the younger sitting beside her.

"You should go get some rest," Mr. Kim said finally. "Yes?"

"Right." Kera stood up and wavered on her feet. When Mr. Kim handed her a pastry from downstairs, she smiled. "You both take such good care of me. What did I ever do to deserve you?"

Mr. Kim smiled and patted her on the back. "I think you know the answer to that. Now, go rest. No more magic tonight, yes?"

Kera hugged him and let him pat her on the back, then did the same with his wife, though more gently, given her condition. "Thank you so much. I'll rest, and I promise I won't just throw myself away, like you said."

They said their goodbyes, and Kera strode out, leaving the couple behind watching her.

When she was gone and the sound of her motorcycle had receded into the distance, they looked into each other's eyes, not bothering to speak. It was pointless to ask how the other felt since they had both agreed on their course of action. The conclusions were obvious.

Both husband and wife had agreed to a sacrifice of their own.

Mrs. Kim pointed out, "She is going to be very upset with us when she finds out."

"Yes," Mr. Kim conceded. "Yes, she is. I'll go tell Sam to go to a friend's house for the night. We have preparations to make."

Several blocks away, Kera was stripping off her leathers and thinking about the Kims' request to be careful when her helmet started buzzing. Frowning, she went over to pick it up and realized it must still be tuned into the police scanner, which was currently filled with anxious voices.

She put it on to be able to hear better, and her jaw dropped open.

"You're absolutely sure?" one of the voices was saying.

"*Yes*," another snapped back. "There isn't much that rhymes with 'We're going to turn the Mermaid into a fucking crater,' is there?"

Kera's knees wobbled, and she gasped.

"The FBI is mobilizing," someone said. "They're claiming they have jurisdiction. They say these people came in from Nevada."

"I don't fucking care where they came from," someone else snapped.

Kera pulled off the helmet, her breath coming in quick gasps.

Think, think, think.

She had just promised the Kims that she wouldn't throw her life away, so what could she do?

CHAPTER TWENTY-ONE

"Okay," Agent Richardson began as he loaded 5.56 NATO rounds into one of his assault rifle's magazines, "I don't suppose we could get a real estimate of how many gang members will be there, do you? We want to know how much backup to have. Our usual philosophy is 'overwhelming force' since it reduces the likelihood that the bad guys will be stupid enough to fight back."

MacDonald shrugged. "No fucking idea. The cops aren't talking. Lamar said he didn't think it was a bomb of any sort, so apparently 'crater' was metaphorical. The number of enemies Motorcycle Man has made is anyone's guess, but Lamar said the Startup told other gangs to stay away, so this is pretty much just…whoever they are."

Richardson sighed as he continued to load magazines. "Okay, whatever. We will bring as many people as possible to be safe and have LAPD SWAT standing by to back us up. And a detachment of regular officers. I don't fucking care what they say about us pulling rank; this is a national operation. We want them to know that resisting arrest is tantamount to declaring war against the United States government."

There were two other FBI agents present, Almeida and

Barker, but they were not talkative. Both were clad in full paramilitary battle gear minus their big, heavy helmets, which they seemed reluctant to put on until it was necessary.

MacDonald looked grim. "We just want to take care of the threat, and no one needs to get hurt. But I suppose if violent criminals are there, it causes problems."

Richardson wagged a hand. "Causes some, resolves others. By the way, HQ settled on a hostage situation as the smokescreen for managing the public."

Agent MacDonald stood to shrug into her bulletproof vest. "The problem will be if Motorcycle Man heads there some way the—" She looked at Almeida and Barker. "Some way our other team can't head him off."

"We'll have to trust them to manage that," Richardson said bluntly. "In the meantime, the hostage situation gives us a pretext to raid the place while also evacuating all the nearby civvies. They won't get hurt, and as icing on the cake, nobody will see anything."

Almeida chortled and hefted his Benelli M4 semiautomatic shotgun. "If anyone gets hurt, it's going to be those scumbags trying to turn a bar into a fuckin' crater. I knew one of them would spin out someday. Just glad I'm one of the ones who gets to be there."

"Yeah," Agent Barker added. He had a Heckler & Koch MP5K submachine gun. "This ought to be wild, kids. The kind of thing I signed up for."

"Roger," Richardson said and smiled, glad the two new agents had left behind glum stoicism for humor. It made for better energy going into the fight.

He left them momentarily behind to duck into the bathroom, where he examined himself in the mirror. After safety-checking his rifle and the positions of everyone else in the building, he held it one-handed, pointing it toward the ceiling while puffing out his chest in his vest and tilting his head in a way that emphasized the vaguely macho sneer on his face and the strong set of his jaw.

"Oh, yeah," he commented in a low, breathy voice. "*Badass motherfucker right here.*" He tapped the Glock 17M, his usual service weapon, at his side, and lamented inwardly that he didn't have a big, scary combat knife to go with the guns and black armor.

He walked back out to see if everyone else was ready. They were standing with a quiet tension that suggested the time had come to rendezvous with the other feds and their contacts in the LAPD.

"Let's head out," he told everyone.

"Would you like a dramatic montage of music?" MacDonald asked. There was a twinkle in her eye that suggested she might have overheard his words.

He maintained as much dignity as he could while he answered, "Yes, please. That would be excellent."

James and LeBlanc discussed their options as they prepared. It was clear they had to head off Motorcycle Man before he—or she—got to the Mermaid. The question was how best to do that.

"So, yeah," said James, "there are all kinds of ways this could go wrong, especially if—"

Something in the scrying bowl glowed green. Both pairs of eyes snapped toward it.

"*That's* different," LeBlanc pointed out. "Faint but steady. An example of far more disciplined magic than what we have seen prior."

James chewed his lower lip as he examined the map. The phosphorescence was coming from someplace a mile or so to the east of their current location, so not the Mermaid.

He acceded, "More disciplined, yeah, but also more dangerous. Do you feel it? It's ominous. I can't put my finger on why."

Frowning, LeBlanc settled into a deep focus. "Yes. There is, as we postulated earlier, an element at work here that we do not fully understand. I think we need to move at once, James. But to where? The site of that, whatever it is?"

"Yes," James said after a moment. "It's our best guess at this point."

"Excellent." LeBlanc put a hand out to him. "James. All we can do now is our best. We *will* keep this person from setting off more than they can handle at the bar. Whether we do that by bringing them on as an apprentice or by shutting down their power is up to them."

James nodded. He couldn't resist a little humorous jab, however. "Okay, but let's not pretend I'm the only one who's nervous here."

"You're most certainly not," LeBlanc said. "This person has more power than most thaumaturges I've seen, and I have seen quite a few. If we want to shut their power down, we'll have to be quick and decisive."

Cevin parked his truck in its usual space behind the Mermaid. When he climbed out, he carried his new shirt on a hanger to avoid it getting rumpled. With one hand, he opened the back door and then hung the shirt in his office, leaving it there as he went through the motions of getting the bar ready for the evening.

Once the essential stuff was done, Cevin went back, redressed, and looked in the office mirror.

Despite the weird, borderline metrosexual color, the cut of the shirt was flattering. It made his shoulders look broader and his posture straighter, and when he rolled his sleeves up to the elbows, it looked sort of...cool. Semi-formal and snappy-casual all at once.

"Huh," he commented in a low voice, hoping the staff couldn't hear him. "Does this actually look decent on me, or am I going crazy? Or was I crazy all along, and this is the beginning of sanity? Ugh, it's hard to say."

His mind drifted to his impending attempt to ask Nadine out on a date.

He would do it tonight, assuming she came in. Jenn and Stephanie and Kera had ruthlessly browbeaten him into submission.

He wondered if he was excited. Generally speaking, excitement was not an emotion he associated with himself, but he had been known to be wrong about such things from time to time.

Of course, part of the problem with excitement was that it was frequently paired with anxiety. The two went together like peanut butter and jelly.

He took a deep breath, then spoke to himself while staring into the mirror.

"Nadine isn't interested in you, you know. Dumbass. A woman like her couldn't possibly be attracted to a dork like you. I mean, did you *see* her, man? Talking to you was just something she was doing out of boredom. Tonight, you'll ask her out, and she'll say no. Which is a good thing. The charade will be over. Right?"

On the other hand, the conversation had been lively. She had seemed enthusiastic. According to the girls, a woman didn't behave that way unless she was sincere.

Cevin attempted not to groan, but a faint guttural sound escaped his throat anyway. Of course part of him wanted to believe that Nadine really did want to get to know him better, among other things, but if, against all odds and common sense, that turned out to be true, his life would become exceedingly complicated.

He would be held to a higher standard. He would have something to lose instead of being able to relax in a consistent state of comfortable mediocrity. It scared the hell out of him.

But that might be a good thing. Maybe. *Possibly.*

"Whatever," he mumbled. "I'll ask her on a date and, uh, see how it goes. It will be fun. I made a good first impression, according to Jenn, so if I can make a good *second* impression, I'm golden."

He smiled into the mirror, then the smile inverted.

"Unless something goes wrong. Unless it's another one of *those* nights, and that rubs off and screws everything else up."

He cursed himself mentally for thinking about that and hoped he hadn't also cursed his chances.

It was true, he *had* been on edge lately, and things had been strange ever since that bizarre incident where someone had shot up Kera's bike. That had been the beginning of all his woes. There was also the bar's growing notoriety, its unwanted reputation as a sleazy establishment that attracted a rough and questionable clientele.

Footsteps approached and then stopped outside the office door. Cevin spun, forcing his face back into a neutral expression so it wouldn't look like he'd been caught doing something ridiculous.

Jenn was standing in the office doorway. "Hey, boss-man. That shirt was worth it. Looks good!" She went on toward the break room.

Cevin breathed in, then out. "Okay, yeah. Maybe they're right, and all will be well. Yes. Everything will be fine."

He adjusted his collar and walked out to check on the floor. "I should relax. It's going to be a *great* night."

CHAPTER TWENTY-TWO

"Zee," Kera said, resting a hand on her bike's shoulder, "we're about to do the right thing, but it's going to be dangerous. Still, I only need you to get me there and probably get me out afterward. You can sit out the worst of it. Okay?"

She took his silence as agreement.

Satisfied, she jumped into the seat, started the engine, and left her warehouse behind. The pack on her back was heavier than usual as she zipped into the dense, noisy traffic of Los Angeles, heading not for the Mermaid, but for the downtown headquarters of what she guessed to be the Startup.

It was twilight. Night would fall in a matter of minutes; she had to hope it wasn't too late, but she doubted it. Somehow, for whatever reason, she felt certain that her enemies' masterstroke would come around "prime time" or later, but likely not after midnight. Peak bar hours.

"Hey!" Kera bellowed through her helmet as some douchebag in a red lifted truck cut her off at the intersection. "Christ, I can see *under* your fucking vehicle. Is your *ladder* secured? Presumably you need one. Cops ought to pull that guy over for excessive liftage."

Of course, no one could hear her over the noise of her motorcycle and all the other vehicles on the road.

At home, she had inhaled every item of food she had available, some awful packaged snack cakes, a cheeseburger, and a nice sugary can of carbonated caffeine. She'd then spent a good half-hour warming up and running through quick drills of every martial arts move she could think of—anything that might help her.

Warming up her mind, as well. Getting into fighting mode, which meant setting the blood to pumping and the brain to blotting out distractions, with the divine powers of the universe on standby for when she would need their help.

Up ahead, there was a miniature traffic jam caused by that worst of all possible road conditions, a red light. When she was halfway down the street, the light turned green, so Kera didn't slow down too much.

However, the other drivers didn't seem to be in much of a hurry.

"Hey!" Kera bellowed. "Did all of you people fall asleep at the wheel or get sudden 'Dear John' texts or something? For God's sake!"

She slowed the bike to a crawl just as the constipated traffic started flowing again.

The ride went smoothly for the next couple of minutes, and Kera's thoughts turned to what the Kims had said, as well as the unspoken implications that underlaid it.

It's like they could see into my head. I feel as though someone saw me naked or something, she brooded. *How did they know? Did they go through the same thing when they were younger? I had assumed that they wanted to live together and be happy. The Kims never had any reason to reach the same conclusions I did. If I can't live a normal life and be with someone, why shouldn't I sacrifice myself and my happiness for the greater good?*

There was something else too, but she didn't want to admit it.

If she wasn't the only one, then someone had stolen her thunder. She wanted to be the sole thaumaturgist who was willing to die for others because she couldn't live for herself. There was something romantic about the idea in a tragic way.

But it was nice not to be alone, either. Others had felt her pain.

Fuck. I was getting used to the idea of eventually being killed in the line of duty or whatever you call it. Now that I'm not sure about that anymore—now that I swore an oath to my friends not to get myself murdered if I could help it—it makes everything complicated again. I'm going to have to re-figure out my whole existence.

First, though—

"Hey!" Kera screamed as the idiot next to her swerved out of his lane toward her before lurching back. "It's barely dark! If you're drunk *already*, the first step is admitting you have a problem. There is help, okay?"

Taking a deep breath, she drove on. Apparently, when she got stressed, she let it out as road rage.

Less of that, MacDonagh. If you get arrested, you won't make it downtown in time.

Inhaling and steeling herself, Kera turned east toward the Financial District and cast a combination cloaking and glamour spell on herself. She was wearing her studded jacket, which, she hoped, would suppress the obvious signature of her magic in case the other thaumaturgists were still looking for her. She needed a disguise.

The enchantment played itself out. Anyone who glanced toward her would see a tourist of South Asian descent in a tiny metro-sized car with a rental license plate, driving confusedly in circles while looking for the Convention Center.

A moment later, she saw the place again. It was the sort of older decently maintained office building that had been converted from something else—a bank, perhaps, or an ornately-decorated factory, much like Kera's home. This one, however, had corporate signage all over the front.

That's it.

She drove slowly past, noting that most of the windows were dark. Hopefully, that would help her narrow down who she was going for. Once she was out of sight of the building, she pulled onto a side street, then parked in an empty lot.

Kera looked down at her handlebars. "You ready, Zee?" She dismounted, breathed deeply, and wheeled him into the shadows, where he would hopefully be safe.

Her hand clutched the small disk in her coat pocket—the relic from the Kims. Believe in it, they had said. Kera had seen and done too much lately to *disbelieve*, so all that was necessary was to have faith in her friends.

As she moved quietly toward the offices, she cast one last spell. It might not work, but it was worth a shot.

A calming spell as widespread and as powerful as she dared invoke, intended to act on anyone she had used the enchantment on before. With luck, some of her foes would be too chilled out to offer much resistance.

She would have to cross the street to reach the building. There wasn't much cover.

Here goes nothing.

Johnny Torrez was thinking. He was also working, though not as fast as he was capable of. They had enough time to get away with a mild delay, provided Pauline didn't scrutinize their timetable too hard.

Sven asked, "Toss me another line of wires, okay?"

Johnny grabbed the rubber-wrapped lengths of copper and threw them to his friend, who caught them and turned back to his work. Sven had experience making high-tech bombs, whereas Johnny was better with basic incendiary devices.

At the other end of the set of offices, Pauline shouted something in that sharp, angry tone of hers, and Lia responded in a soft voice to try to calm her down.

"Yeah," Johnny muttered to himself. "Better to stay cool as we go into this."

But he wasn't cool—or hot, for that matter. Kind of lukewarm. Mixed up.

He *liked* the thought of the Mermaid no longer existing, given how much grief that fucking place had caused him. He liked the idea of Motorcycle Man trying to stop them and going out with a bang. The hood of Johnny's Mustang would be avenged, they would gain a ton of street cred for taking Motorcycle Man out, and Pauline would stop bitching about it.

On the other hand...

What Lia and Sven had said made a lot of sense—that killing multiple civilians was more trouble than it was worth. That it would bring the wrath of God down upon them in the form of every alphabet-soup agency in America, which would only need to know their whereabouts before crushing them like bugs.

That the feds might actually take gang violence seriously this time. They had issued a stay-away to the other gangs, which meant that no one should snitch.

But there was always the possibility.

There'd have to be a snitch, and the cops would have to believe them. Johnny didn't think that was likely.

He hoped not.

Also, given Pauline's total lack of interest in reconsidering, there was the other issue. Johnny suspected it had occurred to all three lieutenants, but it was too dangerous to say out loud.

It was the possibility that Pauline was out to lunch. Two beers short of a six-pack. Ready to be committed. She'd lost her marbles, was *loco en la cabeza*, and other such expressions. Perhaps she had been sane once, but something had changed.

That was a worrisome thought, especially when the two of them had finally been getting along.

Doesn't make me look good, Johnny thought. He had liked the new, bloodthirsty Pauline who said what she meant and solved problems the old-fashioned way, but it was possible that she'd gone overboard.

As he stuffed various household items into canisters of gasoline, a stupid and ridiculous thought occurred to him.

You can call it off. Think about it, Johnny. You're allowed to say, "Nah, I quit," and walk the fuck away. Tell her you conscientiously object or something.

He blinked, and a shudder went over him. Cowardice, disloyalty, and lack of follow-through were *not* traits that helped a man rise in the streets. He hated himself for even thinking about that.

There was a chance that he could get the hell away from the streets altogether. He'd go live in an apartment complex in the suburbs of Muncie, Indiana or someplace like that, go straight, and work a normal shitty job. It would probably suck, but he wouldn't have to worry every waking minute of every day that someone would kill him if he seemed too weak to live.

Except it's not that simple, is it, Johnny? his inner voice went on. *Oh, no. Pauline knows people, doesn't she? Connections. Rich people. Whether they're mobbed up or technically legit doesn't make a difference because the law is just a suggestion for people who have enough money. And Pauline's Russian. Did you ever find out if she was part of the fucking organizatsiya? No, you didn't. And no matter how smart or tough you are, you're not John Wick, and you're not taking on the Russian Mob by yourself if they find out you left one of their princesses in the clutch.*

Sven looked up. "Did you say something?"

"No," Johnny shot back. "Might be my phone. Hold on."

He checked the device. There was a new text from one of his

informants, but it wasn't anything earth-shattering. The guy claimed to have seen a convoy of three or four police cars in the Little Tokyo area. Johnny made a mental note, but it didn't necessarily mean the heat was on. The cops might have just stopped to shoot the shit and ended up racing each other to the donut shop.

If they didn't leave, *then* there might be a problem.

He reported as much to Sven, who nodded and stood. "I'm gonna have a smoke. Care to join?"

"Yeah," Johnny answered, falling into step. "Sure."

Out the side door, near where the warehouse joined with the disused generic storefront, they stood in a pool of shadows and looked out at the patchwork of electric lights around the city. Sven lit a cigarette.

"This shit tonight," he stated, "has to be done with extreme caution. If we're going to do something this big, it's got to be done right. Many, many ways it could go wrong."

Johnny nodded. He was no fool. Sven was expressing his total lack of enthusiasm for and belief in the project, albeit in an indirect way in case Pauline overheard them.

"No shit," Torrez agreed. "I mean, go big or go home, right? Always an element of risk. Little more than I'd like, though. The payoff *might* be worth it."

"Maybe," said Sven. He patted the back of his coat above his waistband, feeling for his Ruger. "You got your gun, right?"

Johnny's hand went to his side, where he was carrying his Beretta semi-openly in a holster under his coat. Sven would have known he had the damn thing, but that wasn't the point.

"Of course. And a spare mag."

Sven inhaled smoke. "Good. Something like this, if the law shows up, it doesn't end with you demanding to talk to your lawyer. It's all or nothing. You have to be *prepared* for that." He tapped the side of his head.

In a way, Johnny appreciated that his friend was giving him

advice and making sure they were on the same page, but it was redundant. He bristled.

"You're not telling me anything I don't already know, Sven. I've been through shit in the barrio, and I have no idea why or how I'm still alive. With Pauline, we're putting a lot on the line, but we have a real chance to go somewhere in life. To—"

He stopped talking, and his and Sven's heads snapped toward the street.

"Wait," the big Swede whispered. "What was that noise?"

Kera had begun casting spells as soon as she'd set foot on the asphalt. She was halfway across the street. A random car came by, and she stood aside, waiting for it to pass. The driver wasn't interested in her, probably because she still resembled a foreign tourist instead of a sinister figure in a black motorcycle helmet.

When she was nearly to the lot where the office lay, she heard someone whisper, *"What was that noise?"*

It was coming from around the corner of the building. The front of the place blocked them from sight, but it meant Kera had stupidly neglected to notice that there was a side entrance, complete with guards.

Enough with trying to seem inconspicuous. I'm not going to waste time criticizing myself for sloppiness, either, she decided, and her hands formed into fists. She dismissed the glamour spell, opting to appear in the form of Motorcycle Man as most people imagined him.

Better yet, a whole gang of Motorcycle Men.

Concentrating hard, Kera cast a ghost-sounds spell in conjunction with three consecutive glamour spells, merging and projecting them into a trio of illusions that looked like her in her leathers and helmet and which were capable of audible footsteps, shouting, and rustling.

No sooner had she completed the task than the soft and rapid footfalls of the sentries moved around the side of the building from different angles. Kera dropped flat next to the curb and commanded her doubles to fan out toward the building.

As Kera watched, a big, pale, heavyset man in a nice black suit appeared from around the corner nearest to her. He aimed and fired what looked like a snub-nosed revolver, and loud cracks split the air twice as the gun's muzzle flashed and small puffs of smoke rose.

The illusion nearest the man wove back and forth as it advanced. The guard was aiming precisely; he was probably a good shot and likely had a low-capacity gun. His brow furrowed in consternation as the bullets kicked up dirt behind the shadowy figure, which did not slow.

Kera made the double laugh maniacally as it moved forward. The man retreated into the building, and a second later, another shot rang out, but she couldn't determine where it had come from.

At the same instant, someone else fired at the other two doppelgangers from around a different corner. The second sentry must have had a higher capacity gun, probably a semiauto pistol, and had snuck the other way around the building. He sprayed half a dozen shots toward the doubles to no avail.

Kera kept an eye out for flashes, focused on the way the noise echoed, and used her augmented consciousness to try to figure out where each of the gunmen was positioned. The big guy had taken cover within the window nearest the side entrance, she was pretty sure, whereas the other one seemed to be firing from behind a trash container near the rear corner of the building.

She made the illusions dart around menacingly as though they had a plan to kill both men. The problem was they could not do anything, only act as distractions. In the meantime, Kera began hearing another sound between the gunshots. A woman was shouting at the top of her lungs in a foreign language somewhere deep within the structure.

The big guy fired his sixth shot. "Cover!" he shouted, and the man on the other side opened fire again, putting another four or five rounds across the lot while his partner reloaded. One of the bullets struck the ground about three feet from where Kera lay.

Shit! I can't keep up this charade forever. What I need is to lure them off or get them both in the same place so I can nail the bastards, then bust up the rest of the party.

Knowing she was taking a severe risk, Kera sprang to her feet and cast a further spell to enhance her speed and reflexes, as well as one to form a rough translucent magical shield in front of her. She pantomimed aiming a handgun at the building and had her illusions mimic the gunshots they had heard from the sentries.

The man near the back corner cursed in Spanish, and Kera heard him eject a magazine to load a new one. Then he sprang out, waving a large pistol and firing wildly at the dark figures.

Kera had the three doubles freeze, then flee toward her position. She directed them toward an adjacent lot where a cluster of small outbuildings and various trees provided more cover.

The man with the snubbie, having reloaded, barked, "Get 'em!"

Kera looked over her shoulder as the dark shapes of the two guards approached, raising their pistols to fire. She repositioned her magical shield so it provided her with full cover.

Both men squeezed the triggers. Sparks erupted behind the witch as the bullets struck; others passed through the illusions to blow chunks off trees or walls.

Kera spun to face them just as the beam of a nearby streetlamp illuminated their faces. She had never seen the big guy with the revolver before, but she definitely had seen the other. It was Mustang Man, his familiar visage twisted by rage and frustration.

Time to end it, Kera thought. *The ringleader might get away if I don't besiege that building in the next ten seconds.*

She contemplated killing them. They had tried to kill her, and what they were planning to do to the Mermaid was unspeakable, but something about the desperation on the smaller, darker man's face and the oddly unthreatening, almost reasonable demeanor of the bigger, paler guy...

Not to mention, she still got pangs of guilt for throwing Deke Anastidis to his death, even though that had been in self-defense and mostly accidental.

No. I won't stoop to their level unless I absolutely have to.

As the men aimed their guns at her face, she flung out her hands and hit them with the strongest incapacitation spell she could muster without seriously weakening herself—a mixture of short-term memory impairment, relaxation, and confusion.

The men staggered back. Their arms dropped to their sides, and they let go of their pistols. The heavyset man stood with his jaw hanging open for a moment, then sat down hard on the ground and stared vacantly into space. Mustang Man wheeled drunkenly in a circle before falling flat on his back, unconscious.

Kera breathed hard in the ensuing silence. The gunshots had been loud enough that someone might already be calling the cops, or a police cruiser might have been near enough to hear them. She had to be fast.

"Okay, boys, let me just take those, and I'll leave you to your rest." Kera picked up their guns and stuffed the little Ruger LCR, which had only three shots remaining, into her pocket. The larger Beretta 92, whose magazine was still about two-thirds full, she put into the rear waistband of her pants after flicking the safety on.

She had fired both guns before, back when her dad had allowed her to take up target shooting as a hobby. Thinking back on those days as the adrenaline faded, she realized her ears were ringing painfully. Tinnitus again.

Trying to ignore it, Kera dismissed the illusions and sprinted toward the building.

I ought to devise a magical earmuffs spell since any gang members left in there are probably going to be armed too, and firing a gun indoors is even worse. Of course, getting shot is the worst of all, so shields get priority.

As she reached the edge of the structure, the first feelings of fatigue struck her. She had used more magic than intended, and she sensed the fight was far from over.

Kera went for the side door and flung it open. As soon as she did, someone opened up with an automatic weapon.

"Goddamn!" she cried out, flinging herself away. Her shield stopped some of the bullets, but others tore up the doorframe and the ground around her, and she could feel the thaumaturgic barrier weakening.

She feigned a groan of pain so whoever had fired would think they'd hit her. Then she cloaked the sounds of her movements as she crept around the front to the main entrance.

Unsurprisingly since it was after business hours, the door was locked. Kera cast a small but concentrated spell that told the metal parts to open and the electronic parts not to send any signals to the alarm system and made her way inside.

Stairs led up to both sides of the lobby to second-floor suites of offices. Her targets clearly lay to the left, the side from which they had fired earlier—but *where*?

Kera listened for any noise, then crept up the stairs.

The place was exactly the sort of corporate nightmare she had been afraid of. She saw posters with motivational slogans using various buzzwords like "Success" and "Teamwork" and "Impactfulness" and "Customer Loyalty." Inside conference rooms, whiteboards held flow charts full of brightly-colored graphics.

"Blech," Kera muttered, and she hurried onward.

She was coming up on a door that had light behind it, and she hastened forward to stand behind it so she would be hidden by it when it opened. Her guess was that whoever had tried to shoot her was still waiting by the edge of the building, but she couldn't rule out that someone was waiting for her.

When Doug and Mia worked cases, it was usually Doug who drove, but tonight, Mia was behind the wheel. Perhaps it was because they weren't technically working.

In fact, both of them were thinking about passing out.

Mia blinked aggressively to keep her eyes on the road. "Doug. Are you feeling more tired the closer we get to the Mermaid?"

Her partner yawned. "Yes."

Knowing she was not alone didn't provide much comfort. There were times when misery did not love company.

Doug added, "I started feeling it right around dark, I think. It's like the thought of going there and researching this shit is, I don't know, provoking the universe to convince us otherwise. Does that qualify as a conspiracy theory?"

Mia narrowly evaded driving through a stop sign and tried to hide her alarm at her diminishing skills. "There are better conspiracies to report on than us being tired, but yeah. This whole trip has been like wading through a lake of molasses. You want coffee?"

"Sure," Doug agreed.

"Good, because I *need* it to get there without us getting killed or arrested." Mia looked for the nearest amenable drive-through and found one less than a minute later.

They purchased java, a medium for Doug and a large one for Mia, and parked the car to drink them. Fortunately, Mia had also asked for a small cup of ice. She shook half of it into her beverage before passing the rest to her partner.

Doug was impressed. "Damn, you're smart. We would have had to wait, like, entire *minutes* for this crap to cool down otherwise. They keep it at a temperature that can smelt iron."

Once both journalists had downed a good amount of caffeine, they continued toward the bar.

"It's weird," Mia commented as the streetlights sped past and cars randomly honked around them, "I don't remember ever being this burnt out. Like, we've always been energetic types, haven't we? Is this what other people deal with, and we never experienced it until now?"

Doug swished the coffee around in his cup. "It's within the realm of possibility, but why would we get struck simultaneously and out of the blue? Like I said, has to be a conspiracy by the universe against our right to report on this story."

Though the caffeine helped, Mia still felt dazed and zoned-out when they arrived at the Mermaid. Business appeared to be slow; there were only two cars out front. She and Doug trudged in, muttering to each other that they would only stay for an hour since sleep was becoming vital.

They seated themselves, vaguely aware of how quiet it was, but it wasn't until they plopped down in chairs that they examined the place.

"Holy crap," Mia exclaimed. "It's *deserted*. Are they closed?"

Doug rubbed his chin. "Nah. The lights are on and the door was open, but it *is* weird, isn't it? Still, at least they set out complimentary mozzarella sticks. And marinara, of course." He gestured at the food before them.

Mia could not recall if the Mermaid pre-served appetizers to their customers. Most places didn't, so it was possible they had accidentally sat at someone's table. Still, Doug was digging in, and food *did* sound good...

There were multiple crashes as men in black armor burst through the front entrance, the back door, and out of the kitchen. The journalists froze as voices shouted and gun-mounted flashlights shone in their faces.

"*Freeze!*" a man bellowed, apparently unaware that they hadn't moved a millimeter.

Mia stared. Most of the paramilitary guys had FBI stenciled on their vests, though some appeared to be LAPD SWAT. A disgruntled-looking woman strode toward them and flashed a badge.

"Agent MacDonald, FBI," she said. "Who are you, and what are you doing here? This place has been evacuated due to a hostage threat. Are you aware of that?"

As Mia's mouth soundlessly moved up and down, Doug exhaled in blatant relief.

"Oh, thank God," he said. "See, Mia? It's not us. Agent, it's okay if we finish these mozz sticks, right?"

CHAPTER TWENTY-THREE

Kera stood in front of the door that opened into the offices. She had done a "vibe scan" of what lay beyond, but she could detect nothing except fear and anger, which was not a great surprise and of little help.

There was nothing to do but go through. She channeled another stream of power into herself, augmenting her speed, strength, and mental acuity at the cost of growing tiredness in the back of her mind that would overtake her in a short while.

She eased the door open and stepped into a short corridor. At the bend on the ceiling was a camera. She had no idea if they were watching her, but she couldn't take the chance of them getting tipped off to her being in the building.

Kera streaked forward, stood on tiptoe, and used a gun to turn the camera. That done, she moved around the next corner into an open area between a series of doors that led to other offices.

Even with her limited knowledge of demolitions, she could tell that people had been assembling bombs, but that wasn't what caught her eye.

Two women were standing behind a heavy, overturned metal

table. One had blonde hair and was holding what looked like an AKS74-U Russian automatic carbine, and the other, with black hair, was aiming a tiny pocket pistol. They opened fire.

Deafening noise and flashes filled the room. Kera dove and rolled toward the wall and the minimal cover provided by a pile of crates filled with wire and components she hoped weren't explosive. The armor-piercing rounds from the blonde's assault rifle could probably penetrate the crates, so Kera knew she'd have to dodge and replenish her shield.

She seized her chance to open the door of one of the offices and tumble inside as both women reloaded. Her ears were ringing so loudly that she could hardly hear, but she couldn't focus on that.

Kera pulled energy from the universe and used it to reinforce the barrier she had conjured. A few gunshots sounded; they were trying to keep her pinned down as they moved to fire at her like a fish in a barrel.

Kera waited, the don't-notice-me spell now gone. She could tell that the two women were closer to being able to fire into the office.

Silence fell after both the rifle and the pistol clicked, empty.

Kera sprang back out, pulled out the snubbie, and blasted at the women. She didn't want to hit them, merely scare them into standing down. She fired a shot over the brunette's head and the other two off to the blonde's side.

The blonde barked out a curse in what might have been Russian, then turned and fled toward the farthest office.

Is that who I think it is? Kera wondered. *No, she looks different from the girl at the bar with Mustang Man, but the unpleasant, disturbing, soulless vibe seems familiar.*

She had no time to explore the thought, however, because the other woman shouted, "Pauline, stay back!" and charged Kera with a keyboard.

Kera shifted into fighting mode. Her opponent was a small

lady of East Asian descent somewhere between twenty-five and a youthful thirty, dressed snappy-casual like an off-duty office worker. The speed at which she moved and the way she held the piece of tech in her hands suggested that she was not a pushover, however.

Kera was feeling the effects of having channeled so much magic, especially after healing Mrs. Kim earlier.

The keyboard lashed at her face as the woman roared and kicked. Kera took the blow from the plastic on her forearm, grunting in pain while sidestepping the kick and punching the woman in the stomach. She let out an "oof" and dropped the keyboard, then moved into a clinch.

Kera realized the other girl had some martial arts training, probably Jiu-jitsu, Hapkido, or perhaps Krav Maga. The two grappled fiercely, each trying to catch the other with a wristlock or joint break between attempts at clawing at one another's eyes or kneeing groin and stomach.

The Asian woman screamed continuously as if she were trying to unnerve Kera.

"What is *wrong* with you?" she demanded, her hands tearing at Kera's helmet and arms, then wrenching the faceplate up. "You moron! She's only making us do this because you couldn't back off and had to be queen bitch of all the gangs. I *knew* you were a chick!"

Kera, though tired, had adjusted to the woman's fighting style, and she was still running high on her thaumaturgic infusions. She saw a gap in her foe's defenses and struck her in the side of the head with an elbow.

Lia fell back, gasping and thrashing, and Kera stepped in to simultaneously trip and shove her. She crashed into the wall with twice the force most normal humans would have been able to muster. The woman crumpled, alive but battered, and probably out of the fight.

Kera looked up as a door clicked ahead of her. The blonde

woman, Pauline, leaned through the doorway of her office, aiming her freshly reloaded rifle.

"You lose," the blonde woman said simply. "And I'm still going to take down your precious Mermaid."

A barrage of hot lead spat from the barrel of her gun, and Kera ran to the side, not only to protect herself but to draw fire away from the collapsed Asian girl. Bullets sparked off her shield as she ducked behind the table the two women had used for their own protection.

And that's it, Kera's mind acknowledged. *I'm dizzy and exhausted. I used too much magic too quickly without bringing a backup energy source, and now this Russian corporate wannabe is going to kill me with Soviet-era military surplus hardware. My faceplate is gone, and I think my other pistol fell out while I was doing cartwheels back there. Maybe I'm not such a badass witch after all.*

She turned and ran, managing to rush, crawl, leap, and stumble her way back to the corridor and into the lobby of the office. It took too long, and she was certain Pauline would appear and put a couple dozen holes through her at any moment.

But she didn't...yet. In fact, it sounded like the other woman had climbed out a window or left through an exit that Kera hadn't noticed. If that were the case, she might get away, burst into the Mermaid, and shoot as many people as she could rather than bombing the place.

And Kera was out of extra energy. Not only would any more magic wipe her out, but she didn't know how long the effects of the Kims' relic would last. She might draw more trouble on herself if she attempted further channeling at this point.

I have to pull through. One way or another, I have to end this now. Tonight.

She looked around, and the first thing her eyes fell on was the office's coffee station. With the desperate hunger of a dog waiting beside the dinner table, Kera pulled herself toward it, grabbed a cup, and pushed the lever.

Only a tiny trickle of blackish liquid came out, barely an ounce.

"God*dammit*," Kera raged. "Cheap bastards." She seized sugar packets—there were only two, barely enough—and dumped them into the cup. Otherwise, there was only one option remaining.

Kera pinched the creamer packs and her mouth puckered. "Fuck. This is one of the grossest things I have ever done. I hate French Vanilla." Swallowing a sudden bulge in her throat, she tore open the paper and added them to her half-assed beverage.

Next, she went to the sink, filled the cup with water, and stirred it with her finger. It was better than nothing.

Outside, shadows were moving. Kera looked up. She couldn't see much of anything, certainly not enough to know if Pauline had come back for Round Two.

Kera tilted her head back and poured the thin, sweet mixture into her mouth. She gulped it fast to minimize the weird taste and shuddered, but she felt the effects within seconds. Calories and cheap carbs were exactly what she needed for a vitality boost.

The outer door Kera had opened earlier crashed inward and Pauline stomped in. Her face, which might have been attractive under other circumstances, was horribly contorted with vicious hate, and her bleached hair was coming loose. Her red-nailed hands clutched the carbine to her shoulder in a way suggesting she was familiar with weapons.

Kera dove behind the reception desk as her nemesis opened fire again, and once more, the agonizing loudness of the gun was made worse by the enclosed space. As her ears rang and debris flew, a single thought filled her mind.

It's her, the creepy woman from the Mermaid who showed up as Mustang Man's date. She was disguised as a basic bimbo, but she's the leader of this whole operation. Mustang Man is just her lackey. I can tell. None of them seem like great people, but I don't think they want to blow up my bar. This bitch is making them do it.

That knowledge, combined with the slight boost from her horrible coffee, brought her back from the brink.

Kera stood up and lunged out from behind the desk as Pauline's AK exhausted its magazine. The Russian tried to reload but dropped the gun after a second, realizing there was no time. Instead, she directed a solid punch at Kera.

It was easy to duck under it, but Kera was too off-balance to counterattack with her own fists, so she swept her leg upward behind her, bending it so it rose past shoulder level. The sole of her boot crashed into Pauline's face.

The woman cried out and hit the wall, then scrabbled at a sheath on her thigh and pulled a knife. Her face looked even more livid with a nasty red mark forming on her cheek. "You lose. I said so before, and I'll say it again. There was only one of you this whole time, wasn't there? You don't have a gang! You're nothing! All you want is to break down the world I'm trying to build—"

Kera fell into a battle stance and raised her hands. The knife made everything more complicated, but some of her augmented speed and strength remained, not to mention everything she had learned from her sessions in the *dojang* with Mrs. Kim.

"You're crazy is what you are," Kera observed.

Shrieking, Pauline lashed out at her with the blade, feinting at her face before making a lower strike at her gut.

Kera raised her arms to protect herself but did not flinch. When the knife went low, she hopped out of range and swept her foot hard at the side of Pauline's knee. The blow connected, but not with much force because Pauline was charging into the next strike.

Still, her knee wobbled, and her thrust at Kera's heart went wide and slashed her lightly along the lower side instead. The blade was terrifyingly sharp, and it cut through the leather jacket to draw blood.

Kera hit Pauline in the jaw with the heel of her hand. The

Russian blonde reeled back, which gave the witch enough time to circle into the most open part of the lobby while forcing Pauline toward the corner.

Kera grabbed the only thing at hand, which happened to be a potted plant, and half-bashed, half-threw it at her enemy's arm and shoulder. Pauline fell to her knees but retained her hold on the knife and surprised Kera with a sudden slash at her legs.

Stumbling, Kera narrowly avoided taking the blade in her kneecap. Pauline pounced on her, bending her back over the low part of the desk, the knife poised to stab her in the face.

Kera caught Pauline's wrist, and their eyes locked as the blade trembled.

"I'm still burning down the Mermaid after you're dead," Pauline promised.

Fear and anger and adrenaline were blotting out Kera's ability to think, and Pauline had pinned her in a way that she could do almost nothing except hold the knife at bay, but something occurred to her.

I could let her stab me and bash her head on the desk. Then she wouldn't be able to do jack shit to Cevin or Jenn or Stephanie or anyone else. But I promised the Kims not only victory but survival.

Kera was strong. She had worked out, trained, and prepared for moments like this. The two women were of the same moderate height and slender build, but Kera was more athletic and a better fighter. She strained against her attacker, pushing upward.

Pauline moved back, and so did the knife. Her bloodshot eyes widened in fear. Kera calmed, focusing everything on the determination—the *certainty*—that she would leave this building alive and walk into a peaceful, intact bar the next time she went to work.

Pauline was no longer in control. She tried to fling herself against Kera one last time, using both hands to attempt to push the knife down, but by now, Kera had moved them both past

Pauline's point of advantage. She pivoted and used the Russian's motions against her, directing the knife down and to the side. The blade hit the desk's surface and fell to the floor.

Kera ducked in a counterintuitive swooping motion, just as Mrs. Kim had taught her, then came back up, her foot striking true. It caught Pauline full in the face with all the disciplined force her body could muster.

Pauline cried out as she was knocked off her feet. She fell hard, and the back of her head struck the corner of the fridge with an awful crunching sound. She flopped to the floor, a red pool spreading beneath her as her hate-filled eyes went glassy. Perhaps for the first time in years, she looked at peace.

Everything was quiet for a moment, aside from the sound of a car passing by outside. Then Kera heard sirens approaching, since automatic gunfire would not go unnoticed for long.

Kera stood, brushed herself off, and exhaled. She was sweating and shaking, hardly able to believe she was alive and Pauline was dead, but it had to be done.

The cops would be here soon, and she had one more thing to do before she could leave.

Kera stood and raised her hands, feeling the vibe-essence of Johnny, and Sven, and Lia, all of whom were unconscious or barely conscious but still susceptible to magical suggestion.

First, she projected a mental image into their memories of her, the dreaded Motorcycle Woman, a figure of terror and aggression who mercilessly doled out retribution. They would remember her that way.

She delivered her message, tying it to the image of her speaking in a deep, booming voice while her eyes glowed red.

Consider this your ONLY FUCKING WARNING. You will not receive another. Like cowards, you went along with a plan that would have killed innocent people. I foiled that plan, and I also marked all three of you. I can hunt you down at will, and I'll disembowel you with a blunt spork if you so much as think of getting involved with a person like Pauline ever again.

As the spell faded, Kera could actually hear Lia moaning from the upper floor of the building. As she darted out the front door and across the street, she saw Johnny and Sven twitching like kids having nightmares beside the tree where she had left them.

They would wake up soon, but if they had to deal with the cops right away, it might interfere with their ability to get the point of the night's events. Kera summoned the last of her magic and wove a final ghost-sounds spell, combined with a minor memory-wipe. The cops would think the gunfire had happened two blocks down the street, and they'd spend enough time looking there that the other three could get out.

She found Zee and gave him a pat. "Thanks for waiting. Sorry it took so long. One more stop before home—*food.*"

CHAPTER TWENTY-FOUR

An hour earlier, Mr. Kim had waved as his son, with a fully loaded backpack of supplies, walked down the street toward his friend's house. Once the boy was gone, his father shut the door and turned the sign out front to Sorry, We're Closed despite it being an hour and a half earlier than usual.

Mr. Kim stood and stared vacantly into space. There were forms of magic that could trace people to other people by following the ties of blood, emotion, and shared experience. He didn't think whoever was coming for Kera would go after his child, but he refused to take any chances, and Ye-Jin had agreed.

Tonight, it would only be the two of them, as it had been back in Korea so many years ago.

His wife came down the stairs, feeling better after a nap, a meal, and some strong tea. She was still not as strong as either of them would like, but well enough to help make the preparations.

"Ah, Ye-Jin." He clapped his hands together. "We should have fun with this as long as we are at it, don't you think? They probably have no goddamn idea what they're dealing with here. We can throw them off with a bunch of bullshit stereotypes and theatrical stuff."

Mrs. Kim made a sour face. "What does that mean? We will distract them with stupid things they might have seen in movies?"

His grin broadened. "Exactly. For all we know, one of them majored in East Asian Studies in college, but probably not. And a class like that would be full of horseshit and know nothing about the tradition we come from. Right? Ha, ha."

Though one was far more enthusiastic than the other, the spouses both contributed to turning their shop and home into a combination of an obstacle course, an amusement park ride, a museum exhibit, and as Mr. Kim put it, "A *Home Alone* meets *Rambo V* trap course."

Their presumed opponents were magicians of considerable power and knowledge, but since the secrets of the miraculous arts in Korea were quite closely guarded against outside scrutiny, the hunters would have to assume that anything unusual was a magical component of great significance or dangerous power.

"So," Mrs. Kim quipped as the nature of her husband's fiendish plan became clear, "this was the real reason you sent Sam away, isn't it? He would die of embarrassment if he saw this."

Mr. Kim cackled and continued to decorate.

They hung veils and tapestries and random prayer cloths everywhere and filled the store with cheap knick-knacks with varying degrees of "Asianness," some of which had nothing to do with Korea: Vietnamese Buddha statues, a crappy reproduction katana they had bought for Sam on his seventh birthday, a poster of Bruce Lee, and some strings of Indian beads Mr. Kim had purchased from a street vendor on a whim last year.

Most of it had zero magical potential, but it would all distract, confuse, and confound, especially in conjunction with the profusion of different types of slow-burning incense they'd ignited. Scents could have a significant effect on the performance of the obscure arts. Using too many or the wrong ones would make life difficult for those who were sensitive to such things.

Further, they pulled apart the shelves and brought in boxes and crates and dollies from the back storeroom, littering the aisles of the shop as well as the hallways and the staircase to their living area with disorganized junk.

"And," Mr. Kim pointed out, holding up a particular box, "we will finally be able to use this ridiculous thing. Ha!" It was a smoke machine he had intended to save for Halloween. "It will probably hurt their eyes and lungs and screw with the scents even more."

Mrs. Kim finally managed a laugh. "We should have opened a party store instead of a grocery store. Business would not have been as consistent, but you are perfect for it. Or the circus."

Beaming with sudden pride, Mr. Kim hid speakers in locations where they were inconvenient to find and deactivate. They would soon blare a jangling profusion of spoken-word tapes in Korean, music of Sam's, and a Halloween CD of scary sounds.

Mr. Kim concluded that unless the people trying to find Kera were the best magicians on the planet, they would have a rough time concentrating on spells amidst this godawful mess.

Mrs. Kim chided, "Careful with that candle. Making them lost and confused will be funny, but it won't be so amusing if the veils get swept into the flames or the burning herbs and we end up with a pile of charcoal instead of a home and business."

"Oh, right," he replied as though he'd just thought of that. He paused. "Are you sure we should not have told Kera about this, Ye-Jin? I don't like withholding things from her."

His wife put a hand on his shoulder. "We did the right thing. She would never have agreed to it."

***

James and LeBlanc, both magically cloaked, stood on the sidewalk, taking in the convenience store. The sign said Closed, but there were dim lights within.

They had searched several times for the source of the magic, and the answer was this place every time. Apparently, Motorcycle Man was prepping for his mission in Kim's Convenience.

James turned to his friend. "Ready?"

"Of course," she replied. He held the door and she went in first, one hand in front of her to ward off anything the rogue channelers might throw at them.

Nothing happened. James stepped in behind her and closed the door, and his eyes bulged.

It didn't look like a grocery store. It seemed to be a cross between a carnival haunted house and a makeshift Asian temple. It also looked like it had been ransacked, or maybe the proprietors had been doing inventory, only to be interrupted in the middle of the process.

Sounds and scents wafted on the air, weird noises and chanting, and the smell of multiple types of incense and herbs. James' brain put up a massive red flag.

God-fucking-dammit. It's not just one person, it's multiple people, and they knew we were coming. They're fucking with us. Were the Motorcycle Man and Mermaid things hoaxes to get the FBI out of the way? I can sense magic. It's faint, but then again, they must have successfully cloaked how powerful they are since the beginning.

They might very well have stumbled onto a coven, and a brief look at LeBlanc confirmed she was thinking much the same thing.

"James," she said softly, "let's *not* split up. A quick roundabout of the store, then we find their living area and see what's upstairs."

His eyes darted around. Veils and cloth had been hung everywhere, obscuring the dimensions of the place. "Yeah. Affirmative."

They circled to the left toward the rear part of the shop where the refrigerators were, pushing aside hangings as they went. James felt something catch his ankle, and he stumbled into a shelf, knocking about twenty bags of chips and cheese curls onto himself.

"For fuck's sake," he hissed as LeBlanc helped him back to his feet. He'd stepped in an empty box that had been left in front of an overturned greeting card rack.

They advanced a few more steps toward the far back corner. Out of nowhere, someone cackled loudly and maniacally, and LeBlanc, startled, blundered into an incense burner.

"Oh!" she exclaimed, hurriedly casting a frost spell to extinguish the flames that began to catch along the edges of her flowing dress. "They'll pay for *that*," she vowed, glaring at the burnt, ragged ends.

There was nothing in the store. The thaumaturges headed toward the counter past squat statues that leered at them in the dim candlelight. Both sensed a considerable amount of power throughout the place, but its nature was elusive. They were dealing with a magical tradition outside their expertise.

A hand-painted banner with what looked like Korean lettering hung over the counter access gate; James thought it might be a curse, so he and LeBlanc climbed over the counter instead. Unfortunately, someone seemed to have spilled vegetable oil on it, and James found himself skidding off and into the opposite wall, while LeBlanc watched in horror as the oil sank into the bright fabric of her clothes.

James sighed as he got up. "I'm hoping these people turn out to be *really* hostile so we have an excuse to nuke them into oblivion."

LeBlanc took a deep breath. "No comment. Come on."

There was no light in the hall beyond the main space, and after they activated a minor illumination spell to create a stationary glow in front of them, a series of black shirts and dark blue shawls hung from wires. They pushed them aside and found a bathroom and a jumbled storeroom, but nothing else of interest.

LeBlanc pointed out, "I think we missed a staircase leading up."

"Probably," James conceded. They retreated, found the stairs, and slowly climbed them.

The profusions of weird, confusing sounds grew louder, as did the smells, and there was more dull orange light. The steps creaked under their feet. They were almost upon whatever was waiting for them in the heart of the place.

James stood before a closed door with his hand on the knob. He looked at LeBlanc, who nodded and raised her hands to conjure a powerful shield or devastating attack spell at an instant's notice.

He pulled the door open, and in leapt his partner.

"Oh, hello!" A man looked up from his dinner. He was short, with gray-flecked black hair. A Korean woman, perhaps his wife, sat next to him. "Sorry about the mess. Please, come in! We made too much chicken."

The thaumaturges stared at one another. The feeling of magic was still here, but the only people they could see were the older couple sitting at the table, enjoying a candlelight supper with aromatic tea.

"Nice Scary Halloween Sounds tape," James said as he stepped inside.

"Thank you," said the man. He sipped his tea.

LeBlanc sniffed the air. "That chicken does smell wonderful. We, uh, apologize for entering without permission, but we wanted to talk to you about something." She seemed to have decided to approach this politely despite her earlier outburst.

She and James glanced at each other again. They could not perceive much of an increase in the intensity of magical power. It clearly emanated from the husband and wife, both of whom were setting the table for more diners.

"You are here searching for magic," the man said. "Yes, yes, we know. Come in."

James said, "We're looking for Motorcycle Man before people get hurt."

"Mmm." The man looked to the side of the room, where a black motorcycle helmet sat on a side table. "As you can see, no one is presently being hurt."

James frowned and turned away, checking his phone. Richardson had sent a terse message indicating that taking the Mermaid had been uneventful and nothing was showing up on scans, although two civilians had blundered in after the place was cleared. Apparently, that had been cleaned up, and so far, no one else had so much as approached the building.

James thought, *I don't like this,* but he could *feel* the signature of magic emanating from this place. He and LeBlanc went over and sat down at the table as the older couple introduced themselves.

"First—" he began, but Mrs. Kim held up a hand.

"Eat first," she said quietly. "You are our guests. You will come to no harm. There is no reason we cannot be civilized, and of course you can check the food to make sure it is safe."

The dinner was one of the stranger events James had ever partaken in, though between the delicious food and the candlelight, it was strangely soothing. Throughout, he could feel the magical signature he had sensed in the Mermaid, centered more strongly on the woman.

When all that remained was empty plates, Mrs. Kim sat in silence, one hand on her husband's arm. The thaumaturges looked up.

"So," Mr. Kim began, in a low, solemn voice, "tell us about the people whose minds you have wiped clean and whose powers you have taken away. We know who you are. There is no need to pretend." He had dropped the jovial facade.

James frowned. He still could not get a proper reading on these two. They were stronger and smarter, yet weaker and less knowledgeable than he had expected, depending on the issue, and every time he thought he understood what he was dealing with, they threw another curveball. LeBlanc seemed nearly as baffled as he was.

She cleared her throat. "First, thank you for a wonderful meal. Second, we are not in the business of harming anyone. In fact, everything we do is to prevent people from abusing their talents or causing unnecessary problems. Our only goal is the common good."

The Kims chuckled. The woman said something in Korean, and the man added, "Ah, yes. Many people *think* they are the good guys, don't they? We *are* pretty good, aren't we? Ha, ha. But there are people who like us and protect us who, you might say, are *not* as good. Dangerous people who wouldn't like it if they came back and found us with our brains melted."

LeBlanc smoothed her dress. She was usually unflappable, but tremors of irritation were going through her.

James tried a different course. "We're not going to melt your brains. We only wanted to assess whether you posed a threat to the general populace and if you were attracting so much attention to our kind that *we* would have to deal with a threat *from* the general populace. Get it?"

Mr. Kim nodded.

James went on, "You two don't seem like much of a threat, but Motorcycle Man *is*, and you two seem to be telling us you're him."

LeBlanc finished for him. "Reckless vigilante actions are a danger to everyone."

The Kims laughed again. "Oh," the man quipped, "that was my wife in disguise. She thought she was dying—false alarm—and wanted to do some good before the end. Have some fun, too. But it looks like she will live, so no point in it anymore."

James and LeBlanc looked at each other, their expressions mirror images of chagrin. They turned back to their hosts.

"And the altercation at the Mermaid tonight?" James asked.

He had checked his phone at regular intervals and knew that nothing had happened. "Your showdown with the Startup? The scanners are clear. How did you defuse that one?"

There was a moment of silence between the couple. They looked at each other.

"That," Mr. Kim said, "is our secret. Simply know that we will only do it again if the gangs make it necessary."

LeBlanc looked down at her lap. James felt her certainty, and to his sadness, he felt the same.

This was not a younger magic-user who would be able to conform to a new system of beliefs. This was a *couple*, one with decades of life experience. Their minds were made up.

Which meant the path ahead was clear.

"You wanted us to join you," the woman said. "That was why you sent us the message. But, no. This is our home."

That settled it. James glanced at LeBlanc.

"I understand," he said.

James focused on the asphalt ahead and the lights above and to the side as he drove through Los Angeles. It would be a short trip, but he had enough time to think. Neither he nor LeBlanc felt like speaking yet.

Each had reasons for staying quiet. In James' case, it was because everything had turned out so...anticlimactic. Their gamble had failed without even enough fanfare to make a proper tragedy of it.

He suspected the reason LeBlanc said nothing was that she was content all was well.

He had to be sure, though. "Did we make a mistake? Was it the right thing to do, wiping the magical ability of a nice couple who gave us half their teriyaki chicken?"

LeBlanc kept her eyes straight ahead too. "No. That woman

was in her forties, or perhaps older. If she has not learned better than to ride around stirring up the whole city by now, she never will."

"I guess." James sighed.

They left downtown and passed into the outer reaches of Little Tokyo. Turning onto East 2nd Street, they found the parking lot of the Mermaid filled with police cars and "inconspicuous" black vans. Things seemed quiet despite the hubbub of so many law enforcement officers running a virtual occupation of the place.

After parking and exiting the Rolls, the thaumaturges composed themselves, prepared to take charge if need be.

James pointed out, "They said nothing happened. I'm starting to wonder if we screwed up worse than we could have anticipated, and *all* this has been a false alarm. Still..."

"Still," LeBlanc said, picking up where he had left off, "we should have a look through the place ourselves. We cannot trust that the FBI will pick up on the same things we would."

James was having doubts about their abilities to pick up on things as well, but he supposed he agreed.

Within, Richardson and MacDonald appeared to greet them right away.

"Hey," the former began, chewing on a mozzarella stick, "what did you find? There's nothing going on here, sadly. We didn't have a *single* discharge of firearms. Did scare the *crap* out of some civilians, but that turned out to be nothing. It turned into a costume party, basically. Good mozz sticks, though."

Scowling, MacDonald confirmed what her partner had said. "I can't shake the feeling that there's more going on than this, or we were duped by *someone*." She narrowed her eyes at the thaumaturgists. "Brief us."

LeBlanc smiled. "We dealt with the problem. It is likely you will have no further issues here. Of course, we can provide more detail than that later, but first, might we have a look around? It's possible that there may be subtle details here you missed, or we did not detect the other evening."

MacDonald looked at James, who shrugged. "Yeah, what she said."

The agents took them on a tour of the place, and they inspected the main floor, the area behind the bar, the public restrooms, the kitchen and storeroom and walk-in freezer, the main office, and the employee break area. The bar's staff had been hustled into the latter, and they looked bored and nervous.

Neither James nor LeBlanc noticed anything of significance. They saw the same traces of magic they had perceived on their first visit, and that was it. Still, while LeBlanc briefly enthralled the agents with a beautifully-spoken assurance that peace would return to their fair city, James did an extra scan.

His fingers contorted in the proper gestures, and he hummed the incantation in his throat to keep it below the threshold of human hearing. The residues of channeling appeared before his mind's eye. It seemed they were slightly stronger here in the break room, but not enough to matter. Otherwise, everything was as it seemed.

He came out of the semi-trance and noticed that one of the bar's employees, a pleasant-looking black woman, was looking at him. "Hi," he said to her. "Consultants. The feds don't pay that great, but it's secure work, right?"

She shrugged, and James turned away from her as LeBlanc completed her speech.

"Thus," the elder thaumaturgist concluded, "we shall take our leave, and trust that there will be no further wild rumors imperiling people. Goodnight, ladies and gentlemen."

MacDonald shook her head. "Our big haul amounted to virtually nothing. Better than the disaster that might have gone down if we had failed, but still disappointing."

"Meh," said Richardson. "At least this way, we can make fun of those pricks who foisted this job off on us so they could go on vacation by telling them we *didn't* get blasted into subatomic particles and got to party in Vegas while we were at it."

Stephanie watched them go. After the strange, mismatched pair had left, she excused herself to go to the bathroom, trying to shake the bizarre feeling that had arisen when she'd watched the geeky-looking man twiddle his fingers while his eyes went vacant. She had seen too much to dismiss it as eccentricity.

In fact, it reminded her of something she had read. Reaching into her bag, she pulled out her bootleg copy of *How to Be a Badass Witch*. She smiled, then slipped it back into her bag and headed out. After the hostage crisis, customers were coming in again to get the gossip.

They might as well try to salvage what was left of the night.

To her pleasant surprise, a familiar face showed up not too long after, and the woman's eyes landed on Cevin. Stephanie gestured Nadine to a table and told her she'd be right back with some water and a menu, then went behind the bar, where Cevin was mixing a drink.

He hadn't noticed Nadine.

"Be cool," Stephanie told him in a low voice. "Your chick is here, and she is looking for *you*."

Cevin froze.

"Get out there," Stephanie said after waiting for more than a reasonable amount of time. "Go, go, go. I'll handle the bar."

Lia began seeing through her eyes again, finally realizing they had been open for some minutes. She gasped, clutching her chest as her heart thumped, and groaned as she got to her feet.

Her memory was a mishmash of terrifying sounds and images, the dark figure who had invaded their headquarters presiding over all of it. The message Motorcycle Woman had left was clear: she was giving Lia and Johnny and Sven a second chance. She hadn't mentioned Pauline.

Lia slowly made her way to the back door. She felt her way along the wall, trying to stay upright. Trying to keep her balance. Outside, in the little manicured park, she passed the two men, who were crawling around in the grass like frat boys after a bender. They were alive, which meant Pauline was still a priority. Lia turned and walked quickly down the sidewalk, hoping no one would stop to look too closely at her. It was clear that all was not well.

Pushing through the front door, she found the reception area devastated.

Pauline had clearly shot up the place, and it looked like there had been a hand-to-hand fight as well. As for Pauline?

"Oh," Lia gasped, turning away. "Oh, my God." She stumbled back outside and crouched, trying not to be sick.

She became aware that she had been hearing sirens for some time. They were nearby, not moving, but there wasn't time for much in the way of emotional reflection.

But two simultaneous feelings could not be ignored. One, horror and regret that her friend Pauline was dead. The other was relief that someone had stopped Pauline in time. Things had gone sideways so quickly, and she had gone from a woman who was coldly calculating but calm in the face of pushback to someone whose icy resolve was matched only by her desire for revenge.

I was such an idiot to think this would go any other way.

But she didn't have time for that now. Lia pushed up and half-ran over to the park, looking for Sven and Johnny. She helped each of them up in turn. They'd lost their guns. That was bad since their fingerprints would be all over the damn things.

The sirens were passing them. Still, the cops would figure it out before too long.

"Johnny. Sven. We need to clear out the evidence and then get out of here. Can you help me with that?"

The men stood, blinked, and drew on their inner reserves.

"Yeah," said Johnny.

"Probably," said Sven.

Lia grasped something else. They too had experienced the nightmare vision and the clear warning about what would happen if they didn't clean up their acts.

They went in through the back door and set to gathering up all business-related documents, memos, invoices, the remains of the bombs they had been making and, so forth to bring with them and later destroy. There was no reason to be sloppy, especially when the state of the office would spur so many questions.

There was enough to fill a briefcase and a half.

After Lia had made sure there were no live cameras trained

on the reception area—they had been disabled the night before, probably a "gift" from Motorcycle Woman—they began wiping down the surfaces they had touched recently, leaving Pauline's body where it lay and trying not to look at it.

"Y'know," Sven said finally, "I think I'm about done with the Russian Mafia portion of my life. From now on, I'm gonna play up my Swedish nice-guy half and go be a fuckin' farmhand or something in Minnesota with all the other overly polite Scandinavian types. After this, I'm out of here. Sorry, guys. It's been nice working together, but I don't expect to see any of you ever again."

Lia nodded. "We understand, Sven. Best of luck with whatever you do." The automatic politeness came out of her, a relic of a different time. It seemed ridiculous to say things like that with a dead body nearby.

She didn't know what else to do, however.

Johnny patted his shoulder. "Yeah, man. We saved each other's asses a couple times, but all good things come to an end, or whatever."

He paused while running a sanitary wipe over the handle of the coffee pot. "I can't stop thinking about it—all of this. I'm not ready to leave town yet. LA has been my home for my whole life, but I'm seeing a lot of things differently. That's all I'm gonna say."

Since Sven was the biggest and had explicitly decided to leave the state anyway, they gave him the briefcases full of papers. He saluted them and shot them a wry smile before trudging eastward. They didn't ask where he was going. He probably had multiple safe houses or old girlfriends within a mile.

Johnny left next, after recovering his and Sven's pistols from the warehouse. He planned to sell or destroy them. They were tainted anyway, and if he needed a new gun, it wouldn't be hard to find one. He didn't bother to take Pauline's compact assault rifle. She had never let anyone else touch the fucking thing.

Waving at Lia, he slunk behind the tree line, keeping to the shadows at first, then strolled casually south toward his Mustang.

Lia, alone, remembered one last thing—the security cam footage. Motorcycle Woman had smashed the camera, but there was still the data stored on Pauline's device in the office. She retrieved and pocketed it and debated whether to throw it in the Pacific or find a nice blast furnace that would do the job even better.

Hurrying west, she went to her car, which was parked on a different street, and took time to study the flashing red and blue lights nearby. The police had raided the defunct art gallery down the road for some reason. If they didn't find Pauline by morning, she would leave them an anonymous tip. Her former friend deserved a proper burial.

Lia drove off and did not stop until she was halfway to Santa Monica. She stopped at an all-night coffee shop and got a small cappuccino to drink in her car, alone with her thoughts.

The terror was receding. Motorcycle Woman clearly possessed astonishing powers of some sort. Lia no longer cared to speculate as to what they were since it didn't matter. The vigilante also had standards and was capable of mercy. She *could* have killed all four of them, yet she had recognized that it had been Pauline who had crossed the line, dragging the rest with her.

It made no sense, but the notion growing in Lia's mind, now that she had time to think, would not go away.

She wanted to find this mysterious person again. And help her.

Mary Mitchell sat in the position she'd assumed at the head of the table. No one had indicated who should sit where, and that seat was open, so she had taken it. The other nine members of the council—minus the two who were off gallivanting in California —were lined up down the sides.

It was 9:16 a.m. Eastern Standard Time. James Lovecraft and

Mother LeBlanc were supposed to have shown up for the next video conference at nine sharp.

Mitchell drummed her fingers on the table, thinking about the dog-sized Venus flytrap she had been cultivating to eat rats and other pests. While they sat there doing nothing, she was neglecting the poor thing.

"They're late," she observed. That was obvious, but she wanted to complain and hear how the others would react. It would make it easier to gauge the opinions she could expect from them as the situation developed.

Rufus chuckled, "It's Los Angeles. They're probably stuck in traffic somewhere. I lived there once long ago, and I doubt much has changed."

Amanda nodded. "Accurate. I spent some time there too. It's an awful place as soon as you have to get behind the wheel. I believe there was an organization who tallied all the available data and determined that LA has the worst traffic on the continent of North America, including Mexico City."

Mitchell felt her molars grinding together. "Well, then they should have accounted for that before they set out. Some of the rest of us have things to do besides wait for them."

A few more mumbles went around the table, then the screen in front of them finally flickered to life. James and LeBlanc appeared on it, squinting into the camera to adjust it. They looked tired, irritable, and less than enthusiastic about the coming discussion. Mitchell was not surprised.

"Hi," James grumped as he took a seat on a couch.

LeBlanc sat down next to him. "Good morning. We apologize for the delay, but traffic was truly abnormal. We had to spend some time on what seemed like a worthwhile pursuit but turned out to be a wild goose chase."

"Oh," said Mitchell. "You might have informed us in advance that you were running late."

James' face curdled. She suspected he was going to argue with her, but before the theatrics could begin, Hugh spoke up.

"As we are running late, please come straight to the point if you would. Did you locate this person, and what happened if so?"

The pair on the other side of the screen sighed in near-perfect unison, and Mitchell braced herself for the news. Most probably, they had failed to find their mark.

James scratched his ear and adjusted his glasses. "Our offer was rejected," he stated. "That's the long and short of it."

Zacharia gasped. "What? How can that be? I sensed nothing of the sort."

James scowled vaguely into the camera. LeBlanc put a hand on his arm and explained.

"The individual, who was not an individual but a couple, did not become combative or anything of that sort, fortunately, but it was abundantly clear that they were not interested in submitting to us and being trained. They have chosen to go rogue. Or *remain* rogue, rather."

The other ten thaumaturges exchanged glances. Their faces were grave.

Mitchell proclaimed, "You know what you must do then as per our traditions, not to mention the personal agreement you made previously."

"Yes," James replied in a flat, morose tone. "We remember the terms. We did what we had to do."

LeBlanc held up a hand. "Indeed, please do not worry. We have erased any memory of *us* but left them with the knowledge of why they no longer have their powers."

Those who had voted in favor of Lovecraft's initiative gave brief condolences.

Lady Mitchell folded her hands in front of her and leaned back. "Well, it is *somewhat* encouraging to hear that you don't plan to do anything else foolish. You have already created multiple problems that should not have arisen and took far longer than necessary to deal with."

Most of the other council members grudgingly concurred. The two errant ones were stony-faced.

"Well," James intoned, "we're dealing with it now."

"Good," Mitchell responded, "but do not think there won't be a reckoning once you return. Clearly, we must all agree on a new set of policies to avoid such entanglements in the future." She flashed them a grim smile.

James, who looked as though he wanted to set the screen on fire, said, "Of course. Looking forward to it."

Kera covered her mouth and turned away from a couple strolling down the lane toward the pond. "Are you *sure?*"

"Oh, yes," Mr. Kim said on the other end of the line. "We're fine. We had a nice dinner. Teriyaki chicken. Chinese, but good enough. Sam spent the night with a friend. How are you? I heard there was some unpleasantness."

She took a deep, rattling breath. "I'm fine. I can't shake the feeling that you're not telling me everything, but I trust you. Please reach out if anything is wrong, okay?"

"Sure," the man responded. "We will see you soon."

Kera echoed the sentiment and hung up. Certainly, nothing *terrible* had happened, or she wouldn't have been talking to them.

She turned around, hugging herself. Hollenbeck Park was nice in the morning sunshine, and the night of sleep—and several breakfast sandwiches—had done her good.

Her phone buzzed again before she could put it away. It was a text message from Stephanie.

"Huh," Kera muttered, swiping the screen. Apparently, Stephanie wanted to talk about something—*and* about Cevin doing even better than before with the woman the waitresses had begun calling "Supermodel Chick."

Kera walked away from the pond toward her bike. "I should go see what that's about. It might be significant. Or Stephanie is just bored."

She'd deal with it later. Right now, there was something she needed to take care of.

Or someone: Christian.

With the memory of him came the avalanche of feelings unleashed by what the Kims has tried to tell her. Mrs. Kim's disapproval of her shutting herself off, and Mr. Kim's concern for her.

Her promise to them that she would make it through the night instead of throwing her life away, which implied she needed to have something to live for.

"God-fucking-dammit," she grumbled. "This is crazy. I mean, I did vanquish the hell out of the person who was causing the worst of my problems, but it's still moronic, insane, ridiculous, and so forth."

She could not be certain, but she suspected that Pauline had been behind most of the attempted hits on her; she had certainly been responsible for the attempts to leverage the Mermaid. With her gone, things might calm down some, but the life of a vigilante thaumaturge was guaranteed to be *complicated*.

Did Christian need that in his life?

Not necessarily, but she couldn't choose for him.

A few minutes later, Kera had been buzzed into the building and stared at Christian's door. She hadn't expected him to answer her call, but he had, and now there was going to be a discussion that might be unpleasant and end with him telling her to get out.

But she was going to be honest.

She knocked on the door, and he opened it quickly enough that he must have been standing there, waiting for her. He didn't look great if she was honest. He hadn't been sleeping enough, and it looked like he had lost some weight. He hadn't shaved for a few days.

She couldn't help but smile at the sight of him, and although he was clearly still wary, he smiled back.

"You said you wanted to talk?" he asked.

"Yeah." Kera stepped inside and let him close the door behind her. "I, uh…I lied before. Now I'm going to tell you the truth."

Hey, readers! To give Michael Anderle a small break since he's been very busy lately, I am writing these notes instead of him. Thank you so much for making it not only to the end of this book but the end of this trilogy!

During the course of these three volumes, Kera has learned a lot about herself, which I'm guessing is what's happened to many of you during 2020. It's been one hell of a year, hasn't it? I needed some records from an event that happened in January, and when I mentioned the date I needed the docs from, my thought was, "Wasn't that, like, ten years ago?"

What did *I* learn about myself this year? <taps lip thoughtfully> Well, I learned that four generations of the family can live under the same roof, even when three members are under covid quarantine. Things get flung up and down the stairs or left in a spot near my mom's part of the house, then the cry goes up, "Hey, I left the (fill in the blank) for you!" "Thank you!" is shouted back. Haven't seen my kids except through a window (they live on the bottom floor, so we see them when we go out down the stairs, out the back door, and around the house to get to the car) for more than a week now. My grandson's smile is always great to see. Quarantine's almost over, and all is well.

I learned that when the going gets tough, DoorDash delivers Dairy Queen Blizzards! I love Reese's PB cups plus cookie dough plus Butterfinger (hey, go big or go home!), husband likes chocolate strawberry with fudge chunks. I had one the night after the election when I couldn't take the tension anymore. Even my nutritionist said that was fine.

I learned that Facebook, no matter what people say about it, is a wonderful place to reach out and touch your friends and family when you can't do it any other way. I also learned that sometimes you just have to take a break for your mental health.

I learned that Michael Anderle and our operations manager Steve Campbell never lose their sense of humor no matter what is happening. Well, I already knew that, but this year it was particularly apparent, and may I say, vital! Also, Mike's and my goal this year was to get Steve to snort coffee through his nose during Zoom meetings by us cracking jokes just when Steve takes a sip. So far I came closest, but Mike made several valiant efforts.

It was so much fun that we will be keeping that game going next year too!

The next part of this series, *How to be a Badass Vigilante*, will be coming to you in February, and it's available for pre-order now. We hope you enjoy Kera's further adventures, and as always, if you have the time, a review would be much appreciated!

Hoping you had a tolerable if not stellar 2020 and that your 2021 is loads better. The world has reshaped itself yet again, and there will be many new adventures to be had—and I'm not just talking about in our 2021 lineup of new and continuing series.

Wishing you all the best this holiday season and in the coming year,

Lynne Stiegler